SURROGATE LOVER

I think you're a dangerous woman to know, he thought wryly. But maybe that was why she set his adrenalin flowing. She was a challenge and Patrick never chose an easy path if he sensed that a difficult one might be more rewarding. That was the reason he would finally either be enormously successful or be destroyed in the attempt.

He could not help himself. If he burned his fingers playing with fire, then surely the pain would seem less grim than turning his back on this powerful and unpredictable female.

The prospect of life without her struck him as extraordinarily dull.

SURROGATE LOVER

A One-Night Stand Becomes a Nightmare

Janet Cameron

toExcel

San Jose New York Lincoln Shanghai

Surrogate Lover
A One-Night Stand Becomes a Nightmare

Published by toExcel
an imprint of iUniverse.com, Inc.

For information address:
iUniverse.com, Inc.
620 North 48th Street
Suite 201
Lincoln, NE 68504-3467
www.iuniverse.com

ISBN: 0-595-09347-7

Printed in the United States of America

SELF-DECEPTION

With compressed lips
And lowered lids
That veil the truth
Within my eyes
How I evade and euphemise.
I think of life the way
I like to see it
And any other way, do not accept it
And so my stubborn mind tries to reject it
And spit it out.

Although I did not rise above
My limitations,
Sad that the saving grace I grasped
Crumbled between my fingers
Spawning complications.

1

Their lovemaking had been terrific. All forty seconds of it!

'Oh Christ! Oh Jesus! Oh sweet Lord Jesus!'

He rolled off her, making her wince as he crushed her left breast, and collapsed on to his back, his pale chest heaving as he gulped great lungfuls of air. Noisily, he expelled them in a series of tormented guttural grunts.

She propped herself up on her elbow, watching him, her full lips compressed into a thin, uncompromising line, as if she had zipped up her face. She found his ecstatic babblings neither insulting nor blasphemous, for what man did not invoke his maker's name, at least inwardly, in these his most vulnerable moments? It was as solemn and sublime an entreaty as was ever offered in the greatest of cathedrals.

No, it wasn't that at all. It was his apology, when it came, that so deeply offended her. She hated it when a man apologised for his performance, like a winded runner tumbling to his knees and giving up the race. Instead of bleating his redundant regrets, why didn't he use his imagination? Why didn't he finish her off?

He was too young, too eager, too raw. Too selfish. He was a mistake. Nevertheless she conceded the blame was not his, but hers, for breaking one of her self-imposed rules.

No gauche, inexperienced kids. Too much trouble and always the danger of further involvement. Look at him. He was lost. Out of his depth. Bewildered by her lack of empathy. Fascinated by it and by her.

'Do you *always* suffer from premature ejaculation?' she inquired of him, half-pityingly, half-contemptuously. She knew she attacked him because she was angry with herself. Now he was angry too, for a delicate, almost feminine, rose-coloured flush infused his transparent skin.

7

'Of course not! It's your fault. You're too much!'

She let out an involuntary 'Ha!' He wasn't telling her anything new. She had always been too much. She had been told many times, on a number of occasions, in a variety of circumstances and by many different people.

She had been told by ecstatic lovers, by confused husbands, by wondering friends, even, albeit sarcastically, by those in direct competition with her. And in her youth, she had been similarly accused by her worried parents and by irate teachers at school.

Not that she minded. It was her trademark and, in truth, she quite liked it. It set her apart, her loudness, her unself-consciousness, her very intensity of being. She no longer cared if it sometimes embarrassed others, made them feel threatened or inadequate or alienated. She had little control over her personality, so she learned to like it, to revel in it, to emphasise it.

If her figure was too curvaceous, big bum, tiny waist, full breasts, then so what! If her hair was a wild tumble, too thick, too black, then she permed it so it was thicker and more intensely black in its abundance. If her eyes held too intimate and too permanent a sparkle, bright sandy eyes, the texture of a wet beach, then let the tide roll in and fill them with the unfathomable mystery of its depths.

And if a lover ever failed, just for a moment, to be transfixed by those extraordinary eyes, he might notice the crowsfeet that erupted from their corners, a small but not unattractive betrayal of her maturity and, even more, a statement of her perception, her experience.

'It'll be OK next time. Honest it will.' His calculating, streetwise eyes implored her. 'It'll be OK, you'll see.'

'*What* next time?' she snapped cruelly and was instantly contrite as she recognised his humiliation. She knew he would be only too willing to satisfy her manually. But she wouldn't ask. Although she would be doing him a favour if she did. He ought to know. At his age, he *should* know. How old was he? Twenty-three, twenty-four?

Not much older than sweet Eddie when he died. Eddie, her freshest dearest love. Eddie had been wrested from her at the tender age of twenty-two, after just one brief year of married life.

8

Yet, in retrospect, his loss now hurt the least. Time had softened, but not dimmed, his memory . . . and because her recollections of him were of a very young man, they had become maternal. She thought of Eddie with affection and without bitterness or rancour.

Eddie, too, had been an impulsive lover. But they had learned together. There had been time, however brief.

There wasn't time now.

'Please don't be angry, Liz. I'm so sorry. It will be OK,' he repeated. He didn't understand. Didn't know that she didn't have time for him to learn to please her. For his own protection, as well as hers, he would have to go. Finish! Over! Kaput!

She swung her lower limbs out of the bed, dainty feet slipping into high-heeled sandals which accentuated the pronounced curve of plump but shapely calves. She always put her shoes on first, so she had to negotiate the flimsy panties with care, so as not to snag them. Determinedly, she buttoned her wrap-around skirt, dragged a T-shirt over her bra-less but firm breasts. Her nipples made two proud bumps in the skimpy material.

She glanced around the room one last time, blank walls devoid of decoration, colourless, ordinary, impersonal. Gathered together her belongings. She didn't feel sad, just bored with the whole affair.

'You're not going?' he whined.

She leaned over him , deposited a sisterly kiss on his forehead, now damp with perspiration. Refused to acknowledge the disbelief in his expression.

'How can you be so impatient, so uncaring? Why can't I have one more chance?'

'Be lucky,' she countered, slipping her huge canvas holdall over her arm as she made for the door.

She knew, by the stony silence that greeted her when she entered the flat, that the kids were going to give her a bad time. She checked her Rolex. Nine-fifteen. Oh hell! She sighed, stowed away her holdall in the downstairs cloakroom, peered into the hall mirror to ensure there were no give-away smudges of lipstick or mascara.

9

Honestly, kids were worse than lovers!

Robbie, dark and diminutive, sat cross-legged on the floor. He was watching television with the sound down, one of those comic strip things with balloons bursting all over the screen, proclaiming POW and KERPLONK and ZAT. Robbie did not look up as she entered, pretended not to notice she was there.

'Hello, darling,' she said brightly. He grunted, but did not move. She pulled a droll face at him, opened her mouth to wheedle him into dropping his defences. Thought better of it. Well, maybe she would get a warmer reception from Charlotte. From the sound of pots and pans clattering and muttered vehement, yet fairly constrained curses, Charlotte was in the kitchen.

The kitchen was reached through a small annexe that led off the main sitting-room, and Liz stood outside for a moment, listening, trying to gauge her daughter's mood. Charlotte needed careful handling at the moment. She was at an awkward age. In spite of herself, Liz had to smile, for she could hear nothing more shocking than an occasional 'damn' or 'blast it'. Obviously deeply frustrated, and even supposing herself to be alone, Charlotte remained for ever a lady.

Liz plucked up courage, peered round the door at her elder child. 'What are you doing, darling? Are you cooking dinner?' she asked, almost nervously.

It certainly didn't look like dinner. There was a huge pile of what looked like nettles on the work surface. Charlotte's slender shoulders were hunched over the cooker, her hair as black as her mother's, but long and straight, hung limply forward, caressing the sides of the saucepan.

'Charlotte, how many times have I told you? Tie your hair back when you're using the cooker.' Fear made her voice shrill, more aggressive than she had meant to sound. A flood of guilt at the thought of what might befall her precious children while she was idly dallying with her lover, propelled her into a further tirade of abuse. 'One day you'll bloody well catch fire. Do you hear me, you little idiot? Do you hear? Do you?'

'What do you care?'

'What do you mean? Of course I care.'

Tenderly, Liz approached her daughter from behind, curled her long fingers around the dark tresses, now damp with steam, gathering them behind the endearingly fragile neck and tucking them into the ribbed band of her sweater. She peeped over Charlotte's shoulder into the pot. Charlotte was stirring something dark green and slimy with a wooden spoon. From the rank odour, the matter on the bottom of the pan had begun to burn.

'What is it?'

'Nettle shampoo.'

'Really! How super! I didn't know we had a budding herbalist in the family.' Suddenly, Liz laughed. 'Did you realise, I made a pun?'

Charlotte didn't laugh. Instead, she replied, 'You're never *here* to know things like that, are you *Mother*?'

Liz flinched at the tone in which she spat out the word 'Mother'. It was an accusation, an insult, a curse. She could not have been more stunned if her daughter had told her to 'fuck off'.

And it was so unfair. She seldom arrived home this late. Usually confined her personal pleasures to times when the kids were visiting grandparents or involved in pursuits of their own. Why should she feel guilty? After all, they should understand that being a mother did not release her from being a woman.

She had heard the women at her firm discussing this quandary often enough, the general consensus being that mothers *ought* to be able to do their own thing. In moderation, of course, and with due regard to the age and protection of their offspring. Women who felt good about themselves, who were people in their own right, ought to be better mothers. Such women were more interesting, more informed and consequently their relationships with their youngsters improved. Self-sufficiency being the goal. And quality being more important than quantity.

Well, that was the theory. In reality, they would prefer to have her here all the time, frustrated, crotchety, bad-tempered, but *here*. Even one occasional evening, no, half an evening, was deemed a betrayal.

'I'm sorry I couldn't be here when you got home, darling. I was working late. But I'm here now, aren't I.'

11

'What was his name?'

Liz froze as Charlotte continued stirring apathetically. 'How dare you.' Liz's voice was low now, her words not an exclamation, but a statement.

For the first time in her life, she came close to hating her daughter. For making her feel so bad. For failing to appreciate the efforts she made to support her and educate her in a manner that surpassed what could normally be expected of a single, working mother. For forgetting about the visits to the theatre, the outings to the seaside, the barbecues in the country every fine Sunday afternoon. For being fourteen and minding about baby-sitting her young brother just once in a while. Whatever had happened to Charlotte?

She had become so detached, so stand-offish. Just like her father, John, when he was alive. She was dark, like Liz, and John had been Nordic in colouring, but apart from that, they were two of a kind, father and daughter. The same way of appraising anyone who might threaten or challenge them, the narrowed eyes, the supercilious lift of the chin. With every gesture she intimated that she was one apart from the human race, charmed, special, an entity unto herself.

And if she could put you down in the process, that made her even better, didn't it? Like father, like daughter.

'What was his name?' indeed.

Yes, Charlotte was too cute by half! If Liz had really been working late, maybe that would have been acceptable in her daughter's adolescent mind, But her mother as a sexual being! Well, that was something else.

For protection, Liz retreated into the mundane.

'Have you both eaten?'

'Yes,' said Charlotte, still stirring, her eyes downcast.

'OK, then, I'm going to bed. I hope you'll be in a better frame of mind in the morning when I shall, of course, expect your apology. In the meantime, do watch that hair of yours. Because I do love you very much, whatever you might think.'

Charlotte remained inert, the stirring had ceased and the spoon stuck up in the glutinous mass like an exclamation mark.

'This looks more like frogspawn than shampoo,' commented

Charlotte in her cool, precise voice. But Liz was relieved to spot a small tear roll down her cheek. She was still her much-loved daughter. And she could still reach her; however thin the threads of communication had become, they were still there.

Poor Charlotte. She was just going through a bad patch. We all did, from time to time, didn't we!

She hustled a protesting Robbie off to bed and retired gratefully to her own bedroom, her sanctuary where she sat on the edge of the huge divan, running her fingertips sensuously over the smooth dark gold silk of the quilt cover.

This bedroom was sheer indulgence on her part. Pure Hollywood. The Hollywood of years ago, when men were men and women were women and bedrooms were bedrooms.

It was a large room, with space to frolic, a white room, the coving embellished with intricate gilt plasterwork, its corners ostentatiously scrolled. The carpet was thick and woollen and cream and her feet sank deeply into the pile. Her wardrobe ran the length of one wall, its sliding doors gleamingly mirror-tiled.

It would have been a wonderful room to make love in.

But she had never brought a lover back here, to sleep with her in this beautiful bed. That was another of her self-imposed rules, that the children should never be subjected to a string of uncles.

She studied herself in the mirror tiles. Not bad. Not bad at all. Half-imagined the figure of a handsome and distinguished man sitting on the bed behind her, his lips hot on her neck, his arms encircling her, fondling her breasts.

Not that she had any trouble in attracting the sort of men to whom she was attracted. At least, not for the last six years or so.

Not that she had ever been exactly what one would call a mouse. But it had taken a while for maturity to add the finishing touches, the self-awareness that enabled her to express herself to her best advantage. In a way, that had made her a late starter in the charm stakes, learning how to develop the nuances of style that had changed her effervescent personality into a dynamic one.

And she had made up for lost time. She had done very well for herself.

She mulled over the events of the past few years. It was as if a

13

hand had guided her, smoothed out the paths for her. As if an unknown spirit had put all the right words into her mouth. There was only one thing missing, just at this moment.

She slipped her hand between her legs and began gently, with featherlight fingers, to manipulate. It was ages since she had had sex, proper, fulfilling, abandoned, satisfying sex. She was going to need someone soon.

Of course, sex with love was great, but since she had decided, for her own reasons, to dispense with love, then sex without it was better than no sex at all. With or without emotion, sex was an appetite, and so she had to compromise, to settle for someone she *liked* to satisfy her yearnings.

There were still enough hills to climb ahead of her without the distraction of sexual frustration being included among them. Liz was practical, so she concentrated on bringing herself to climax.

It seemed unjust that the satisfaction brought about by self-treatment seemed so short-lived, left one incomplete.

She got up, put a John Williams tape on her personal stereo and tried to think of other things.

2

'Well, of course you *must* know that Patrick Evans in Credit Control fancies her like mad. Although I can't see why myself.' The bleached blonde head with the ginger roots inclined closer to the colour-rinsed black tulip with the spiky tufts on top. 'But with a past like hers, you'd think he'd have a bit more sense.'

'What past?' breathed the black tulip.

'She's had three husbands, you know.'

'What happened to them?'

Reluctant to admit that her information was limited to these bare facts the bleached blonde stopped and considered. 'I don't know if I should tell you,' she volunteered eventually.

'Oh please, Cora, do tell . . .'

'The crux of the matter is,' the blonde paused to heighten the dramatic effect of her words, 'they all died in Very Suspicious Circumstances.'

As Liz paused behind them, studying the tops of their heads as if they were a couple of alien beings, a darker girl at the desk in front of the blonde ceased her hesitant typing and turned as if to ask a question. As she caught the tail-end of the conversation, her brain registered Liz standing there, statuesque in navy pinstripe, scarlet lips pursed, her huge mane of jet twists standing out like a satanic halo. Indecision ghosted the girl's features as if she wanted to offer a warning to her workmates. Her eye caught Liz's and she thought better of it, turned back to her desk, fumbled for her dictionary instead.

'And, of course, she goes through lovers like the rest of us go through tights. Using them and then throwing them away.'

As she listened, Liz felt more contemptuous than angry, more rattled at the waste of company time than threatened by

15

their slander. The bleached blonde would have to go for a start. She was a troublemaker of the first order, would never have been hired had Liz not been ensconced in Chamonix on a skiing holiday when the vacancy arose.

'Haven't you two girls got anything better to do than waste your time in idle gossip? Get on with your work immediately.'

The black tulip cringed over her typewriter, the blonde shot her a terrified look, began to grovel apologies and excuses, but by this time, Liz was gone, marching assuredly to her office at the far end of the typing pool.

Before entering her office she always paused momentarily, almost as if to reassure herself it was still there, shining brightly: the nameplate that she had fought so hard for. Mrs E. Carlton, it proclaimed, Personnel Manager. It needed a polish. She'd have a word with Dinah about that.

Dinah was her secretary. She worked in a small ante-room immediately behind the door with the plaque. To get to Mrs E. Carlton, you had to get past Dinah first. Liz liked it that way. It gave her status. And exclusivity. Only the MD, George Pascall, enjoyed a similar set-up.

'Morning Dinah,' said Liz brightly as she entered the ante-room.

'Good morning Mrs Carlton.'

'Could you come straight into my office, please.'

Dinah followed her, tall and chic, in a slim-fitting pinafore and crisp white blouse, her light brown hair high in a coiled chignon. Her notebook and pencil at the ready, she settled herself in front of the large teak double pedestal desk and appraised her boss. Liz smiled at her briefly as she sat down, her briefcase spread out on the desk in front of her.

Dinah's face was pleasant and relaxed. Liz sometimes thought that Dinah must be the only female in the whole of this huge outfit who wasn't intimidated by her. Well, they had worked together for four years now. Dinah had watched her boss climb to the top in this male-orientated firm, admired her determination, her ability to manipulate, her innate cunning. And Liz appreciated Dinah's loyalty and expertise. The two women understood each other perfectly.

'OK, Dinah, so what's new.'

Dinah looked down, started doodling on her notepad.

'A man's been trying very hard to contact you this morning. Not someone I know, but he's been very persistent.'

Liz looked shrewdly at Dinah, detecting an edginess to her voice; her eyes dropped to the notebook which was being decorated with borders of tiny flowers. Dinah's displacement activity, a dead give-away! For some reason, Dinah was under stress.

'Such are the rigours of working in an area where the supply so greatly exceeds the demand,' countered Liz lightly.

'I think it's more than that, Mrs Carlton. He's been calling every ten minutes since nine o'clock and it's now ten-fifteen. And he won't leave his name or a message, although I promised him you'd ring back immediately you arrived.'

The phone rang again. 'That'll be him!' announced Dinah with such reluctant confidence that Liz felt a sudden heaviness in the pit of her stomach.

Dinah picked up the receiver. Liz watched the expressions on her face as they altered in stages from mild annoyance to barely suppressed rage.

'I cannot put you through to Mrs Carlton unless you tell me who you are and what it's in connection with. No, I'm sorry, it's not company policy. It's up to you if you want to go over my head and write to the chairman. I must insist you tell me who you are. Edward, yes, Edward what . . .? And could you tell me the nature of your call? You couldn't. A personal call. Would you hold on a moment, I'll have to check this out with Mrs Carlton . . .'

'All right, Dinah,' said Liz, 'put him through.'

The sense of foreboding increased as she picked up her receiver, her eyes on Dinah's tactfully retreating back as she returned to her own office. 'Hi,' he said. He sounded almost chirpy now that he had got his way, not desperate like Dinah had intimated, just chirpy.

'Who is it?' she hissed, to give herself time, although she knew very well the identity of her unwelcome caller.

'Don't you remember?' his tone overtly impertinent, now

took on almost a sinister undertone. 'Don't you remember? Soft white thighs and heaving bosoms . . .'

'You have no right to contact me here. How did you know how to reach me? Who told you?' She could hear her own voice quavering. Mustn't lose her cool. She had never lost her cool before, here in this office. Mustn't start now.

'You left your calling card. Literally.'

Her business cards! She kept them in her wallet. One must have fallen out when she had gone to her wallet to check she had her car keys.

She lowered her tone. Dinah was discreet, she trusted her secretary's integrity implicitly, but after all, she was only human. Liz could almost imagine Dinah's ears flapping at this unexpected, juicy exposé of her boss's private life. 'What do you want? Just tell me and then get off the line.'

'I want to see you.'

'It's out of the question.'

'No it isn't.'

'You are ridiculous.' She said it in her 'let this be the end of the matter' voice, but he came back at her immediately as if sensing that she was about to replace her receiver.

'Then I shall have to come up there and get you.'

'Piss off, creep!'

The clearly audible sharp intake of breath over the earpiece imbued her with a sudden small surge of triumph. She smiled to herself, smug at having so effectively abandoned her victim's role with a few choice words. Slowly, gently she replaced her receiver so that he would not hear the click, and would continue to rant at his supposedly captive audience. She imagined his frustration as he ultimately discovered that he had no such audience, then his subsequent indignation that she had dared . . .

Either it would incense him to further abuse or maybe he would give up, leave her alone. Whatever happened, she had won the first round, crude though her tactics had been, and she hoped his reaction would be one of capitulation. She could certainly do without the hassle.

Served him right, didn't it?

18

Liz always considered the health of her mind as concurrent with that of her body. Cowardice, fear, withdrawal, all such negative reactions were no more than a gathering of poisonous white corpuscles, mutually supportive. Until those implacable red blood cells, the mantle of the aggressor, descended upon them, encompassing, crushing, annihilating.

She would have to wait and see. Thirty minutes had passed and he hadn't phoned back yet. The communicating door between her and Dinah's office was slightly ajar. Had it been like that all the time? Had Dinah been less discreet than usual? Could she have left it open deliberately? Not that Dinah would ever sit in judgement on her. She was too nice for that. But she had seen the respect often enough in Dinah's shrewd grey eyes and she didn't want to lose that respect.

He had reduced her to this. To worrying about what her secretary might think of her. She who had never ever made excuses for herself to anyone . . .

Forty-five minutes. Fifty. She fiddled uninterestedly with sheets of notes on her desk. Shoved a batch of documents in a tray for filing. Wiped off the ring her coffee cup had made on her desk, where she had absent-mindedly missed the saucer.

An hour. A whole sixty minutes had passed.

What was it her old gran used to say? The proof of the pudding was in the eating. That was it. And in terms of personal survival, she had always got the ingredients right before.

She could handle it. She always did.

'Dinah,' she called out, 'Can you chase up the printers for our new supply of Termination of Contract forms?'

'Certainly Mrs Carlton. Right away.'

Of course, what she really needed were some Termination of Bitter Love Affair forms. She smiled wryly to herself. If only it were *that* easy.

Liz had worked at Pascall House for seven years, having started as assistant to the Transport Manager, after taking a thirty-day intensive secretarial course. She had not bothered to learn Pitman's, but she had taken to Speedwriting with considerable dexterity. It served its purpose. She did not intend to stay a secretary for ever.

The first two years she had spent in observation, sometimes irritated, sometimes amused by the interaction of office relationships, the intricacies of company protocol. She began to involve herself, make herself useful, gaining experience in other areas. There was plenty of scope.

Although the Pascalls were millionaires, they had never stopped being entrepreneurs. And while the entire Pascall administration was housed within the building, it was in the guise of separate units. There was a wine importer's, a shipping merchant, a building construction company, an advertising agency, a packaging company.

Each outfit was autonomous in its management and running, linked only by a common Board of Directors – and Liz. Liz was Personnel Manager for all eleven units, she was the one link apart from the lofty and aloof Pascall men. This gave her a very special sort of power.

Of course, she had a unique relationship with the chairman, Sir George. He had helped her, not because of any reasons of sentimentality, but because he recognised talent when he saw it.

Sir George had three sons. Jeremy was the eldest, smart, smooth, slick and mean. Jeremy had everything: seniority, intellect, drive and a beautiful Italian wife. Liz had no rapport with Jeremy.

The middle son, Martin, a bachelor shortly to become engaged, was a different matter. He too, had an an attitude of authority, endorsed by his swarthy, rather intimidating, dark good looks and his position and involvement in the companies. But he didn't have Jeremy's killer instinct. In a different set-up maybe that would not have mattered, but Martin seldom, if ever, won a point over Jeremy.

As for Trevor. No one took Trevor seriously anyway, least of all Liz. Trevor was only interested in fast cars, fast women and fast drinking. In that order. Trevor was the thorn in Sir George's side.

Sir George had once confided to Liz that Trevor could have

done with a couple of years in the army. Square-bashing. Painting the coal white. Learning about discipline. Liz could not have agreed more.

She had learned how to handle them all. Jeremy she handled with extreme caution, guarding her conversation, holding back from revealing too much about herself, her relationship with his father and her ambitions. Martin she treated with a slightly deferential respect, sensing that in him she might find an ally if the chips were ever down.

Trevor she tolerated because she had to. She did not believe in wasting her energies worrying about matters she could not change.

3

'Did you truly love my father, Mummy?'

Liz's hands flopped forward at the wrists and her long fingers hovered over the pastry dough she had, a moment ago, been so vigorously kneading. Charlotte's question had caught her off-guard. After all, her daughter had hardly spoken to her for two days except in monosyllabic response to her own efforts at communication. Her hands dropped into the bowl like two hanged corpses cut down from the gallows.

'Of course I did,' she replied, without turning round, 'You know that.'

'Did you love Robbie's father too?'

'Yes. I did.' Anxiously she shook the flour from her hands, wiped them down the front of her apron leaving two dusty trails. She took a deep breath, aware from Charlotte's tone that there was more to come.

'Whose father did you love the most?'

Slowly, she turned, forcing herself to meet her daughter's deep brown eyes, earnest, questioning eyes, eyes that sought answers that only she could give. Eyes that desperately needed reassurance because they saw so much that defeated understanding.

'I loved them both equally, in different ways and for different reasons. Because they were individuals, just as you and Robbie are individuals.'

'My friend Samantha says that a woman can only truly love one man in a lifetime.'

'That sounds very romantic, darling, but you see, love has no restrictions, no limitations. It is all-embracing, it grows and grows. So you see, I loved them both, as much as I was capable of loving each one during the time I was married to him. Just as I love you and Robbie, each of you totally as if you were my only child.'

'What you're saying is that love feeds off itself,' Charlotte's small face suddenly glowed with something that looked suspiciously like approval. A flood of relief welled up inside Liz and tears stung her eyes. Relief that maybe she had found the right words, that maybe she had not failed her daughter, just this once.

She began to smile through her tears, but her expression froze as an unexpected, bewildered grimace flitted across Charlotte's face.

'In that case, a woman could love two men at the same time. Or even three.'

'I don't think her lovers would care too much for that.' Defeatedly, Liz began to knead her dough. Why was it all so damned complicated?

'But is it possible, Mummy, is it?'

'I don't know. For some maybe, but I doubt it. One love at a time is a pretty demanding pastime. For a start, it demands loyalty and faithfulness.'

'That's only social conditioning,' countered Charlotte and Liz fancied she could feel those dark eyes boring into the back of her neck. 'In fact,' she continued, 'if love really has no limitations as you say, it seems perfectly logical to me that . . .'

Liz crossed the kitchen, not looking at Charlotte, fumbled in a drawer for the pastry cutters.

Charlotte tried again. 'It seems perfectly logical . . .' She paused, stared hard and lingeringly at her mother.

'Wait till you're older, Charlotte, then you'll understand.' Liz felt suddenly very tired, almost apathetic. She made a tremendous effort and for the second time she forced her eyes to meet Charlotte's.

She didn't like what she saw. You're lying to me, Mummy, said Charlotte's eyes. You're lying, dressing it all up in clever, pretty words to shut me up. You really don't know *anything* about love, do you? You're a sham, Mummy.

Deftly, out of habit, Liz rolled the pastry into a smooth flat circle, then slammed the blue plastic ring into the dough, one

23

tart, two tarts, three tarts, concentrating all her energy on these mindless actions.

How could she ever explain to Charlotte that her one true love, the love of her lifetime, had not been her father, or for that matter, Robbie's father? It had been her Eddie, her first husband, her first lover, the one and only incomparable Eddie.

Eddie, both her lover and her child. Eddie, who had left her with no hang-ups, just a flooding infusion of warmth whenever she thought of him. She still visited his grave at Easter and Christmas and on his birthday, wept soft words of motherly reassurance into his tombstone, grateful for the gentleness and freshness of his memory.

If only she could have had a child by Eddie . . .

Her Eddie had hurtled to his death at one hundred and twenty miles per hour astride a roaring 650cc-powered mass of gleaming red and black metal. A streak of lightning. Followed by blood and thunder.

It was a Norton. The in-bike of the Sixties for a lad with an image to maintain.

She tried not to think about it any more. At least, not that part of it. She'd erased it from her mind. Because she was a survivor. Because she had will-power. Only the weak and self-indulgent dwelt in the past, harped on the negative, but she wasn't like that. She remembered the good times, the constructive elements of their short but rewarding love affair.

Only, afterwards, it had been tough. The hardest part to bear. The fingers pointing, the accusations that were never openly declared, but were there all the same. The under-currents of hostility she had subsequently had to endure.

As she had sat amidst the cow parsley, beside the railway track, she had plucked a lacy flowerhead. Perfection, then decapitation. Like Eddie's poor mangled head under the wheel of the ten twenty-three from Charing Cross.

Systematically, she had picked off the florets, one by one. Three four five six. Fifteen sixteen. Twenty-two. One for each year of Eddie's life. How many florets did a head of cow parsley have? Had she counted some twice over?

He loved me, he loved me not, he loved me . . .

'Did you dare him, girl? Did you? Was it a dare?'

She had heard him speaking, but had not registered the meaning of his words. Confused, she looked up. He was an extremely large policeman and his face seemed so high above her. She focused into his eyes. His eyes wanted to be kind. Only they weren't.

'Come on, miss. did you dare him to race the train?'

She blinked, buried her face in trembling hands.

What was he saying?

Was he accusing her?

The silence lasted for what seemed an eternity. It incriminated her in the policeman's ordered mind. 'Come on, miss,' he barked, 'I want an answer.'

'Of course not,' she whispered. 'Of course not. He was my husband. I loved him.'

Her numbed lips sought the rough stem, now bereft of its snowy glory, and she chewed on it, crushing it, mangling it between her teeth.

'Come on, miss,' said the policeman eventually, in a softer tone. 'Come on. We have to contact your parents now, come on.'

Liz had just removed the tarts from the oven, placed them on a wire rack to cool, when a small hand slipped tentatively into hers.

'I'm ready for bed, Mummy. May I have a story?'

'Of course you may.' She smiled down at her small son.

'And a tart?'

'And a tart.' Solemnly she surveyed the array of goodies on the kitchen table, tarts, a flan, a sponge, some fairy cakes, a bread pudding. Her penance for being a rotten mother.

'Which story would you like?'

'The Wobblyglucks,' crowed Robbie, enthusiastically, his face lighting up. The Wobblyglucks were Liz's own creation. They were green and roly-poly. They lived in caves in Folkestone, Robbie's favourite seaside resort, and supped each day on tasty seaweed pies. Robbie much preferred them to any of the fairytale characters in his storybooks.

She followed him to his bedroom. He had to keep tugging up his pyjama trousers because she had forgotten to replace the elastic. Because the top was too short, she caught glimpses of the line where the whiteness of his small bottom met the bronze of his suntanned back. He gave an extra hop and lost the trousers altogether. Smiling, she leant forward, gave his delectable little backside a crafty pinch. He collapsed into giggles on the floor and she had to carry him the rest of the way.

He bounded into bed, pulling the quilt up to his chirpy, pointed chin. Liz removed her apron, flexed her arm and face muscles. Robbie liked plenty of action to accompany the story and for that she needed a rubber face.

And so she began, watching his enraptured face, as his eyes became circles absorbing in wonderment her crazy tale of the Wobblyglucks' escapades, their triumphs over adversity. Those circles traced each movement of her lips, each grimace, each frown, each smile, each gesture. As she drew closer to him, he became drowsy and her ear became a conch shell, trapping his gentle breathing as the sound of the sea.

'I'm so glad you're here, Mummy,' he murmured as his eyes closed.

Liz left him sleeping and wandered aimlessly around the flat for a while. It was a large and expensive flat, a penthouse flat, in a much sought-after area on the borders of Surrey and Kent – the stockbroker belt. There was space here; she needed space.

The flat was sumptuously carpeted throughout in natural wool, light creams and beiges. The gold velvet curtains were lined and hung in rich folds from ceiling to floor. The furniture was conservative mahogany, enhanced by the occasional antique that added character to the decor.

It was tasteful, understated, with the occasional hint of frivolity she found amusing. Not that Liz was a snob, she was far too self-contained not to set herself above such trivial notions. In pride of place in her lounge stood a Victorian what-not, painted black and topped by an ugly orange vase which contained a bunch of plastic, out-of-season poinsettias.

Robbie's last Christmas gift to her. And she loved them. Not just because they were a gift from a child.

She went to her bedroom, stood for a time looking out of the window at the vista of parks and houses and lawns. Dusk was beginning to fall. The nights were drawing in.

She lay back on the bed, flinging off her shoes, buried her nose in the freshly laundered pillowcase. Mrs Oakes had done her stuff to make everything perfect for the weekend.

The weekend! It had seemed it would never come.

Since the telephone call from her so-called lover, Eddie – that other Eddie – it seemed she had run the gamut of emotions from A to Z.

Lust. He had seemed so attractive at the time. How had she mistaken the cunning in his eyes for devilment, the confidence of his patter for sensitivity, his sharp wit for a sense of humour?

But he had reminded her of her Eddie. The real Eddie.

Maybe it was the faint hint of a Brummie accent that had fooled her. The long, gangly body, the way the light hair curled into the nape of his neck. The handsome long face with the high cheekbones and the interesting hollows.

Then disappointment. He was so gauche in the end, so mundane. Detachment as she had left him, without malice, without interest, a brief sisterly kiss as a consolation prize.

And in the few brief moments of their telephone conversation there had been alarm, fear, anger and finally triumph. Followed by three days of anxiety, culminating in an immense flood of relief that he had not seen fit to contact her again.

Now self-disgust sidled up and nudged her. Usually she felt good about her love affairs, however brief, remembered her lovers affectionately by name, not number.

But she hadn't even known his name was Eddie, till that fatal telephone call. What had she been thinking of!

Oh hell! Hell and damnation! What a wally he had turned out to be. Even more, what a wally she was, for having entertained him in the first place. But she was entitled to one mistake, wasn't she? One fleeting one-night stand that was now a part of her past, one minor error of judgement.

She rose from her bed, went to her dressing table and began plastering her face with a thick layer of cold cream. Methodically, she cleaned the muck of the day from her face, the debris of the week from her mind, and kicked self-disgust firmly out of the window.

4

Liz dressed with particular care for Monday morning. She dressed to do battle, to clear up all the niggling, unpleasant bits and pieces she had been too bemused to deal with last week.

Her clerical grey, with its straight skirt, fitted waistcoat, a jacket that lightly skimmed her voluptuous body. Energetically, she poked out her wiry curls with a wide-toothed comb, pinned a diamond brooch on to her lapel, old-fashioned but classy.

When she arrived at Pascall House, Johnny Morris, the commissionaire, greeted her with his usual half-there grin.

Johnny liked Mrs Carlton. Indeed, he liked her very much. Whatever they said, as far as Johnny was concerned, she was every inch a lady. Needed a man to take care of her, keep her in line, that was all. A steady man. Maybe a man like him. But Personnel Managers did not get involved with commissionaires. More fool them! that's what Johnny said. A good working-class man like him could show her a thing or two, if only he had half a chance.

'Morning, Mrs Carlton.'

Johnny was always careful to address her as Mrs Carlton whenever others were present. Out of respect. But if she ever lingered for a few moments after work to inquire after his welfare, he fell back on the more familiar 'Liz'. After all, she had been Liz when she had first started work as a secretary at Pascall House just a few years ago. New and nervous, she'd been. He'd told her not to worry about a thing.

Who would have thought she would rise so high, and so fast? She hadn't even started as a director's secretary, she'd merely worked for the Transport Manager, way, way down in the office hierarchy.

'Nice day, Mrs Carlton.'

He wondered if she noticed his diplomacy. He hoped she realised that he denied himself the privilege of using her Christian name in the interests of office protocol. Because of 'how it looked'. That showed he was discreet, a gentleman.

She seemed remote, disinterested, lost in a world of her own as her high heels clattered across the shining sweep of marble floor.

'Morning, Johnny,' she said briefly, without smiling, more out of habit than interest. He felt a stab of disappointment.

As he watched her retreating back as she approached the lifts, he admired her short jacket. It was what he had called a 'bum freezer' in his youth, the way it skimmed over her waist, jostling with the alternating swellings of her hips as she moved, showing off her figure. A right sexy piece was Mrs Elizabeth Carlton.

God, how he missed having a woman in his bed each night. Ever since Maud had died two years ago, indeed, even before that, he had imagined . . .

Oh how he had imagined!

'Thank heavens Monday's over,' breathed Liz fervently. With one sweep of her arm she gathered the pile of papers she had been sorting into an untidy pile.

'You look peaky, Mrs Carlton,' commented Dinah with gentle concern. Liz smiled at her.

'I am tired, but I'm pleased with my day. That's an entirely different kind of exhaustion. Now, be a dear, Dinah, and file this lot in the waste-paper bin.'

Dinah obligingly made a cradle of her arms, into which Liz stuffed her pile of what she called 'dead wood'.

'That's that,' she said with satisfaction, 'that's tidied up my desk no end.'

'Don't you think I'd better check this lot, make sure you're not dumping something you're going to want tomorrow?'

'Rubbish, all rubbish. All obsolete rubbish. Don't know why I harbour so many useless bits of paper.'

'You've got a filing tray,' said Dinah reasonably, 'If you used it, then I'd soon deal with it for you and then you wouldn't accumulate so much junk.'

'True,' replied Liz in a suitably chastised tone.

'And if I do dump this lot,' continued Dinah, 'without scrutinising it first, you'll be sure to ask me tomorrow for something or other I'll spend three hours searching for in the files, and then you'll say, "You must have thrown it away, Dinah".'

'Oh, Dinah, give me a break.'

'Well that's what happened last time you had a clear-out.'

'I can't stand people who are always right,' grumbled Liz. 'OK Dinah, you win, I'll try to be a bit better at delegating in future.'

'About time too. Well, Mrs Carlton, I'll be off now if that's OK. My husband's taking me to the theatre tonight and I've got to do something with my hair. Is there anything you need before I go? Right then. By the way, Patrick Evans just buzzed through on the intercom. He said he wanted to see you just for a few minutes. I said that would be all right.'

'Patrick . . .' mused Liz. 'Wonder what he wants.'

'See you tomorrow,' said Dinah and Liz was suddenly discomfited by the hint of a sparkle in Dinah's eyes.

God, she was hot. She delved in her bag, got out her cologne spray, gave herself a couple of blasts behind her ears. As she heard Patrick Evans's knock on the outer door she pressed her buzzer to indicate that he could enter. She heard his footsteps, slightly hesitant, as he passed through Dinah's office, called out a cheery 'come in' at his tentative knock on her door.

'Hello, Patrick. How nice to see you. What brings you here at this late hour?'

'Well,' said Patrick looking bashful. 'You, actually.'

'Me?'

'Yes,' said Patrick, beginning to pace the room, uncomfortable beneath her questioning gaze. 'You,' he repeated as much as if to reassure himself as to inform her.

'Hmmm ' muttered Liz, nonplussed.

There followed a long, pregnant pause, while Patrick contemplated his feet and Liz admired the top of his thick

31

thatch of violent red hair. He intrigued her, this large, eager man with the precise BBC accent and the direct way of speaking his mind.

This was ridiculous! She had to do something, say something, to break the spell, or they would both be here like this tomorrow morning, a couple of zombies, frozen in time . . .

'It's strange, Patrick, even your name seems a contradiction,' she said, and as she spoke, she realised that by including the word 'even' she implied that her thoughts dwelt upon him sufficiently to note other ambiguities about him. He did not miss the implication, glanced down at her and grinned beguilingly.

'Oh, you mean the Irish first name and the Welsh surname. Well, I'm seventy-five per cent Irish. My mother came from Dublin and my father was half-Welsh. So you see, despite the fact I have eliminated all traces of my ancestry in my diction, I am predominantly Irish and too thick to take no for an answer. So you might as well let me take you out for a drink.'

'That's a new line in blarney.'

'It's not blarney. I think you're the cat's whiskers. I know you outrank me at the moment, but not for long, Mrs Carlton. I'm going places, you know. I'd certainly like to go places with you.'

'This conversation is becoming too personal.'

She was beginning to get cross with him. Who did he think he was, in heaven's name?

He was undeterred. 'I won't apologise for that,' he informed her. 'My request comes straight from the heart and I don't believe one should ever apologise for a heartfelt request. Do you?'

'No, but . . .'

'Of course, you'd like to know my credentials. Let me put you in the picture. I've never been married, but that's because I've never met anyone quite like you. I did live with someone for three years. She was a live wire. I wined her, dined her, took her to all the best nightclubs. Then one day, she left me for a cabaret act.'

'A cabaret act?' she repeated weakly.

'Yes, a cabaret act. A comedian. Short, tubby verbally somewhat pornographic and not nearly as handsome as me. But he made her laugh and that sealed my fate . . .'

'I can't stand this,' groaned Liz.

'So there you have it.' He spread his hands, palms uppermost, to show he had left nothing out, that he had laid it all on the line for her. 'I'm free and I'm pretty sure you're free too. Two lonely souls with nothing to lose. Just a quick drink and see how it goes. What do you say, Liz, why not?'

'Too close to home.'

'Nonsense. We're both adults, we can be discreet. Meet out of the area, if you like, at least until we know if we've got anything going for us.'

'Patrick, I think you're a nice man and I don't want you to build up any hopes about me.'

'Sorry, you can't stop a man from hoping. But I won't pressurise you. Just one quick drink would do for now, but if, on the other hand, you really don't want to . . .'

Liz decided she wanted to.

'OK,' she stood up, smoothing her skirt. 'Just one quick drink.'

In the lift, they were separated by the homebound crush of bodies. She found that by angling herself sideways and slightly bending her knees, she could glimpse his large face through the muddle of shoulders, hair-dos and profiles. His face was blank, as is the wont of those forced into close physical contact with strangers. It was, of course, impossible to be on speaking terms with more than a smattering of Pascall staff, partly due to their number, but also because of the diverse operations employed by the Pascalls.

His impertinence simultaneously amused, intrigued and provoked her. Going places, was he? And he had it in mind that he would one day outrank her. Did he have any idea who he was talking to?

She had, of course, earned her élite status. Her uncanny judgement of character and ability, her pragmatism with regard to hiring and firing. She didn't enjoy firing people, but she didn't believe in procrastinating either. If it had to be done, than it had to be done.

33

Her secretary was better paid than anyone else's in the whole outfit, with the exception of Sir George Pascall's girl, Julia. She was even paid more than four of the Pascall general managers. Dinah too, was the élite.

And Liz was the Pascall hatchet-woman.

She half-smiled to herself as she dwelt on Patrick's precocity in intimating his intention to equal her in status, perhaps even top her. Not that she minded. Not really. Let him enjoy his little fantasy. He would soon learn. After all, it had been she who had hired him in the first place, cheeky young pup.

It was strange how, in repose, his face seemed simultaneously worldly and innocent. It was the sort of face you could imagine in boyhood. Smooth-skinned cheeks, just a little plump, that fair skin peculiar to most redheads, a smattering of freckles over a short, broad nose.

And those incisive eyes, curious hazel-coloured eyes which refused to be diminished by the alarming, shaggy eyebrows that protruded forward, almost apelike, belying the boyish features.

As they stepped out of the lift he waited for the crowd to disappear and for her to hesitate and glance around for him. He took her by the elbow, guided her to one side, away from the busy lifts and the milling people.

'Liz, I'm bursting to tell someone about my coup.'

'Oh?' she raised her eyebrows.

'Pascalls have acquired another company. A very good company. A company that makes surgical instruments. You haven't heard anything about it on the grapevine I suppose?'

'No,' she replied coldly.

If he noticed the fleeting glint of annoyance in her eyes, the tightening of her cheek muscles that made a small pucker in her chin, he did not show it. With a great effort, she reassembled her face into the appropriate expression of mild anticipation, to disguise her indignation that it should be he who imparted such a vital piece of information to her.

'The terrific part of it is,' he continued, 'that I alone am responsible for it. Their account went overdue for payment, so of course, I was on to it straight away. I paid them a visit,' his

34

voice positively crowed with self-satisfaction, 'and what is more, they were in deep trouble. *Deep* trouble.' Smugly he crossed his arms and leaned back on his heels. 'Mismanagement, that's what it was. I know those guys so well. But the set-up was good, the potential . . . you know what I mean.'

'Anyway, I had a quick word with old George Pascall. And he thought so too, agreed with me one hundred per cent. And Liz, you know how the Pascalls appreciate initiative? I'm sure it'll mean a seat on the board as a junior director.'

'That'll depend entirely on how much money they make out of this new company. The Pascalls are businessmen first, innovators second and philanthropists last.'

'Well, that's as it may be, but Sir George led me to believe . . .'

'Congratulations, Patrick, you did well,' she said coolly, wanting to be pleased for him. But she wasn't and she hated herself for it.

'And that,' concluded Patrick, baring his teeth in his usual broad grin, 'is what gave me the courage to ask you to come out with me.'

After he had bade goodnight, with his customary respectful inclination of the head accompanied by an ingratiating smile, to the last of the Pascall sons and Sir George's disdainful young secretary, Johnny Morris removed his commissionaire's hat. Set it down in front of him on his desk.

He was sticky. He ran his palms over his head, feeling his thinning hair, wet with perspiration. He tugged gently at a few strands as if to reassure himself that they were still securely rooted in his scalp.

As he spotted Liz's wild black mane, distinctive amidst the layered haircuts and bobs of the throng spilling from the third lift, he quickly put his hat back on. One couldn't be too careful!

Now he would find out if that grim young man with the flowers was anything at all to do with Elizabeth Carlton. Johnny didn't like the look of him. He was a rum one, if looks were anything to go by. Skinny, sullen in expression, sly clever eyes. Not at all the type one would expect Liz Carlton to go for!

What made Johnny suspicious was the strangely hunted quality in his demeanour. Not that Johnny could have articulated his unease, or the reasons for it. He just knew that something wasn't quite right. The man held the flowers as if they were no more than a carrier bag, his slender, artistic-looking fingers coiled around the tissue-covered stems, the blooms pointing to the floor. As if he wanted to dissociate himself from them. He must feel a right berk, thought Johnny, hanging around Pascall House with a bunch of bloody flowers.

His eyes sought Liz. Liz deep in conversation with that carrot-top Paddy from Pascall Packaging. They had almost disappeared behind the huge artificial rubber plants in the far corner, like a couple of illicit lovers. Johnny snorted. What could you do with her? She was like a bitch on heat and now Paddy had jumped on the bandwagon too.

The grim young man was approaching his desk.

'Excuse me,' he said politely to Johnny. His voice was peculiarly resonant for such a slim, ineffectual-looking young man and Johnny automatically straightened his back. 'To your knowledge, has Mrs Elizabeth Carlton left the building yet?'

Aha! He'd thought as much. Frigging little upstart!

'She'll be along in just a moment.' Johnny's anxious eyes involuntarily swivelled sideways, like a couple of magnets, in the direction of Liz and Patrick.

'Ah, I see her now. Thank you so much.' The young man rose on to the balls of his feet, then rocked back on his heels. Eager. Impatient.

They both studied Patrick and Liz through the plastic greenery which interfered with their view. Even so, Patrick's excitement was obvious, from the way he was throwing his arms about. Johnny wondered if he was trying to persuade her to date him. Or worse . . .? He was faintly reassured by the way she suddenly stepped backwards a pace, as if overcome by the enormity of Patrick's proposition.

Satisfied, Johnny looked back at the younger man, and was thrown into a flurry of confusion and unease by the manner in which he was being studied. Ice-blue eyes bored into him. Knowing eyes, that could see right into Johnny's mind, his thoughts, his fantasies, his self-deceptions. All his guilty little secrets.

Thoroughly disconcerted, Johnny broke eye contact by coughing falsely into his hands. His own perspiration assailed his nostrils, he sniffed at it. It was human and comforting.

'She's a little cracker, isn't she?'

'I suppose so,' replied Johnny insincerely, 'if you like that sort of thing.'

The other man laughed. 'Oh I do,' he assured Johnny, 'I certainly do.'

Liz and Patrick slowly crossed the foyer towards them, her speculative gaze centred on his laughing Irish eyes. As they passed the desk, apparently oblivious, she automatically lifted her hand in farewell, then glanced over at Johnny.

Her face dropped, her mouth gaped. Johnny could see her wet pink tongue, was mildly aroused. Then she swayed a bit, and for a second time, Johnny was disconcerted until he realised that he was not the reason for her reaction. Indeed, why should he be? It was this strange young man. Johnny wished she would close her mouth. She looked so silly. Not like a sex symbol at all.

But she was transfixed by him, mesmerised, helplessly in his control. Suddenly Johnny shivered and wished he was somewhere else.

'Hello! Liz, *darling*! How perfectly wonderful to see you.'

He stepped towards her. 'I thought I'd give you a surprise and I see that I have. Come on, Liz, I'm real, not a ghost you know.' He held out the flowers with all the panache of a knight of old courting his lady. Johnny almost expected him to drop on to one knee.

As the tissue-wrapped spray was upended, the blooms hovering a few inches from her nose, she visibly stiffened. It was the smell that hit her first. That faint, collectively pungent odour, never forgotten, the stuff of a thousand nightmares. With a sudden sharp movement, she flung her head back. The tops of her eyes showed great ovals of white as her eyeballs

37

rolled reluctantly downwards, the pupils dilating and darkening.

'Cow parsley,' she breathed. 'You've brought me a bunch of *cow parsley.*'

The young man laughed delightedly, as if he had done something very clever. 'Private joke,' he remarked, to no one in particular.

Patrick's arm encircled her protectively as she began to sway again. 'What is all this?' he barked at the skinny young man, the man he had thought at first to be his rival. What was he, this bringer of flowers that were no more than an insult? 'Liz, are you all right?' he whispered.

'I'm all right, Patrick, don't worry, just came over a little faint. I think they've turned off the air conditioning. Eddie's right. It's just a harmless private joke between old friends.'

'Obviously you work her too hard in this joint,' remarked Eddie as if it was all Patrick's fault. 'What she needs is a nice cold beer.'

'If you don't mind . . .' began Patrick, annoyed.

Liz turned to Patrick, put her hand on his arm in a gesture that was meant to be both reassuring and pleading.

'I'm so sorry Patrick, I had forgotten that I had a previous engagement to see Eddie. Please do excuse me this evening.'

The pain in his expression cut through her like a knife. Suddenly she longed to gather him to her, press her lips against those endearingly shaggy eyebrows. Instead, she leaned towards him, whispered that it was all his fault, for wasn't it only his Irish charisma that had made her forget her commitment?

'Tomorrow?' he whispered back urgently.

'Tomorrow,' she assured him.

'She don't half pick them,' grunted Johnny begrudgingly as Eddie escorted Liz out into the bright sunlit street, the bunch of cow parsley lying forgotten on the corner of his desk.

5

He took her to a wine bar, a stone's-throw from Cheapside. He was careful to walk on the kerbside of her; as they crossed the road, he glided behind her to the outside of the pavement. A small touch on the elbow for her benefit. A perfect gentleman. He kept sneaking triumphant sidelong glances at her. He strutted, like a young cock. His manner was possessive. With each small gesture, he implied ownership.

She felt the resentment welling up inside her like a poisonous gas.

She asked for a Beaujolais. He ordered likewise for himself.

'You left your flowers behind, darling,' he commented, with cloying familiarity as he sipped his drink. She choked on hers.

It had to be a coincidence, the cow parsley. Just *had* to be. Despite her present predicament, her mind wandered back to that railway track, banked each side with a profusion of soft, off-white flowerheads.

She thought of the head she had picked. The twenty-two florets, one for each year of her husband's short life. She had chewed on that mangled stem till her parents had come to fetch her from the police station. Her father had had to prise it from her fingers.

What could this gauche kid know about all that?

How *could* she explain his extraordinary behaviour?

Cow parsley, indeed. A poor joke! A sick pun! What else would a twisted mind like his deem suitable for a woman he considered had acted like a cow? Cow parsley of course. What else?

As she reasoned with herself, she began to feel a little better.

'Shows how little you think of what I do for you.'

She glanced up. 'What?'

39

'Leaving your flowers behind.'

'Look here, I haven't got much time . . .'

'Of course, the kids.' He lingered on the word 'kids', making a protracted drone of the vowel. She sensed malevolence. Dismissed it. Mustn't over-react. What did he really know about her? He didn't know where she lived, with whom she socialised.

He could find out, though, couldn't he. Worm his way into the confidence of someone at Pascall House. Johnny Morris maybe. He was so *plausible*. After all, even she had been taken in, and it was her job not to be.

There had to be a rational explanation, a way of dealing with him for once and for all.

'I was so sorry about Robbie's father,' his features took on a hangdog expression. 'So sad!'

For a moment it seemed her heart ceased to beat and she had difficulty in drawing breath. She slammed her wine glass on to the table and its contents spilled. They made a brown sticky puddle, trickled in a thin stream over the side and on to her skirt. She watched the stain expanding over her knee, like blood.

Her head jerked upwards. 'Just who are you?' she spat out her fear, her anger. As fear consumed anger, leaving her once again, weak and helpless, she slumped, touched her fingers to her forehead in defeat.

'I'm Eddie,' he said softly, so softly. 'Drink up your wine, sweetheart. As much as I am loath to leave you I do have another engagement this evening.'

He smiled at her, the corners of his mouth crinkling upwards into deep crevices, as if he really meant it. Like that other Eddie. So young and so old. Charmingly evil and evilly charming.

'Please leave me here. I'd like to sit for just a few moments longer,' said Liz. In truth she longed for escape back to some safe, familiar haunt, but doubted the ability of her legs to carry her far.

Like a dutiful suitor, he gave her a peck on the cheek and left. Still strutting, the lines of his neat behind clearly visible in the tight corduroy trousers. Funny, she hadn't really noticed his clothes before. But wasn't he wearing just the kind of garb the first Eddie had favoured?

She gazed down into her empty glass.

'Hello Liz. Are you OK?'

'Patrick!' the welcome in her eyes evoked a reciprocal brightness in his. 'Patrick, please could you get me another drink?'

'He may be a friend of yours, Liz,' said Patrick as he placed her drink in front of her and quickly took a mouthful of his own, 'but I don't care too much for your taste. I had a feeling that young man was trouble. Thought I'd hang around, make sure everything was OK. He's upset you, hasn't he?'

'It doesn't matter. All that matters is that you're here now,' she took another sip of wine. 'I'm going to need this. I shall be in dead trouble with the kids when I get home for not ringing to tell them I'll be late.'

Patrick leaned forward, put a large square hand over hers. 'Liz, I know it sounds presumptuous, but let me come home with you tonight. I'll make it all right with your kids, honest I will. I'm great with kids. It's only with beautiful women I can't seem to make out.'

'Oh Patrick!' In spite of herself, she had to laugh. He was priceless, a one-off. They must have thrown away the mould when they made Patrick. 'Honestly, Patrick, you don't know them. They're unnaturally possessive of me, like a couple of maiden aunts.'

'We'll see about that. Come on kid, drink up. Let's boogie on home.'

Patrick's technique with her children was unusual to say the least, if ultimately quite successful.

'Don't say a word,' he instructed her as she put her key in her front door, 'however offhand they are, button your lip and leave it all to me.'

'On your head be it.'

If Patrick seemed a little awestruck by the beauty and lushness of her home, he certainly did not appear too enamoured of her children. Since their response to his polite 'hello' was pointedly unenthusiastic, he proceeded, pointedly, to ignore them. He settled himself into her best armchair with a cup of tea and a large piece of bread pudding left over from the weekend. Robbie was sitting at the table, demolishing a large plate of fish and chips which Liz had bought on the way home. Charlotte, out of pride, had declined hers. It was her way of getting back at her mother. She liked to indulge herself in a little dramatic fantasy, imagining herself as a frail, wan creature, unable to eat, unable to sleep, emotionally bereft. A shadow of her former vivacious self. Then they would all be sorry, wouldn't they? 'They' being Liz.

Uncharacteristically, Charlotte was sprawled out on her stomach on the white goatskin rug, doing her homework. She did not cluck and complain and ask questions as she usually did. A stony silence was more appropriate to the occasion.

'Let's play Scrabble,' said Patrick.

'I don't want to play.' Grumpily Robbie set his knife and fork together on his plate and trotted out to the kitchen with it.

'I don't have time for games,' sniffed Charlotte.

'I was asking your mother,' retorted Patrick easily.

She beat him at the first two games without effort. It seemed he had a highly creative approach, but this was severely restricted by his spelling, which was abysmal. Robbie came over to watch, in his pyjamas, crowed victoriously each time Patrick produced some new howler.

'You'd get a 'D' minus for spelling if you were in my class.'

Eventually Charlotte rose, stuffed her books back into her schoolbag. She sat opposite Robbie, on the floor, watched the action on the coffee table with pretended disdain.

'He's done it again.' Robbie slapped his thighs with delight at Patrick's latest *faux pas*.

Charlotte could stand it no longer.

'Don't worry, Patrick,' she proffered reassuringly. 'I'll help you.'

'That's not fair on Mummy,' protested Robbie loyally.

'I'll just help him with his spelling, not his ideas. Otherwise he goes off on entirely the wrong track and misses opportunities.'

'I hate to miss opportunities,' agreed Patrick.

'All right then,' conceded Robbie, 'So long as I can help Mummy. Otherwise it's two against one.'

'It's only about one and a quarter against one,' corrected Charlotte. 'It's up to you, Robbie. If Mummy doesn't object to you hindering her, then go ahead.'

'What's "hindering"?'

'See what I mean,' said Charlotte smugly.

They played three more games. Patrick won one, with Charlotte's help, then Liz won one with Robbie's. Patrick won the decider.

Eventually, Liz insisted it was bedtime. Robbie raised his eyebrows at Charlotte, who returned a knowing grimace. So the grown-ups wanted to be on their own.

'Come along, children,' said Patrick. 'I'll look after your mother. Make sure she doesn't get bored or lonely.' Charlotte giggled and Robbie flung his arms around Liz and bombarded her with a shower of quicksilver kisses. Then, without hesitation, planted a quick goodnight kiss on Patrick's cheek. With studied refinement, Charlotte too kissed her mother, a light, hardly there, brush of the lips on the side of her mother's face. She straightened and Liz could sense her sudden indecision. What to do about Patrick? Oh, the agony of being only fourteen and not knowing what was expected of you.

He solved the problem for her by rising quickly to his feet and dropping a brief kiss on the top of her dark head. She looked pleased, then slightly embarrassed.

'I hope we meet again,' she said politely as she followed her brother out of the room.

'That didn't go too badly,' commented Liz in congratulation.

They played three more games. He beat her hands down. His spelling was perfect. He managed to get all seven letters out three times, twice on a triple.

'You're a fraud, Patrick Evans.'

'You've sussed me out, Liz,' he agreed, as if she had paid him a compliment. Which she had.

They passed a pleasant hour, chatting about trivialities,

43

nothing too personal, just people at work and attitudes and ideas. A pitiful howl interrupted their flow.

'Let *me* go,' said Patrick.

Liz looked uncertain. 'I suppose it'll be all right,' she agreed. 'I think it's Robbie in the bathroom. Turn left out of the door, third on the right.'

She remained seated, listening to the insistent high chirping of Robbie, the low gentle buzz of Patrick's comforting responses. Eventually Patrick returned, a bundle of striped material in his hand.

'Could you direct me to the washing-machine without asking any awkward questions?'

'He surely hasn't wet his pants?'

'That's the trouble with mums. They have such suspicious minds.'

'Oh come on, Patrick, what's happened?'

'All right, if you insist. But don't you dare to breathe a word to him that I've told you. It's all my fault, anyway, for buying him lemonade and keeping him up so late.'

'He's wet his pants!'

Patrick's large face assumed a droll and doleful expression. 'It's not quite like that. The poor little lad was so tired, but he wanted to do a very big wee-wee, so he decided not to stand up at the lavatory, as he surely would collapse with exhaustion. Then, when he sat down, he realised, too late, that he had forgotten to take his trousers down first.'

'Oh, no!' convulsed with sudden, helpless laughter, she rested her head against Patrick's hand, which had come to rest on the back of her chair. It felt good to laugh so unrestrainedly, to laugh about the trivial, crazy, family things that made life worthwhile.

Suddenly Patrick dropped to his haunches and his arms went around her. She leant against his shoulder, smelt the warm muskiness of him through the linen of his shirt. As their laughter subsided something else took its place, something warm and tangible and infinitely more demanding . . .

With a croak of anguish, she shoved him aside.

'No,' she growled. 'No, it's no good. You have to go.'

44

'Liz!'

'No, please go Patrick, if you know what's best for you.'

He took a deep breath, drew back, avidly searching her face for clues. Her eyes were wild and haunted and dark with fear, her skin had grown florid, uneven in tone, She had drawn back her lips in an almost animalistic snarl which produced, in the pit of his stomach, a sense of hot, churning liquid. As instantaneously as she had reacted, she now withdrew, so that he felt he was looking at her through a mist. He was both alarmed and moved by the vulnerability which he sensed beneath her outburst.

'All right, Liz, as you wish. It's been a hell of a day, but let me tell you this. I'll be back. We *have* to talk about this. You know that, don't you?'

She didn't answer, refused to look at him. She leant forward, her shoulders hunched, began to replace the Scrabble squares back in their bag, one by one, needing to perform some mindless task that would take a long, long time. It was entirely instinctive, a kind of occupational therapy.

Patrick appraised her for a few moments, bewildered, afraid for her, then silently, defeatedly, he left her.

Eventually, when the Scrabble squares were all away, she folded up the Scrabble board and stowed it away in its box. Then she put the bag of letters on top, patted them down and replaced the lid.

After a while, she took off the lid, tipped out the letters and started all over again.

6

On Tuesdays, Liz had a regular appointment.

So, at five o'clock, after Dinah had left, she quickly sluiced her face, renewed her make-up and rode the lift down to Sir George's suite.

Their routine was always the same. They met after hours to enjoy a period of discussion uninterrupted by visitors and the nuisance of telephone calls. To make sure, Sir George would disconnect his direct line.

He would start by pouring her a glass of very fine pale sherry and himself a lemonade shandy. She found his boyish partiality to shandy enormously endearing.

He used her as his sounding-board. She knew exactly what he was talking about, never interrupted till he had finished, could converse on any subject relative to the smooth running of his business empire. Took an interest in his dabblings on the stock market. It was a combination on which he now depended. And, in addition to all that, not only was she discreet but she was very easy on the eye! A most unusual mixture in a female, in Sir George's slightly chauvinistic opinion.

Sometimes, he even took her out to dinner afterwards. They both had a passion for Indian curry.

'Liz,' he exclaimed, his old crumpled face lighting up with pleasure at her appearance. 'Sit down, my dear. How would you like your sherry?'

'Dry please, Sir George,' she said, as she always did. It amused her the way that he never presumed, and was certain that if one day she asked for a double whiskey, he would still, out of habit, pour her a sherry.

'How's life treating you?'

'Fine,' said Liz and because her reply was automatic, businesslike, it sounded sincere. 'Although,' she continued, eyeing him craftily as she sipped, 'as you are aware, my activities are diversifying more and more each day.'

'Isn't that what you want to happen?'

'Oh yes,' she replied quickly. 'I'm delighted that I am being encouraged to widen my scope, both in finance and general admin., only . . .'

'Only what?' he prompted, regarding her speculatively.

'Only I don't feel that my business title is adequate to describe my new status. I am having to delegate much of the functional and routine side of my personnel duties in order to rise up to my new challenges. So I thought you might be prepared to create a new job title for me.'

A small smile lifted the corners of Sir George's broad mouth. 'Ah, I see. So the position of Pascall's Personnel Officer isn't good enough for you any more?'

He waited for her to make excuses, perhaps even to contradict his blunt interpretation of her meaning. Liz, being Liz, did neither.

'No, Sir George,' she replied coolly, 'it is not.'

Sir George's smile broadened. He scratched at his scalp through his fine white wavy hair. This woman never ceased to amaze him. Her honesty was remarkable, her ego every bit a match for his.

'And what would you consider to be a more fitting title?'

'Administrative and Financial Consultant,' said Liz grandly. 'That just about covers everything.'

'Until you talk me into giving you a directorship?' His light blue eyes twinkled, 'Eh, Liz?'

She grinned back at him, knowing she had won.

'That's right,' she said, 'but I felt it was, perhaps, a little too soon to ask you about that.'

He clinked his glass with hers.

'Congratulations on your promotion, Administrative and Financial Consultant Carlton,' he toasted her. 'But I trust you will be patient and not expect us to update all our stationery before our old supplies are exhausted.'

47

'Of course,' she agreed happily, treating him to her most dazzling smile. 'I wouldn't dream of causing such a waste of company profits.'

'Fancy a chicken curry?' inquired Sir George affably.

He telephoned her again on Wednesday afternoon, while she was dictating her report to Dinah from her scribbled notes.

It had been a day that had stretched her to the limits of her business acumen and expertise and patience. She had interviewed a number of applicants for the new vacancy selling shipping space for P & L Maritime, had been so disappointed by the abysmal lack of talent available that she had refused to make a short list.

She had just instructed Dinah to telephone the *Evening Standard* and book a further three days' advertising space, when Jeremy Pascall dropped by.

'I'm not even sure that's the answer, taking on new sales staff,' said Jeremy, depositing his elegant body in her visitor's chair. He was an austere and immaculate man in his middle thirties, dark in colouring, dark in personality. A closed book. Because he was so graceful in movement, so precise in every gesture, he was sometimes falsely rumoured to be a homosexual.

He was the most ambitious of the three brothers, the most devious and the most perceptive. For a few moments he sat before her, contemplating his perfectly manicured fingernails. When he spoke it was in the soft, measured tones of one who was not being totally straightforward. This would have fooled almost anyone except for Liz, who studied him covertly beneath lowered eyelids.

'Liz, I want you to do a time and motion study on P & L Maritime.'

She was surprised. For some time, and with good reason, she had considered herself to be much more than merely a Personnel Manager, for the confidence she had managed to instil in her bosses had brought about a number of requests for her assistance in tasks outside her area. But this was something different.

'Of course,' she said automatically. Her policy of always rising to the occasion was a long tried and tested one and had always paid off before. Whatever it was, she could handle it. She would worry about details later.

A slight smile lifted the corners of Jeremy's thin slit of a mouth.

'Of course you can.' She had the strangest feeling he was mocking her. 'Actually,' he continued conversationally, 'although ostensibly I'm asking you to conduct a time and motion study, it is a little more than that. It hasn't been going too well just lately for P & L and I want to know why.' Then, lest she assume he was asking her to do something he himself could not handle, he added, 'Obviously, if I start poking around, the staff will close ranks immediately and the investigation will subsequently be messier and much more time-consuming. I don't want to stir up a hornets' nest at this stage.'

She could not resist feeling flattered that he deemed it pertinent to justify himself to her. 'I understand,' she murmured, lowering her eyes to conceal the twin rays of triumph she was sure glowed out of them like beacons. Don't let him think he had paid her some great compliment! Don't ever be too grateful!

'Personally, I think the problems stem from the top.'

'Hmm,' Liz considered, idly drumming on her front teeth with her index fingernail, aware of his cold, calculating gaze upon her, weighing her up, as if trying to decide just how frank he could be with her.

That was it! Trevor Pascall, the youngest of the Pascall sons, the profligate, the rebel, was being allowed to cut his baby teeth on P & L Maritime under the dubious guidance of one Damien Lambert. Damien, Liz knew, was ambitious to be one of the favoured few outsiders admitted to the Pascall board. In return for his considerable experience in the shipping industry, his connections and his know-how, and also for taking young Trevor under his wing, he had been offered just two small carrots: one was the inclusion of his initial in the company title, which, since he was a social climber, pleased him immensely, the other a bonus related to the overall amount of shipping space sold by him and his staff.

It was the size of the target set for him that had reduced the desirability of that particular carrot. And the fact that young Trevor took a great deal of organising.

Liz knew that. Everybody associated with Damien and Trevor knew it too. Surely it had not escaped the notice of the astute Jeremy Pascall. A worried frown creased her forehead and, as if reading her thoughts, Jeremy bounced back at her.

'I want the truth, Liz. Why isn't P & L making out? Obviously we are not prepared to carry the business for ever. In my own mind, I don't believe Trevor's to blame, but if he is, then I want to know. This isn't political, Liz. I'm here under my father's instructions. Your report will, of course, remain entirely confidential.'

Liz almost laughed out loud. Did he think she was born yesterday? Trevor not to blame! Well, that was a moot point to say the least. And as for his father initiating this exercise, that was so much eyewash. Sir George was far too direct a man ever to indulge in a ploy of this nature, setting one son to spy on another. Because that was exactly what he was asking her to do. To bring about the downfall of little brother Trevor. No, Sir George would never involve himself in such skulduggery; his way would be to get his son on the carpet and browbeat him into submission, face to face and eye to eye. At least everyone know where they stood with Sir George.

And as for the confidentiality of her report, if she managed to uncover the unpalatable details that Jeremy obviously suspected, it was surely going to result in another hatchet job. From the point of view of her popularity rating in the firm, Liz was sufficiently self-assured not to let it worry her. But politically, it could be very dangerous for her. He had no right to ask her to set herself up as judge and jury in a power struggle of this nature, especially where the antagonists were members of one family.

'Of course, it's not a pretty task to have to perform. If you want to chicken out . . .?'

'I'll do it,' said Liz, disliking the cheap psychology he was

50

employing to manipulate her, disliking him with his smooth unctuous manner, his black crafty eyes, the way he sat with his legs crossed as if he was modelling his suit.

Of course she'd do it, she always did, didn't she?

She had done it that afternoon. Trevor and Lambert were both out on business, which gave her a good opportunity to snoop without too much interference. It hadn't been difficult.

Jeremy had led her from office to office, with a brief introduction, which was entirely unnecessary since everyone knew who she was, and a short, rehearsed speech to the effect that they should give her every possible assistance. Access to their books and records, full and detailed answers to her questions. None of their jobs were at risk, repeat, this wasn't a witchhunt.

The sole purpose of her inquiry was to ensure that the company was run as efficiently and profitably as possible, which must ultimately benefit everyone concerned.

The staff of P & L were not convinced. By the time he had finished, Liz could feel the hostility boring into her like a hundred knives.

After Jeremy left her there, with a parting glance and a brief touch of his hand on her arm, a gesture meant to convey both complicity and reassurance, she felt as if both legs had been cut out from beneath her.

She began to ask a number of questions which were, on the surface, irrelevant to her true purpose, but which were calculated to confuse. If people were sidetracked, they were subsequently disarmed.

Examination of the petty cash vouchers revealed a great number unsubstantiated by official receipts, drawn by Trevor Pascall and authorised by Damien Lambert. Liz's shrewd eyes flickered with interest, for minor discrepancies often indicated trends. And how did Trevor justify his petrol allowance? Did he expect the auditors to believe that he did about eight hundred miles a week?

There was evidence of at least three 'business' trips abroad for Trevor within the past two months. None for Damien

51

Lambert, the young executive who had been set the unenviable task of acting as mentor and guide to the youngest Pascall son.

There were several more irregularities. Trevor hadn't bothered to cover his tracks at all. Either he was plain stupid, or just did not care.

'Jane,' she said finally, to the senior accounts clerk, having asked a number of seemingly innocent questions about the P & L method of credit control, 'what do these codes mean on the cheque stubs? RB40 for instance, that seems to appear quite regularly.'

'I don't know,' said Jane evasively.

'I think you do, Jane.'

She watched with detached amusement as Jane struggled with her sense of duty, which was obviously in direct confrontation with her loyalty towards her young boss. She cracked under Liz's direct stare.

'Sometimes,' she proffered, 'companies have to buy their business.' Discomfited, Jane twisted a tress of platinum hair around her little finger.

'It's quite common practice, Mrs Carlton,' she continued imploringly, 'it happens all the time, you know.'

'I'm quite aware of that,' soothed Liz, 'but Jane, can you tell me who actually draws the cash made out to RB40?'

'Mr Trevor,' said Jane miserably.

'What code does Mr Lambert use?'

'He doesn't have one,' admitted Jane.

'Hmm,' pondered Liz. This was getting interesting. Very interesting indeed! Damien Lambert was far more closely connected with P & L's key accounts, where such payments might be justified, than was Trevor Pascall. 'Cash payments to TP passed off as backhanders,' wrote Liz in her notebook in her spidery Speedwriting.

Trevor was milking the company systematically by every means possible, but not without Damien Lambert's co-operation.

Jeremy Pascall had not been exaggerating when he had voiced his suspicion of a hornets' nest, thought Liz.

So what was Damien Lambert getting out of it? Alternatively, what did Trevor Pascall have over him? It would be interesting to find out.

On the way back to her own office, Liz bumped into Trevor Pascall. Literally. It was her fault, for she erupted from P & L's offices like the proverbial volcano, almost sending him reeling.

'Its OK, Mrs Carlton,' he said insincerely, although Liz had not, of course, apologised. Not to *him*. Resenting the inference that she should apologise at all, Liz glared at him.

'You must slow down, Mrs Carlton. Take one thing at a time. If you're finding your job a little too much for you, please let me know and I'll have a word with my father.'

So stunned was Liz at his impertinence that she was momentarily unable to retaliate, and he was gone. She caught a whiff of the whisky on his breath, glowered resentfully after his neat, pin-striped back as he swung into P & L Maritime's reception, briefcase in hand. His fair hair was far too long and untidy, curled over his collar in unruly wisps.

Liz could not understand it. Could not understand how his father and elder brothers allowed him to get away with it. Surely, between them, that capable trio could have *done* something about their parasitic relative?

One day she would give that trumped up, good-for-nothing a piece of her mind! And perhaps that day was not too far away.

Hooligans, especially rich and privileged hooligans, ought to be put in their place.

Liz smiled to herself as, clutching the file containing the copious notes she had gathered on Trevor's misdeeds, she retraced her steps back to her own office.

She had only just sat down behind her desk when the internal phone buzzed. It was Jeremy Pascall. She gave him a brief resumé of her findings, and could not disguise the satisfaction in her voice.

'You've done well, Liz,' he congratulated her. 'Although it does seem there is a lot more to this than meets the eye. Could you have your report sent to me by ten o'clock tomorrow morning?'

'Certainly, Mr Jeremy.'

She made a few last-minute amendments to her copy, then called Dinah so that she could dictate directly from her sheets of scribblings. Dinah sat waiting patiently for her boss, pencil poised at the ready.

'This report,' said Liz, 'is highly confidential, Dinah.'

'As far as I am concerned, all of your work is confidential,' Dinah assured her.

'I know, I know, I'm not doubting your integrity, Dinah. Just asking you to take a little extra care if someone comes into the office. It mustn't be left lying around.'

Liz took a deep breath and opened her mouth to begin. And that was when he telephoned.

Dinah took the call and as recognition dawned on her delicate face, her full, pink mouth turned down in distaste.

'It's that man again,' was all she said.

Dinah retired to her own office, mincingly, almost on tiptoe, as if to make her supposedly tactful exit appear less obvious. For a moment, Liz was irritated at Dinah's slightly reproving affectation. It would have been better if she had merely marched out and slammed the door.

Poor Dinah! It was a tricky situation for her. Nothing at secretarial college had ever prepared her for this.

The insides of Liz's thighs were wet and sticky from perspiration. Her hands felt clammy and cold. She stared at the receiver, as if she didn't quite know what it was. She could just make out the cracklings of his vituperative bleatings. Eventually, with reluctance, she placed the receiver to her ear. She did not speak.

'Are you there, Elizabeth? Boy, am I hot for you! Seems such a long time since we last met, a lifetime since I had your lovely body all to myself. Why are you angry, Elizabeth? Was it because I had to cut short our last meeting? I'm sorry, baby, I'll make it up to you.'

Still she remained silent, tried in vain to control her breathing. Couldn't get enough air. Pressed her hands hard into the smooth curve of her soft stomach to control its involuntary heaving. Her whole being demanded air. She

54

capitulated, took a great gasp as her stomach spasmed. Reassured that she was there, his rantings continued . . .

'I wanted to give you the opportunity to apologise for being so rude to me last time I called.' He spoke now in a modulated, conversational tone. 'You haven't been very nice to me, have you darling? Walking out on me after our lovely screw, now that was downright inconsiderate. And as for leaving my beautiful flowers on the doorman's desk! Well! You really ought to be punished, but of course, I know you don't mean any of it. You're just playing hard to get, aren't you, sweetheart? When are you going to make it all up to me? You'd better you know, or it will be the worse for you.'

'If you don't leave me alone, I shall call the police.'

He laughed his deeply resonant masculine chortle. 'That's what attracts me to you, baby,' he told her, 'you've got spirit. But you don't *mean* that, do you? It wouldn't be wise. Look, I'm so sorry but I really must go now. In the meantime, be sure to take care of that beautiful, pulsating body of yours, till I come for you.'

And this time *he* put the phone down on *her*.

Johnny Morris watched out for Mrs Carlton. She was late, much later than usual. Normally she just couldn't wait to get home to her kids.

Eventually a lift panel flashed from 8 to G and, as the lift doors opened, she was standing there, looking dejected and alone. Since the main body of the Pascall staff had already departed the building, he waited for her to stop and exchange a few words with him.

She was preoccupied. She did not hurry but passed across his line of vision as if he didn't exist. His disappointment quickly turned to acrimony as he watched her pass through the tall, smoked glass doors and vanish on to the street.

Stuck-up bitch! That's what she was, a bloody stuck-up bitch! Johnny wondered why he had ever wasted his time on her. Worrying about her and encouraging her during her tremulous first few months at Pascall House. Charting her progress through the years. Bloody women! All the same. Ungrateful and self-centred.

Johnny shifted angrily in his seat, went back to his *Hustler* magazine, discreetly concealed inside a copy of *Country Life*. It really got him going, looking at these saucy pictures of beautiful girls making out together. 'Lesbian Paradise', the colourful display was entitled. Wow! Mentally he included Liz, naked and voluptuous among the scintillating scenes, for Johnny was essentially a voyeur. Not that he didn't know what to do with it. Oh no, just let him loose among that lot! They'd soon lose interest in each other once he got going!

You would have thought she could have turned around and said goodnight.

7

The kids had gone off to stay for the weekend with Robbie's grandparents, and Liz wondered how she was going to fill the empty hours. She had dressed for comfort in a light, softly gathered floral skirt and a crisp white cotton blouse. Her legs were bare, her aching feet pushed into a pair of frivolously fluffy mules.

She cursed when the doorbell rang, took her time to go to the speaker button. 'Who is it?'

'It's me,' said a familiar voice. 'Please could I come in?'

'Patrick!' She hadn't intended to sound so pleased. He stood on the doorstep, a bottle of wine in one hand, a spray of flowers in the other.

'I hope they're not cow parsley,' she couldn't help commenting.

They were chrysanthemums, bronze and golden and darkest red. She smiled her thanks and kissed him lightly on the cheek and he followed her inside.

'You look lovely. Light and carefree and casual,' he commented, approval shining in his eyes. His red hair was tousled, strands fell forward over his forehead. They seemed to annoy him, for he kept brushing them back. 'I can't do a thing with it when I've washed it,' he told her, in mock-female tones.

She poured the wine and they sat down together on her huge comfortable sofa. He smiled his beautiful open smile, a smile that bared all his even white teeth, producing deep vertical creases in the corners of his mouth. She took a mouthful of wine then put down her glass on the coffee table, her thumb and index finger encircling it, stroking it gently, idly, up and down.

'Don't do that with your glass,' he breathed. She smiled and

57

a devil inside her made her continue to caress the phallic-shaped object, then her index finger travelled the rim of the glass, which caused him to make a peculiar, agonised noise in his throat. She desisted her teasing and met his eyes with hers and the tension between them electrified them both.

He was so handsome. He looked overtired and a little desolate. His cheeks were slightly flushed. He was simultaneously predatory yet approachable, a challenge and an enigma.

Liz was essentially a realist, so she had not expected the earth to move the first time he had her. But it did.

'Where are the children?' he'd asked.

'Away for the weekend,' she'd replied. The instant hungry anticipation in his eyes had immediately aroused her. Well, why not? Maybe this time it would be all right. There was something so . . . so *invincible* about this beautiful Irishman.

'Would you like to make love to me?'

His face lit up with such radiance that she had to laugh. He followed her to her bedroom, her glorious white and gold sanctuary, where he opened his arms to her and she nestled inside his jacket, pressing her nose to his chest and drinking in his healthy masculine odour.

They stood for several moments on the brink of awareness, the tension between them every bit as demanding as it had been that time before. That time when she had so abruptly rejected him.

'Did you think I would?' she could not resist asking. She loved his response.

'I wasn't sure but I'd hoped.'

He did not hurry. He took his time, undressing her slowly, carefully, folding each item of her clothing and placing it in a neat pile on a chair. Her blouse, her skirt, her slip. He performed these small actions automatically, for his eyes never left hers until he deftly unhooked her bra; and then they travelled downwards, absorbing the sight of her full pointed breasts.

'You have beautiful breasts.'

58

His control was remarkable, almost calculating. By the time he drew off her brief Kanga panties, she was helping him, lying back and lifting her bottom to aid his progress. 'You are a goddess,' he said as he saw her naked for the first time. 'You are a nude by Botticelli.'

She was enchanted. And as Botticelli was a master in painting, so was Patrick a master in the skills of lovemaking. She had never been with a man who had made it all so easy, so effortless, so natural. He coaxed her gently with kisses, persuaded her with caresses and although her reticence was in no way due to false modesty or any sense of morality, but to fear of the violent attraction he invoked in her, it gave her, ironically, a deep sense of womanliness. Of being pursued, of being hunted. She felt suddenly very young and very submissive.

She sat up, naked and with the same unhurried care, performed the same service for him, removing his tie, undoing his shirt buttons. When she slipped off his shirt, leaning over him as she did so, his tongue gently explored her nipple. Then he rose to his knees and bore her on to her back, their eyes held in a direct and challenging stare.

She cried out as he entered her. This was what she was for, the ultimate, the pinnacle, her *raison d'être*. Her head jerked from side to side, her small hard heels bore into his back as he pounded into her. His lovemaking was unique. He brought her almost to orgasm, then let up just a little, so that she gasped for more. Thus he both prolonged their pleasure and, at the same time, drove her to wilder heights of ecstasy until, at last, she begged him for satisfaction.

So he hammered her relentlessly until she felt she was disintegrating. Shock waves ran through her, his lips were inside her mouth, her hands clasped behind his head, her legs clenched around his torso, tightly, as tightly as she could, she held him.

He was beautiful. So beautiful. He had all of her, every bit of her. Mind, body and soul. It was a physical, spiritual and emotional experience. It was Karma. It was The Perfumed Garden. It was everything . . .

'I love you, Liz,' he gasped as his juices flowed into her.

'Eddie! Oh, EDDIE!' she screamed as her body shuddered in response.

She turned on to her stomach, pressed her face into the pillow, pushing its ends around her head to muffle the sounds of his frantic preparations for flight. She bit hard into the soft, cotton-covered feathers in an attempt to contain her sobs, but somehow, from deep inside her, erupted a terrible animal sound, as if all the agony of human suffering had centred like a vortex inside her body and was about to explode into a myriad of red-hot pieces.

Although she clung desperately to her pillow, it was suddenly wrenched from beneath her, jerking her sideways. Roughly, he grasped her shoulder, forcing her on to her back.

'It's no good behaving like the three wise monkeys, all rolled into one. At some time in your life, you have to learn to be honest, Liz, with yourself as well as with other people. You have to face the truth, Liz.'

'I don't know what the truth is any more,' she choked piteously, rubbing her broken jig-saw cheeks with her fingers, mildly surprised to find, in fact, that they were still intact.

She tried to focus, but his image was blurred through her tears, wavy, undulating, indistinct, like watching someone floating under water.

The impact of his weight shifted the position of the bedsprings. She rubbed at her eyes. He had donned his white casual slacks, but his chest was still bare. Smooth heavy shoulders, strong muscular arms, a column of shaggy ginger hair that marched from his collarbone and disappeared into the waistband of his trousers. Half-dazed, she stroked the ginger hair. She was grateful when he put his hand over hers.

'Who is this Eddie?' he asked gently.

Although his inherent self-control enabled him to conceal his feelings behind a blank expression, she sensed in his voice an unexpected compassion. Even in his compassion, he let her off lightly, for he offered her no cheap pity, but a compassion dignified by the depth of his empathy for her, his willingness to understand, even to excuse.

'Who is he?' repeated Patrick patiently but insistently.

But he wasn't asking her who Eddie was in the sense of personality identification. He thought he knew. He was asking who, exactly, was the Eddie with whom he was already so briefly and so painfully acquainted. He was asking what was the hold that this Eddie had over her . . . and why? Therefore, her reply threw him off-balance.

'He was my first husband. He was killed in a motor-cycle accident when we were both very young.'

Patrick let out a huge sigh of relief.

'So it's nothing to do with that obnoxious kid who upset you.'

'Nothing at all.'

'Obviously you and Eddie,' he paused as if needing to get it all straight in his mind, 'you and Eddie, Eddie your first husband, had something very special.'

'Yes, we did. But it was all a long time ago. I don't think about it that much now. Don't think I don't care deeply for you, Patrick, because I do.'

'Did you pretend, Liz? Did you pretend that it was Eddie making love to you?'

'Of course not.' Her reply was so emphatic, so immediate, that he felt himself compelled to believe her. 'Truly Patrick, I don't know what makes me do it. Made me do it,' she amended hastily, dropping her eyes.

'So it's happened before,' he countered shortly.

With a strangled croak, she buried her face in her arms.

'Look, Liz, if you can't bear to look at me, that's OK, but I do need to know.'

She did not speak for a long time, but he waited, immobile, not touching her although she could feel his eyes centred on her naked back. Defensively she drew the quilt up over her exposed flesh and hesitatingly she attempted to explain.

'It happened with my second husband, John. It happened on our . . .' she stumbled over the words, 'on our wedding anniversary. It had always been all right before. John was a good lover. But on our wedding anniversary, I was just a little drunk and heady from all the excitement of the day. And, of course, consumed with passion for my husband, which always

61

breaks down one's defences.' She paused, as if afraid she was revealing too much, maybe hurting him further with her candour, but he merely stroked her hair in encouragement.

'After it happened, he was naturally beside himself with hurt and rage. He left me so fast it was as if there was a pack of rabid dogs at his heels. I heard him start up the car in the garage, the squeal of the tyres as he cornered and shot out of the drive. Then, within a few brief seconds, there was a tremendous screech of brakes and a terrible crash. Indescribable! Metal against metal. John had wrapped his car around the third lamp-post from our door. I never knew if it was an accident, or suicide.

'That's why I tried to reject you in the beginning. You can't say I didn't try to warn you. I'm not very fortunate with the men I love, Patrick, and they are even less fortunate than I. I'm a jinx, you see. So that's why I never allow myself to get too deeply into a relationship. But you wouldn't listen, Patrick, would you? You simply wouldn't listen.' In her agony, her voice had grown shrill, accusing. It didn't sound like her.

'I'm listening now, and it doesn't make any difference.'

'I don't believe you're real,' she muttered weakly, now turning on to her back and closing her eyes. He ran his little finger under the long, curling lashes, reaching almost to the tiny red veins in her cheeks, a small imperfection he had never noticed before, but which only served to endear her to him because he cared so deeply for her.

'If you need someone to help you lay Eddie's ghost, then I'm your man.'

'What have I done to deserve you?'

Desperately he yearned to pump her further for information. The circumstances of Eddie's motor-cycle accident. And how had Robbie's father, Liz's third and last husband, met his death? How did you handle a woman, twice, maybe thrice, violently widowed?

But she was not ready for further revelations just then. And for that matter, neither was he.

'I'll make some coffee.' He rose, put on his shirt. His clumsy, awkward fingers fumbled with the buttons, so she sat up, helped him, helped them both, by doing something together that was basic, facile and deeply ritualistic. A confirmation of their mutual support despite obstacles that threatened to consume them, yet that seemed to exist outside of themselves, beyond their ultimate understanding.

I think you're a dangerous woman to know, Liz, he thought wryly. But maybe that was why she set his adrenalin flowing. She was a challenge and Patrick never chose an easy path if he sensed that a difficult one might be more rewarding. That was the reason he would finally either be enormously successful or be destroyed in the attempt.

He could not help himself. If he burned his fingers playing with fire, then surely the pain would seem less grim than turning his back on this powerful and unpredictable female.

The prospect of life without her struck him as extraordinarily dull.

8

When Liz awoke on Saturday morning, it took a few moments for her to acclimatise herself to the fact that there was a body lying beside her in the bed. As the events of the previous night flooded into her mind, she sat up, startled by her own recollections. Gnawed anxiously at her knuckles, wondering if he would feel so magnanimous towards her in the cold light of day. Was afraid to look at him.

She could smell her own body sweat mingled with the unmistakable odour of the sex they had shared to its cloying conclusion, and she knew from experience that it was a combination he would find attactive if he still cared for her, but which would repel him if he did not.

Uncertainty made her slip from beneath the quilt cover and pad naked to the en-suite shower.

She turned the shower up very hot, so that the jets of water on her strong, voluptuous body were almost painful. She thought about Patrick, what he had said, what she had said, playing and replaying the scene in her mind, dissecting it, analysing it, re-analysing it. Tried to calm herself, to concentrate solely on lathering her soft skin, to enjoy the expensive perfume and creaminess of her scallop-shaped ivory soap. Tortured herself by turning her face up so that the hot spray drew the blood to her skin, crowding out the burning in her brain with the burning on her face.

She felt a sudden hard but slippery pressure as he came up behind her, cajoling her, rubbing his naked body against her back, secure in the power of his masculine sexuality. It startled her, for she had not heard him enter. He had slipped through the perspex door so carefully, so craftily.

She was about to spin round and confront him when his

64

fingers exerted gentle pressure on her shoulder blades. As she groaned and allowed her glistening body to curve forwards, he was enveloping her from behind, bending over with her. His sly tongue probed her ear, a sly knowing tongue, knowing well of the nervous conductor of pleasure that flowed direct from that orifice deep into her loins.

She supported herself, palms and elbows flat against the pale gold tiles. Gasped as he parted her legs from behind. He grasped her hips in his strong, greedy hands and with a grunt, impaled her on himself.

'Harder,' she moaned, 'harder, harder, harder . . .'

As she reached her climax, he whispered in her ear. 'Did *he* ever screw you like this?'

'Oh, Patrick,' she moaned as they let go together, she crumpling against the tiled wall, his body a welcome crushing weight against her own.

He turned off the water, stroked the tight wet mat of curls, buried his mouth in her neck.

'I have to leave you now, Liz,' he said softly, 'but I couldn't bear to go without first hearing my name on your lips. For that, I thank you, darling.'

Before he left the shower he slipped her huge white bathsheet around her shoulders. Cocooned, she sat in the corner of the shower basin, like a small child, dazed with the intensity of it all. He didn't say goodbye, but she heard him whistling as he dressed, and the slam of her door behind him was an exclamation of triumph.

Vaguely, she sensed that he needed to leave her wondering, just a little. Half-smiling, she began to dry herself. She couldn't deny him that, could she?

To her dismay, Patrick failed to contact her at all the following week. Refusing to torment herself with false hopes, she flung herself into her work, organising projects, setting up new systems and finally installing a huge visual forward planning chart which took up a great deal of her office wall-space, but which compensated by endorsing her status in the company.

Nothing, after all, looked more important than a huge

colourful visual aid with lots of little red stars and thin yellow strips on it.

As she left on Tuesday evening, she saw *him*, Eddie, waiting for her, talking to Johnny Morris. She didn't like the way they were so deep in conversation. Eddie looked like an overgrown street urchin, torn baggy jeans, a ragged T-shirt covered in slogans. As she vacated the lift, she hung back, allowing others to go before her and shield her from his view. By a tremendous stroke of good fortune, she heard the welcome 'ping' of the adjacent lift, so she slid to the side, waited for it to disgorge its human contents and rode it back up to the eighth floor.

Once safely installed in her office, she intercommed down to Johnny Morris.

'Johnny, I want you to do me a favour,' she said quickly. 'Now please don't say anything. Just listen. There's a man down there with you that I don't wish to see. Could you tell him I left an hour ago?'

'That's a bit difficult,' Johnny responded in a harsh, conspiratorial whisper. 'I've already told him you haven't come down yet.'

'Oh, drat!' her brain raced. 'Listen Johnny, don't hang up. Could you say that you've just remembered that I had a day off today? Will you do that?' She could hear the desperation quivering in her own voice. Mentally berated herself for it. He was just a stupid kid, after all, a stupid kid whose initial infatuation with her had turned to malice. 'Will you do that, Johnny?' she repeated urgently.

'Certainly, Mrs er . . . Jones.'

Johnny put down the receiver and grinned nastily.

'That was Mrs Carlton,' he informed Eddie, 'she says to say she's not in today.'

Eddie grinned. 'No sweat,' he said easily. 'Next time you see her, just tell her I'll be back.'

That evening, while Charlotte was out on a hack with her riding instructor, Liz took Robbie for a stroll over the fields. She felt she needed it, and so did he. She had never known him so pent-up, so fatalistically morose. He ambled behind her in silence, kicking aggressively at roots and stumps. He seemed to have grown thinner. His small body was lost in his bright blue tracksuit.

She hung back, fell into step beside him. Pointed out to him how beautiful the sky was, its whiteness highlighted with jagged streaks of glowing pink. And hadn't the rain made the grass so wonderfully green? She reminded him of Walt Whitman's lines from *Song of Myself* . . . A child said *What is the grass?* He had always loved the bit about its being the handkerchief of the Lord.

But today Robbie was unimpressed. Liz sighed and drew her anorak tightly around her. It was getting chilly.

Suddenly from out of the woods bounded the largest golden retriever Liz had ever seen. He bounded up to Robbie and took up a playful stance, down on his front paws, his mouth gaping in a wide doggy grin, his rear in the air, feathery tail aloft. Robbie screeched with delight and fell on to his knees, his small arms embracing his frisky new friend.

It was a scene that Liz would carry in her mind for ever, the outline of Robbie's small bottom jutting out of his blue tracksuit as he leaned towards the dog, against the vivid green of the grass. The contrast of his shiny black head against the soft gold of the dog's coat.

The boy and the dog gambolled and Liz watched entranced the changing patterns of blue and gold against the green backdrop of the field. She was angry when the dog's master called him away. And Robbie's face dropped. And everything was back the way it was.

'What's the matter, darling?' she asked anxiously.

'Nuffin,' said Robbie and refused to be drawn.

The next day, she asked him again.

'What's the matter, soldier?'

Robbie still looked exactly how she still felt, which was a pity, since it was the last day of the summer holidays. She had wanted to take the whole day off, but there had been the meeting to attend this morning. To the children's chagrin, she had failed to get back for lunch. Mrs Oakes had hastily fed them beans on toast, then departed on her annual package to Ibiza.

Robbie's moroseness must be due to something more than her tardiness. Normally, she could coax Robbie out of his moods and he never held a grudge for more than five minutes. Never mind, eventually it would all come rushing out in a torrent of explanation. He just needed a little time to lick his wounds.

On the face of it, her meeting this morning had been fairly successful. She had used her old ploy of asking for something insignificant to get them into the habit of saying yes, then worked her way upwards to what she really wanted.

Thus her office was to be repainted (dark powder blue, a nice, strong 'power' colour) and Dinah was to have an IBM word-processor to replace her five-year-old Adler. Liz's Volkswagen Scirocco was to be updated to a BMW. So far, so good.

Everyone knew, of course, that George Pascall had a soft spot for her, a fact endorsed by the manner in which his sharp eyes appraised her from the folds of crumpled flesh that made up his craggy face. None of this affected his businessman's judgement, for Sir George recognised ability when he saw it.

Although some might prefer to think otherwise.

Liz herself knew that she deserved everything she requested and, more important, she knew that Sir George knew it too. He expected and she accepted that Pascall's would reap the benefits of rewarding her.

All three Pascall sons had been present. The two older dark ones sat solemn and attentive, the fair one, in character, fidgeted and spent a great deal of time studying his reflection in the window opposite.

Later in the meeting, they had discussed the wage reviews for the draughtsmen in P & P Civil Engineering. Liz produced cross-comparisons with other parallel units, analysed scales above and scales below. Salary reviews were very much a political issue, as critical to the health of the companies concerned as the balance of nature was to the environment.

Her report, analyses and recommendations were precise and to the point. At the conclusion of her question time, she sat down, pleased with herself. She had answered them all, managers and directors alike, with all the panache and authority of a seasoned trouper.

As she sat, so Jeremy rose. He was sitting on the right of his father; Liz was positioned opposite, on the left, with the middle Pascall son, Martin, between her and Sir George.

Jeremy traversed behind his father's chair to reach her and with overt familiarity, slipped his index finger inside one of her springy curls. As she recoiled, the curl was drawn outwards and then released to bounce prettily back into place. She stiffened, resentment welling up inside her.

'Well done, Liz,' he murmured unctuously, with a slightly lecherous wink which she caught with her brief upwards glance. 'Liz,' he remarked to no one in particular, 'managed to produce *this report* just five days after I requested it. Well done, Liz,' he repeated.

The other Pascalls and the five managers present muttered their agreement with grave nods of their heads. Her eyes flew to Martin and she fancied she caught just a glimpse of discomfort in his expression. But it was Trevor who spoke.

'Well done, Liz,' he repeated his brother's words and she did not need to look at him to be conscious of the mockery in his eyes.

Open hostility, she could handle. But this . . .

Her face burned. Jeremy Pascall never flirted with her in private. In fact, he never flirted with her at all. Yet with one calculated action, one short sentence, he had effectively reduced her to the level of the little secretary who had made good. She smouldered her loathing in his direction as he returned to his seat. He affected not to notice, idly performed a couple of arm-tensing exercised as if to show his total lack of concern.

Suddenly, she thought about the report, that *other* report, the one he had commissioned her to compile about P & L Maritime. She shifted uneasily in her seat.

She was grateful when Sir George pronouced the meeting closed. With an uneasy backward glance at Jeremy, she made her escape.

As she wended her way back to her office, Liz was intercepted in the corridor by Martin Pascall. She slowed her pace to allow him to fall into step beside her. Vaguely noted that his suit needed a press. Like her, Mr Martin was working too hard lately.

'I want you to know, Liz,' he said in his slow, ponderous way, 'that Jeremy's performance at the meeting was out of taste and in my opinion, quite disgraceful.'

She stopped short, surprised that he should take such a strong line against his brother, especially to an employee, however well considered. In his intimidating, heavily featured face, his eyes had grown soft and cowlike, betraying his open admiration for her.

'It is a pity for me you did not speak out, Mr Martin,' she said reproachfully, unable to help herself. He did not take offence at her tone.

'I felt it was better treated with the contempt it deserved. It is best not to attach too much importance to such behaviour,' he replied defensively.

She bit her lip. That was an easy way out, wasn't it. Martin Pascall was no con-man, she knew that, but what was the point of having a strong moral sense if you lacked the courage of your convictions? Did Martin ever take a stand over anything slightly controversial? He was hardly a chip off the old block, was he? Oh no, not Martin! For all his burly appearance, his strong, silent stance, he was overshadowed by his wheeler-dealer elder brother, his solid outspoken father. And as for his younger brother, well, no one with any sense took Trevor seriously anyway!

Martin Pascall looked so woebegone she felt a sudden sympathy for him. It would have been difficult for him to stand up for her. It would have been misconstrued as something else. And from the look in his eyes, he was wise to be careful in his dealings with her. Martin Pascall was to be married in the very near future.

Of course, Martin had problems of his own. And he owed her nothing. She should be glad of his interest in her welfare, however small.

'You're very kind.' Impulsively she rested her hand on his

arm. His eyes fell and they both stared at her slender, beringed fingers encircling his arm, thrown by the sudden intimacy of her gesture. Carefully avoiding eye contact, she withdrew her hand and took her leave of him with a brisk smile. As her heels clip-clopped along the corridor, she could feel his gaze following her, could sense his naked magnetism towards her.

Maybe Martin Pascall would be worth cultivating after all. There was nothing like a strong physical attraction for giving a man the courage to make waves on one's behalf.

At home, there had been the usual family confab about what to do with this last important day, now racing well into the afternoon, before the commencement of the autumn term. Liz was in trouble with Charlotte once again for promising to be home by one-thirty and not arriving till two-fifteen.

As usual, there were a number of ifs and buts from Charlotte, but an uncharacteristic vague indifference from Robbie. They settled for a visit to Liz's parents in south-east London, followed by a Rambo film for Robbie. Liz had suggested the film, hoping it would bring a smile back to her little boy's face. She was mildly surprised by Charlotte's easy acquiescence after the preceding bickering. Perhaps she too had sensed her brother's sad mood, needed to see him happy again.

The drive to the suburban council estate in New Cross where the elderly couple lived was depressing, as green fields and large gardens and well-spaced houses with pools and old-fashioned lamp-posts, gave way to busy streets and traffic lights and grey terraces. Strange that one could live in a flat, albeit a very beautiful flat, yet feel stultified by driving into the suburbs. Yet they had space where they lived, in what was actually little more than an overgrown village. They had an open aspect, it was just a few minutes' walk to find yourself among woods and fields.

Their Georgian-style block was a mere five storeys high, not so high that it could not be reached by the questing branches of a huge copper beech. Each morning there was birdsong outside the back patio windows which opened on to a concrete balcony complete with window-boxes in colourful display.

'I'm glad we don't live in town,' commented Charlotte thankfully. 'I do wish that Gran and Granddad would move out a bit, near to us. A little bungalow would be so nice for them. No stairs to clean for Gran.'

Liz was touched. Sometimes Charlotte could be thoughtful. 'You're wasting your breath, darling,' she said sadly, 'other people have different priorities from ours.'

'You mean bingo and the neighbours!'

Disquieted by the contempt in her daughter's tone, Liz shot her a sharp look, but Charlotte stared straight ahead. She peered in her rearview mirror at Robbie. What was the matter with him?

Ensconced in the small living-room, her father lay back in his chair, snoring, his chin slumped onto his chest. He was wearing his check, brushed cotton working man's shirt. No longer a working man, by any stretch of the imagination, he nevertheless retained the uniform. No, her Dad wasn't going to do a thing he didn't have to. He was going to *enjoy* his retirement.

Her mother, on the contrary, tiny, birdlike, her only pretension to vanity the soft blue rinse she had had put in her hair, was born to serve. And serve she would till she left this life for the better one in heaven she knew she had earned. Earned it, looking after *him*.

'I'll just show Robbie the garden, Mum, while you're making tea. Go help Gran, Charlotte,' she added quickly.

She took her son's hand, led him out into the pocket handkerchief of a garden. The antirrhinums her mother had planted were now past their best, but there were a couple of small rose bushes which were coming along nicely. She sat on the grass beside one, pulled Robbie down beside her.

'What's the matter, Robbie? Please tell me. I can't bear worrying about you and not knowing what's wrong.'

'It's going back to school tomorrow,' said Robbie, picking anxiously at the hem of his trousers.

'But you love school.'

'It's that man,' said Robbie. 'I'm afraid that man will be there. The one that keeps waiting for me and asking me about my father.'

'What man?' she felt as if her stomach were disintegrating. The fear in her voice made him tense.

'It doesn't matter, Mummy.'

She fumbled with her handbag. She had to know. She took out her wallet, opened the plastic pocket section where she kept her credit cards. From behind her American Express card, she extracted a tiny photgraph. It was of a very young man astride a Norton motor-cycle. Although the snap was in black and white and very old, you could see how proud he was of his machine, you could tell that it gleamed, you could sense its power.

'Robbie,' she whispered, 'did he look anything like this?'

Robbie took the photograph, squinted at it, his mouth turned down. 'Yes, Mummy, he did look a bit like that. Only, only . . .'

'Only what?' she prompted.

'Only more . . . more cruel.' Robbie's big dark eyes met hers, full of questions and wonderment. Grown-ups were truly incredible. How did Mummy know! How did she come to have this photgraph that looked just like that man he was so afraid of?

She held him close to her, aware of how infinitely precious he was now that he was threatened. Her maternal instinct told her to reassure him. And worry about the details later.

'It's all right, Robbie. Leave it to me. Just you forget about it now and let me deal with it.'

His small arms went around her neck, his kisses, precious as gold-dust, rained warm and wet on her cheek. Sweet summer rain. Infused with their warmth, for a moment she forgot her fears.

After Liz left, obviously uptight about her meeting, Dinah breathed a sigh of relief. Mrs Carlton's early departure would give her a chance to catch up on a few projects of her own. At the moment, her boss was like a cat on hot bricks. Dinah smiled to herself as she filed away the very long 'short-list' for the new set of interviewees for the shipping space salesperson's job.

For sure, thought Dinah, tomorrow would be full of surprises!

Suddenly, she felt a cool finger brush smoothly up the back of her thigh. It lingered on the bare flesh above her stocking top, then boldly twanged her suspender.

'I'm so glad you've been a good girl and left your tights at home.'

'Oh Jerry,' she giggled coyly, turning towards him. 'Oh Jerry, do stop that! Someone might come in.'

'They won't. I've locked the door. Come on, angel, you know nothing turns me on like a girl in a prim business suit, with a set of sexy suspenders underneath.'

'You're the boss and you know I aim to please,' she countered girlishly, as he lifted the back of her skirt and squeezed her bottom beneath the filmy nylon of her panties.

9

'Blip, blip, blip, POW!'

A youth, his hair bleached an unlikely shade of orange, hunched over the space invader machine. A crowd of men cheered raucously as someone aimed for and hit a triple on the dartboard. A plump girl in tight knickerbockers made her selection on the jukebox amidst squeals of contradictory promptings from her pals.

'Christ! It's noisy in here! Can't here myself think!' Damien Lambert up-ended his glass and his Adam's apple worked overtime as he swallowed rapidly. He was rotund and very pale, and although only in his late twenties, his hair had already begun to recede. He sported a beer gut, the legacy of his conviction that the best business deals were negotiated over a drink. This philosophy was right for Damien, for what he lacked in appearance, he made up for in personality, and was more at home propping up a bar than anywhere else. Nevertheless he was a worker.

This evening he seemed rather subdued, thought Patrick. had sat in silence while the two men had downed their first pint.

'Like another, Patrick!'

'Cheers, Damien,' said Patrick chummily. Damien rose, picked up the two empty glasses and strode to the bar.

'Two lagers with lime, please.'

'With *lime*! That's sacrilege, sir, putting lime with our lager.'

Damien smiled. 'In my business, the customer is always right. Even when he's wrong.'

'And what might your business be, sir?' inquired the bartender conversationally, holding the glass up tight to the tap, just slightly on the tilt, to produce the right amount of head.

Instinctively Damien lowered his voice to prevent Patrick from hearing, and possibly challenging him for his presumption.

'I have a shipping company,' he said. It sounded good. Gave him quite a fillip. From the respect in his eyes, the bartender obviously thought it sounded pretty good too, for Damien's lowered tone had given the impression of an executive so secure in his position that he did not need to throw his weight around.

'So long as you're making a crust, that's the main thing,' said the bartender and Damien returned to the table with the two drinks. Patrick was smiling a small triumphant smile as if he had a secret. Damien wondered if he had heard his conversation with the bartender. Wished he had not been tempted to boast.

It had been Damien who had instigated this meeting with Patrick. 'How about a drink after work,' he had said earlier that afternoon, 'but not round here. I like to wind down a little after work, don't you? I like to get right away from the Pascall influence.'

Of course Patrick knew that wasn't the reason Damien had driven him out of the city, down the Old Kent Road to this Bermondsey tavern. Damien wanted a nice, long, informative chat, right away from prying eyes.

It wasn't as if they were exactly mates, after all. They nodded to each other as they passed in the corridor, occasionally shared a smoke in the canteen. Businesswise, their paths never crossed.

What was bugging Damien? Patrick waited. For a while they made polite conversation, their investments, the economy, then Damien commented on the promotion of two women politicians within Mrs Thatcher's cabinet.

'It's happened none too soon, if you ask me,' said Patrick. 'Women have hardly been well-represented in the government. One can only surmise as to why Margaret Thatcher has waited for so long.'

76

'Talking of high-powered women,' said Damien suddenly, 'what do you think of Elizabeth Carlton?'

So *that* was what this had all been leading up to! Damien was gazing down into his drink as if he might find the answer within the amber liquid.

'I think she's done very well for herself, but I've only worked at Pascall's for just over a year. I'm hardly in a position to comment,' replied Patrick evasively.

'Of course, you realise that she and Sir George are like this,' Damien made a circle of his thumb and middle finger. His meaning was obvious, his tone insulting. Liz had got where she was on her back!

Patrick felt his hackles rise. Obviously Damien Lambert knew nothing of his affair with Liz and although he did not like what Damien was implying, he could not afford to lose his temper with the other man.

'Sir George has a great respect for anyone who shows leadership qualities,' he said, trying to make his defence of Liz sound neutral, objective. 'And I don't believe anyone could cast any doubt on her abilities.'

Damien sized him up. Decided to take his remark at face value. 'Agreed,' he said, 'and she's outstripped us all. But I don't know what to make of her. She used to work for me, you know, before I got landed with that bloody Trevor. She was a good worker. But nothing special.'

Patrick smothered a smile at Damien's blatant display of professional jealousy. Damien took another swig of his lager and his Adam's apple popped once more. Drink was beginning to loosen his tongue.

'She was poking around P & L the other day. I don't know what the hell she's up to and I don't like her nosing around when I'm out of the office.' His voice took on a whining tone. 'I wondered if you knew anything about it, what with you being so well in with the old man these days. I'd like to know, Patrick. Man to man. Between these four walls and all that . . .'

'I've no idea,' said Patrick truthfully.

Damien sighed. His lower lip stuck out petulantly.

'There's something ominous about that woman,' he said.

As he drove back to his Sanderstead flat, Patrick thought about what Damien had said. Felt a sudden sneaking sympathy for Liz, a woman in what was still, basically, a man's world. No pally drinks with the boys for Liz, with a deal thrown in here and there. No matey promises of mutual support. There were no precedents for Liz to fall back on. The 'you scratch my back and I'll scratch yours' syndrome was still very much a male preserve.

Little wonder she was a tough nut, professionally. Had she always been like that? Manipulative, wary, calculating? Patrick did not think so, for hadn't he drowned in her warmth, her sensuality? Seen the softness in her eyes as they lingered upon her children?

It was all there, beneath that hard exterior, waiting to be set free. Yet, he sensed it had been a traumatic climb for Liz to get where she was. No doubt she had had plenty of time to work out her own recipe for survival.

She could not afford to show one chink in her armour. Unlike a man, she would never be forgiven for it.

And who was he to interfere with that?

Damien Lambert was not the only person with Elizabeth Carlton on his mind.

Gina Pascall was not your typical Italian senora. For one thing, she was fair in colouring, just a whisper away from blonde. For another, she had become anglicised both in her views and her attitudes to life. So much so, that when she returned annually to her family for the summer holidays, it seemed she had nothing in common with them. She found their world narrow, restricting. They found hers more than slightly shocking, a fact which both she and they found distressing.

The only typically Italian qualities to which Gina subscribed were her passionate Latin temperament and her deep-rooted love for children.

She had met Jeremy Pascall in the gardens of Pascall Lodge one fine day, fourteen years ago, when she was just sixteen. It was her first day as au pair to the Pascall household.

Jeremy and Gina had fallen madly in love. Or so it had seemed at the time. He had been twenty-one, the epitome of sophistication and English style in Gina's inexperienced eyes. She had been flattered. Amazed. Had nearly fainted when he had asked her to marry him.

And so had his mother, Lillian Pascall. For although Gina had come from a good, God-fearing Catholic family, well-to-do and well respected, as far as Lillian was concerned, her son was marrying one of the servants.

That hadn't stopped Jeremy and Gina. And Sir George had taken the wide-eyed Gina to his heart, gladly given his blessing, acted, as far as he was able, as mediator and peacemaker between his wife and the young couple.

Sometimes, she wondered why she had ever been so bloody *grateful*. She didn't feel grateful any more. Jeremy was a difficult husband, distant and deep. However alien her family in Milan might seem to her now, at least it was warm and loving and caring. Not so this family. If it wasn't for Sir George, and Martin's young fiancée, Alexia, Gina thought she would probably succumb to insanity.

She knew Jeremy better now. At least, she knew about him. She doubted if anyone, ever, had really known him. Jeremy always had a bee in his bonnet about something. Made it his business to know exactly what was going on. He dignified his innate curiosity to Gina by calling it 'research', and over the years his research had proved invaluable in many respects. He prided himself that he missed nothing, and what was not available, he could deduce quite accurately anyway, thank you very much.

He had a quick and agile brain, so that while his small black buttons of eyes darted here and there, assimilating, his brain sorted and stowed away the data for later, instant recall. He had a photographic memory, for Jeremy could scan a sheet of copy and in less time than it takes for most people to half-absorb one-fifth of the information, Jeremy would have taken a mental photograph, complete with every comma and semi-colon for future reference.

Despite his privileged background, Jeremy's early education

had left much to be desired. A forward and precocious infant, bored with the slowness of his class at school, he had lost interest and had consequently become a disruptive influence on the rest of his school-fellows. Not surprisingly, he was unpopular with his teachers, who lost interest in coaching him.

For the following few years, he was in and out of various fee-paying schools. If he was not expelled, he ran away. His parents almost despaired of him.

But once out into the big wide world (Sir George had wisely not allowed him straight into the family business before gaining experience outside it), Jeremy had quickly made up for lost time. absorbing everything around him with a speed that was almost unnatural.

The only thing Jeremy really loved was his bloody dog!

Gina went into the bathroom, took off her clothes and stepped into the shower. She had already showered twice today. It wasn't that she was obsessively fastidious, it was just something to do. She was bored with reading, bored with music, bored with everything. She needed a sensation that was purely physical. So she took another shower.

She had just turned off the water, when she heard the insistent bell of the phone.

The dog yelped as, rushing to the phone, she stepped on his outstretched paw. She cursed as the bell stopped just as she reached for the receiver, her left hand still clutching the purple bath-towel to her body. Ignoring the animal's whimpers, she lifted the receiver and tapped out the number of Jeremy's direct line to the boardroom, her wet hair dripping spikily on to her shoulders.

She let out a sigh tinged both with relief and impatience when her husband answered.

'What time do you call this?' he snapped. His reply did not please her, for she began to pace, the earpiece in one hand, the handset clutched to her breast with the other, still supporting the towel.

'I was in the shower when the phone rang. It stopped before I could get to it. I thought it was you. Silly, silly me!'

She could feel rage welling hotly up inside her and her

stomach spasmed. She sat down on the telephone seat. 'I don't care if I'm interrupting a board meeting. I'm fed up, fed up, d'you hear? I'm stuck here inside these four walls waiting for you and just the dog for company. No, I don't want to go and talk to your mother. No, I haven't fed the dog. He's your bloody dog. You come home and feed him.'

The 'bloody dog' surveyed her mournfully with soft brown eyes, then got to its feet and slunk away, its tail between its legs. She glowered after it.

'What's so important anyway, that it needs to be discussed at this time of the night? Tell me, what's so important? What are you plotting, Jeremy, the downfall of Elizabeth Carlton?'

Her stomach spasmed again, as she realised what she had said. Because she wasn't supposed to know about things like that. Matters of business were not her concern. Jeremy had always made that fact abundantly clear to her. It was another way of ostracising her, of keeping her down.

'I didn't mean that,' she said quickly, 'Jeremy, are you there . . .' She trailed off, as she realised she was talking to herself. 'You *dare* to put the phone down on me,' she hissed.

She was sorry now that she had retracted her accusation about Elizabeth Carlton. She liked Liz. Liked her exubereance and directness and did not understand Jeremy's animosity towards her. In that she could identify. If she envied Liz just a little because she had achieved, by hard work and application, what Gina had gained by marriage, it did not alter her regard for the other woman. Gina was the first to admit she was a little mercenary, nevertheless she had a strong sense of fair play about certain matters.

And Jeremy did not play fair. Not ever. Not with her and not with Liz.

She had overheard things. One or two vague remarks to his father. A telephone conversation, which from his tone, she suspected was to a woman. A woman he seemed to know just a little too well for Gina's liking. A woman who had his confidence.

There was nothing she could actually put her finger on. But she sensed that Liz was threatened. Wished she had the courage to warn the other woman of her suspicions.

As she rose to her feet, the towel slipped from her fingers. Catching sight of herself in the wall mirror, clad in nothing but a pair of high-heeled fluffy slippers, she inspected her body, critically, objectively.

She had a great figure for a thirty-year-old. Not an ounce of superfluous flesh anywhere, breasts firm and high, trim waist, legs long and lean, newly waxed, bottle-bronzed. She took good care of herself. Three sessions a week working out at the studio in Floral Street. Tap on Mondays at the village community centre. Fruit, crispbread, cottage cheese and no chocolates. And it showed!

'What a damned waste of time,' she intoned to herself and began sensuously tracing one scarlet fingernail slowly from the smooth valley between her breasts, over the slight swell of her stomach, allowing it to rest momentarily in the bush of pubic hair, which was slightly darker than the moist, highlighted tresses on her head. 'Who notices, except me?' She ached. For Jeremy, or just for a man. A warm, kind, loving man.

The phone rang again. For a crazy moment, she thought it might be Jeremy, calling back to apologise. Then laughed inwardly at her own foolishness.

'Hi, Gina.' Alexia Potts's bright voice brought her down to earth. 'I've been trying to get through to you for ages. Martin was supposed to call for me at eight. I can't imagine what's happened to him. Is Jeremy home?'

'They're at a board meeting, Alexia, playing tough guys. You know the scene. James Cagney and Humphrey Bogart in Savile Row suits.' She laughed falsely at the forced humour which disguised her hurt.

'Who?' asked Alexia innocently.

'Never mind, Alex. You're too young to know or understand.'

'Only joking, Gina. I watch the old movies on television too, while I'm waiting for Martin to remember we have a date. Playing tough guys, are they. I only wish Martin would come here and play tough guys with me.' Alexia sounded wistful. Sadly Gina wondered how long it would take till the boredom and loneliness of being involved with a Pascall would fester into resentment and acrimony.

'We must meet soon for lunch,' said Alexia before she rang off.

Gina towelled her hair into fluffy dryness, all the while watching herself in the mirror. Then, trailing the towel behind her, making believe it was a mink and that Jeremy was escorting her to a very important function, she catwalked into the bedroom.

10

'Dinah, I'm taking the afternoon off, both today and tomorrow. I'll see all the morning applicants for the shipping position, but could you contact my afternoon appointments and put them off till next week?'

Dinah raised her eyebrows. 'Yes, Mrs Carlton,' she murmured demurely. 'Oh, by the way, I have taken the liberty of making an additional appointment for you this morning.'

'Oh Dinah!' snapped Liz crossly, 'you know how busy my schedule is at the moment.'

'Yes, I know Mrs Carlton.' Dinah's tone was conciliatory. 'But I really think you should see this young man. He's not on the short list because his application arrived too late to include him in the first round of interviews. However, his experience seems excellent. Apparently in a previous post he was involved in selling shipping space to the American Military.'

'Household removals, I suppose,' muttered Liz, 'An entirely separate field, Dinah. Not in the least applicable to our requirements.'

'But he's very bright,' insisted Dinah with rather more enthusiasm than the situation warranted. 'His CV is superlative. Nine O levels, five As and he has an HNC in business management.'

'When is he coming?'

'I slipped him in first, so he should arrive on the dot at nine-thirty.'

'All right Dinah,' sighed Liz resignedly, 'but don't you dare ever pull one like that on me again.'

'Sorry, Mrs Carlton.' Nervously Dinah tucked a loose strand of light hair back into her chignon. Liz stared fixedly at the blank white sheet of her desk blotter. During the whole of their exchange she had not looked directly at her secretary once.

The intercom buzzed.

'OK, Johnny,' said Dinah, then to Liz, 'he's on his way up.'

'Let me have his details.'

She glanced quickly at the top of the form. The words leapt out at her from the foolscap printed sheet. No, it couldn't be! Edward. Edward Smith.

Sweat broke out on her forehead in tiny beads. Her hands shook. Stop being stupid, Liz. Edward was a common enough Christian name. She checked his date of birth. Twenty-four. There might be quite a number of twenty-four-year-olds called Edward. After all, wasn't that just about the age of the Prince? There was nothing like the birth of a royal baby for setting name trends.

Dinah's buzzer interrupted Liz's flow of reasoning. The next moment, he was standing there before her. Lean and angular in a dark navy business suit, crisp white cuffs erupting from the heavily buttoned sleeves. Light hair slicked back, like the new wave of pop stars. Same hollow cheeks. Same pallid skin. Same shifty grey eyes that glinted at her from their deeply shadowed sockets. Insignificant eyebrows that gave the impression of a too-high forehead. Everything about him was predatory and supremely in charge.

'Good morning, Mrs Carlton.' He offered her his hand. She stared at it with distaste. To think that she had once allowed that hand to caress her. To caress her so intimately. It was a weak, ineffectual hand, not a sensitive hand, like her Eddie's hand.

'What do you think you're doing here? How dare you gatecrash your way into my office! How dare you!'

'I'm only after a job,' he replied with contrived innocence.

'GET OUT,' she yelled, no longer caring if Dinah overheard her, no longer caring about Dinah's opinion. Her image was now of secondary importance. The only thing that mattered in the world was to get this loathsome creature out of her office, off her territory, by whatever means she found necessary.

'Come on, Liz. You're gorgeous when you're cross, but I can do without the hassle.'

'Touché,' she barked. 'Now get *out*!'

'I need a job,' he held out his hands, palms uppermost, imploringly. 'My qualifications are excellent. Just look at my CV.'

'I don't believe a word of it. Now, *skedaddle*.'

She rose, her palms on her desk, her face pushed forward, sandy eyes blazing with fury. She had intimidated many a cheeky upstart in the past with such a forceful pose, but he merely settled himself in her visitor's chair and proceeded to drape his long legs across the corner of her desk, so that his Gucci shoes rested in her filing tray.

She sat down. 'Please,' she whispered, 'please leave me alone.'

'That's not what you said when you came back to my place,' he leered. Nonchalantly he extracted a long Panatella from his pocket, tapped it and lit it. 'Of course, what I really need in this situation,' he commented, 'is a Hamlet.'

'Look here, Eddie,' she began reasonably, 'I admit I made a mistake and I'm sorry if I've hurt you. But it's over now. I'm just not interested in little boys.'

She sensed that the sudden flash of anger that tightened his thin lips and creased the protruding flesh around his eye-sockets was the first genuine response she had evoked in him. He had a weakness. She knew that, only she had temporarily forgotten. People could be exploited through their weaknesses, she knew that too well enough. It was worth the risk.

'Why don't you just clear off, little chap, and find someone your own age? Someone who doesn't know too much. Someone you can handle.'

His feet withdrew from her desk-top so fast she was hardly aware of it. Suddenly he was on his feet, leaning over her desk until their faces almost touched. His breath smelt rank. She held his eyes, steeled herself not to move, fearing his anger, misplaced as it was. Gradually, he brought his anger under control, slowly his eyes took on the mantle of their original slyness.'

86

'I can't leave you alone, Liz. You're so desirable, *such* a challenge. All I need is one more chance to prove myself. Relax, Liz, we've got plenty of time. Eddie and Elizabeth! How well our names go together, don't you think? Tell you what, why don't I take you for a ride on my motor-bike? Don't you like riding pillion?'

She couldn't take any more.

She didn't want to hear about his motor-bike.

She didn't want to know what colour it was.

She didn't need to know what make it was.

Her chair tipped back as she rose and crashed to the floor. In her haste, she banged her thigh hard on the desk-corner. He started towards her, but she skipped past him and she was through the door that connected her and Dinah's offices. Her flight was stopped short by a sudden dark force. She cried out. Gradually her eyes focused on the yellow and black knot of Jeremy Pascall's old school tie.

'What on earth's going on?' exclaimed Jeremy, exasperated. 'Who is this man?'

Liz's mouth worked uselessly, as she stared up into Jeremy Pascall's flared nostrils. She was distantly aware of Eddie standing behind her, his hand on her arm, as always, marking possession.

'I'm just on old friend of Liz's. Sorry old man. Just a small disagreement.' And in a trice, he was gone.

'Mrs Carlton,' Jeremy Pascall spat out her name as if it was a curse. 'Mrs Carlton, it is quite bad enough to know of the rumours of your young lover hanging around in our foyer, but it is a sorry state of affairs to find him here, in your office, involving you in personal petty squabbles.'

'I'm sorry, Mr Pascall,' Liz stuttered. 'I'm sorry, believe me, but you don't really understand . . .'

'I understand well enough,' retorted Jeremy, his lips barely moving, 'and I would strongly suggest that you put an end to it once and for all, before my father gets to hear about it.

Jeremy Pascall turned – literally – on his heel and marched out of Dinah's office without a backward glance. He was just like the Gestapo in all those old war films. Liz shuddered.

The buzzer sounded again. 'Dinah,' croaked Liz, 'if this is my next candidate, could you take him to the canteen for a coffee? Give me about twenty minutes.'

'Of course, Mrs Carlton,' agreed Dinah sympathetically. 'Goodness me, everything happens all at once, doesn't it!'

Liz was late for her appointment. She drove as fast as she felt to be within reasonable safety limits. Since this was some twenty-five miles per hour over the speed limit, her eye was constantly on her rearview mirror, checking that she was not being pursued by an eager traffic cop. She did not fear reprisals from the police, only the loss of her time. A mother's time was never more valuable than when her children were at risk.

Mrs Margaret Hawkes was the epitome of Liz's mental image of the old-fashioned, archetypal headmistress. She had black hair, cut severely short, so that it showed a horizontal crease in her neck as Liz had followed her into her office. She had *waited*, she told Liz, but she had had *pressing* matters to deal with in the staff room.

She enunciated in a shrill, jarring voice, in sudden bursts, so that every point she made was an explosion from her pale, pursed lips. Obviously she believed that one spoke to parents in exactly the same tone as one spoke in order to subdue their children.

'Mrs Carlton,' she began, as she took her position behind her huge, antique desk. 'I am afraid I do not have much time. since you were expected twenty minutes ago . . .'

'I'm sorry, Mrs Hawkes,' said Liz, standing on the red and black rug by the desk, where she imagined countless pupils had stood before her, shivering in their shoes. 'I was unavoidably detained.' She waited for Margaret Hawkes to invite her to sit. Since no such courtesy was forthcoming, she pulled up a chair, positioning it carefully to Mrs Hawkes's side, so that the older woman had to turn to speak to her.

Liz had read all about 'power positions' and no one, least of all this trumped-up schoolmarm, was going to treat her like a naughty child.

'I too have a tight ship to run.' Liz was faintly amused at the petulance in Mrs Hawkes's tone. 'Would you kindly state your business?'

'I'm worried about my son,' began Liz.

'Yes, I have his file here. I see that you are a single-parent family. Yes, Mrs Carlton, as we all know very well, the consequences of broken homes on our children do leave scars, don't they?'

'I am a widow, Mrs Hawkes,' Liz pointed out.

'Hmm, yes.'

'And in any case, my visit is nothing to do with Robbie's mental stability.'

'Would you please get to the point, Mrs Carlton?'

Liz valiantly stifled a sudden impulse to wallop this old biddy over the top of her head with her handbag, reminding herself that she needed her co-operation.

'My son has been harassed by a man who waited for him outside the school gates last term.'

'Then why haven't we been informed before?'

'I wasn't aware of the fact till my son told me yesterday.' Liz suddenly felt somewhat inadequate, could almost imagine her writing in Robbie's file, 'lack of communication between child and his mother', as soon as she left the office. She pressed on. 'Obviously other children besides my son might be at risk. I feel it would be advisable to inform the police and I naturally think such an action might come more favourably from you, as headmistress.'

Her overt flattery in implying that Mrs Hawkes's approach might be more seriously received than her own, worked as she had intended. Margaret Hawkes's mouth relaxed from its expression of total disapproval into one of mild severity.

'I shall, of course, deal with the matter.' Liz breathed a sigh of relief. If she was any judge of character, Mrs Hawkes would not only inform the police, but she would bring the matter up at the staff meeting, the PTA meeting, and the governors' meeting. As far as Liz was concerned, the more people who knew of and were concerned about Robbie's danger, the better protected her son would be.

'However,' continued the headmistress, 'I must point out to you that the safety of the children once they leave the school gates rests squarely with the parents.'

'I quite agree, Mrs Hawkes. I did think that you might be able to suggest another mother who might be prepared to collect my son for me. For the appropriate payment, of course. You see, I work.'

'I would have thought that would be of secondary importance under the circumstances.'

'Mrs Hawkes,' Liz fought to keep the irritation from her voice, 'if I lose my job, then I shall hardly be in a position to meet your extremely high fees.'

The headmistress spluttered. Liz sat patiently, her hands resting motionless on her handbag, immobile, poised and wondering how many parents had been reduced to cringing ghosts of their former selves by this old harridan. She would like to give her a piece of her mind, but Robbie was happy at the school, loved his teachers, was making progress. It was worth the small sacrifice of biting her tongue.

'Try Mrs Doughty,' said the older woman eventually. 'Mrs Robin Doughty. She's the mother of Benedict Doughty, a *friend* of your son.' Her intimation that Liz was unlikely to be the sort of parent who knew about her son's friends did not escape her. 'Oh Ben, of course,' she rejoindered, flashing the headmistress her most glamorous smile to disguise her discomfort, her sudden sense of wretchedness. 'Thank you so much. Goodbye now.'

'Good-day, Mrs Carlton.' She smacked Robbie's file closed as if to speed Liz on her way.

So Robbie had a special friend called Ben. She must ask Robbie about Ben. Oh dear, maybe Margaret Hawkes had assessed her more accurately than she had judged herself.

Liz waited with a group of mothers outside the school railings. Perhaps their children were younger than Robbie. Boys were so sensitive about being collected by their mothers. It demeaned their masculinity, exposed them to the tauntings of their peers. Especially when they were ten years old.

She watched carefully, her eyes searching for any man remotely resembling Eddie Smith. She stiffened as she saw someone loitering by a tree, one of a row of limes that marched up this pleasant avenue. But it was only a man allowing his dog to relieve itself in the surrounding earth.

Eventually the children spilled out of the school doors and the noise of their whoops and chatter filled the air. Robbie bounded up to her. He didn't look demeaned by her being there, only terribly happy to see her.

'Robbie,' she said as he bounced along beside her, 'who's Benedict? Is he your best friend at school?'

'Yuk,' Robbie pulled a face, the point of his long pink tongue curling round his chin. 'He's *wet*. I can't *stand* him.'

She knew she should have scolded him for being so uncharitable, But she didn't. She laughed and hugged him, twirled his forelock affectionately around her finger. 'You'd have told me about him if he was your friend, wouldn't you?'

''Course I would.'

'But you wouldn't mind if I arranged for his mother to collect you after school? So you won't have to worry about the man.' She held her breath, waiting for him to express indignation and horror. But he acquiesced readily enough.

'OK,' he said simply.

Her heart went out to him. His easy acceptance was an indication of how uneasy he felt, how threatened. The anger rose inside her. She was sure it was Eddie. But how could she prove it? And what would be the consequences for them all if she did? She, too, as very afraid of Eddie.

'Robbie, I don't want you to worry about this, because you'll be safe now. But tell me, exactly what did this man say to you?'

'He kept asking what happened to my father.'

'You must never talk to strangers. I've told you that a thousand times.'

'But I didn't. It's just that he walked along beside me and kept on asking. On and on. But I couldn't have told him, anyway, could I Mummy? I don't know, do I?' he gazed trustfully up at her for confirmation.

'Your father died of a heart attack, Robbie,' she told him

91

gently, 'without pain and very quickly. And he certainly would not wish for you to be worrying about that now.'

'All right, then, I won't,' said Robbie brightly. Liz never ceased to be enchanted at the manner in which he took everything at face value, never looking for problems. He was an open little boy, without guile or cunning.

It was a pity that he would have to change and that she, for his own protection, would have to help him in the transition. It's a big, hard world out there, Robbie, full of people with whom one has to battle on their own terms. You learn about it at school, Robbie. It's called the lowest common denominator.

11

On the drive back, Liz thought over her life and the influence upon it of her three husbands.

From husband to husband, she had gone up in the world, just a bit. Not that she had planned it that way. Not knowingly. She hadn't been as calculating as that in those days.

For the most part, she had followed her instincts. Only later had life finally taught her the value of strategy, the inevitability of consequences.

Eddie, despite all the beauty and glamour of his memory, further inspired by a young girl's dream and softened and romanticised by time, had been a simple plumber's apprentice.

Not the type to start up his own business. Eddie wasn't ambitious, except when it came to his motor-bike. Eddie's only ambition was to be the speed-king of his gang. Superlative, unchallenged, unchallengeable. To Eddie, such things were inherently masculine, as to many young lads of his age.

She had met him at the local Palais. The 'fleapit' as it was known locally. On Saturday mornings, he took her to the Ice Cream Parlour in the Old Kent Road. The Ice Cream Parlour at that time was definitely the in-place for Saturday mornings for all the local young rebels, a fact endorsed by the scores of motor-bikes illegally parked thereabouts, a sore point for the despairing local constabulary.

Love's young dream had been cruelly put down by Liz's own mother, who had spotted her young daughter and her Lothario while doing her weekly shopping. She had bustled past, pretending not to notice them, but later had challenged her daughter.

'Who was the long-haired yob I saw you walking down the road with?' she had inquired with heavy sarcasm, 'holding hands?'

At the time, Liz had not recognised the apparent contempt in her voice for what it was. Envy. Jealousy. Had, for once, because the relationship was so new, so special, so tender, been too embarrassed to reply.

They hadn't been exactly over the moon about the marriage either. Except Liz was becoming such a handful, it would be a good thing when she was no longer their responsibility.

Only now could Liz begin to sympathise with her mother's disparagment of herself and Eddie. It had never been easy for Liz's mother, living her own life of servility to her boorish, pub-orientated husband. A life lived in an overcrowded council estate with all the accompanying problems that such a life encompassed.

After Eddie's death, she had gone home to live for a while. She felt bored, restricted and depressed. Finally she persuaded her aunt to lend her her ancient portable and she taught herself to type with two fingers.

After two years, in the summer of nineteen-seventy, she decided that stacking shelves in the local supermarket was not all it was made out to be. She applied for a job in a large advertising agency in Holborn. As a secretary! Failed her test abysmally, but they needed a receptionist. A looker. A charmer.

And so she met her second husband, John Adams.

The company was an American-owned outfit, very progressive at that time in comparison to its European counterparts. Its middle-management were treated and rewarded most generously. John, a rising and talented young copywriter with more than a flair for art, showed Liz how the middle-class lived. A large, four-bedroomed semi-detached in Kent, their avenue lined with laburnum in the spring, gardens alive with magnolia and conifers, grass verges wider than the pavements. No yellow lines in the road.

Neighbours who dropped in for coffee. Jumble sales and Tupperware parties and Young Wives groups.

Suburbia at its most comfortable.

Ten months later, Charlotte was born.

Life was fairly idyllic for three years. But when the novelty wore off, the novelty of having money and beautiful friends and lots of spare time, she decided she didn't really love John. She found him exciting, but she didn't love him.

Maybe it was because he was such a prig.

Maybe it was because he had never really been her friend.

Sure, he liked to show her off. Complimented her when she looked nice. Never kept her short of money. Was attractive, presentable, interesting.

It was just that she had had the feeling any woman with a nice figure and a winsome personality would have suited John just as well as she. She wasn't *special*. She thought she should be. Everyone needed to be special.

Like a boil about to burst, the situation finally came to a head on the eve of that fatal wedding anniversary. Their third. The day that John had unceremoniously wrapped his car around the lamp-post.

The eve of that wedding anniversary, he had taken her to a business function. The Agency's Annual Ladies' Night. That was a joke for a start! More business dealings were wrapped up on that night than at any other time of the year. All on the pretext of cosseting the ladies!

She remembered it all so vividly. The silver embossed invitations, boasting the name of a top London hotel. Requesting that they wear evening dress. Two bands, a cabaret, carriages at one.

The gilded, glamorous ballroom, reminiscent of the faded glories of the past. John, tall and blond. John and his cronies, all smart, slick-talking businessmen.

They were greeted by the chairman's lackey and announced to the gathering. They had their photographs taken along with everyone else, the men resplendent in frilly shirts and stiff bow ties. Their ladies sparkled at their sides, baring their teeth in the obligatory, slightly self-conscious manner of females aware of their roles as ornamental appendages to their mates.

There were few people there that Liz knew from her working days. The Agency had a fast turn-around of staff and most of her old acquaintances had left or been sacked. Only the directors and the senior management remained constant.

In the beginning, John had sipped on a Perrier water, anxious not to start drinking in earnest too soon. He had to keep his head clear during this important function. Liz, however, already bored, had no such compunction. She was aware of the warning in John's eyes, but ignored it.

God, she had thought those speeches would never end. It seemed to her that the so-called Ladies' Night was little more than an excuse for the senior men to hand each other rhetorical bouquets. Everyone had to jump up and down like yo-yos, toasting this and toasting that, amidst much back-slapping, hand-clapping and 'hear hears'.

To be fair, there had been the obligatory toast to the ladies and their charm, the usual ladies' gifts, in this case a delicate Wedgwood vase, and then the sprays of autumn flowers for the Chairman's wife and the Organiser's mistress. To their credit, all the ladies managed to look suitably entranced, as custom demanded. It had been such a relief when it was finally all over and the band struck up a foxtrot.

'Why do they always go to the loo en masse?' inquired John in amusement, as the other women at their table trooped off, clutching their inadequate evening bags. Liz glared at him. Why was he always so damned patronising?

'It's another social occasion to us girls,' she told him, her grammar slipping, as it always did when she became inebriated. 'A chance to dish the dirt.'

John rocked back in his chair, puffing on a cigar and eyeing her disapprovingly as he recognised the signs of her deterioration. Surely she wasn't going to let him down tonight. The one night of the year when it was so important to impress.

Clients, potential clients, staff, his superiors at the Agency.

They were all here. And Liz, damn her, was getting sloshed and it wasn't even seven-thirty.

The meal, when it arrived, was a feast. And finally the management and their wives were replete, having worked their way through five courses, gazpacho, rollmops, Duck à L'Orange, followed by a sponge, meringue and cream concoction cleverly moulded to resemble a swan, this last refused by Liz, since she felt the calorific content did not justify the pleasure she would derive from eating it. Finally there were grapes, cheese and biscuits.

Liz felt better having eaten. But John, tense from worrying about being shown up by a drunken wife, had merely picked at his food. For the same reason, he had made up for his earlier restraint and downed several double whiskies, chased down by an assortment of liqueurs. By the time the tables were cleared and the DJ replaced by a live band, their positions were reversed. Liz's head was clear. John, probably for the first time in his perfect life, was decidedly the worse for wear, his belly full of wine, whisky and Bailey's.

'I'm going to dance with my wife.'

Liz started and straightened her back. Yes, it was John's voice and not just a figment of her imagination. The bushy blond brows were raised, the steely eyes a little glassy. The cleft in his left cheek deepened as he smiled, no, *leered* at her. There was a claret stain just beneath the knot of his bow tie.

John leaned over and flipped her under the chin with his index finger, running his tongue lecherously along his bottom lip. Surprised, Liz cleared her throat. Someone giggled. A fluttering started up in the pit of Liz's stomach.

That some old conflict. He still turned her on. No matter how detached his day-to-day treatment of her, just one knowing look still drove her wild.

She slipped into his arms. They danced silently for a while, in perfect rhythm. She knew they were a stunning couple. In those days she wore her hair long and straight, as Charlotte did now. Her dress was black and slinky, like her hair. As the tempo changed to a waltz, she encircled his body with both arms, possessively, marking him as her mate, feeling the music, feeling him. The hardness of his erection against her body almost brought her to orgasm

'This way,' she felt his spittle as his lips moved against her ear and she followed him, half-protesting, out of the ballroom, along the plushly carpeted corridor, and into the swish reception, where red velvet drapes vied for attention with huge, apparently natural plastic cheeseplants on low glass-top tables.

'We want a room,' he demanded, somewhat aggressively, making the clerk's hackles rise.

'Have you made a reservation, sir?'

97

'No. We thought our friends had done it for us,' interrupted Liz. 'We've just found out they didn't.'

'Where's your luggage, sir?'

'We don't need luggage. We sleep in the raw,' announced John scathingly. Two impossibly glamorous young women were standing behind them and they began to titter. They were joined by a couple of balding, bespectacled middle-aged men, who bore them away, still twittering like a couple of exotic birds of paradise.

Liz drew a deep breath. 'It's in the car. We'll bring it in later.' Her tone brooked no argument. 'My husband is unwell. If you can't help, then I want to see the manager.'

'Perhaps you would care to leave your driving licence, sir? Just for identification purposes, you understand?'

Liz began to feel annoyed at the way in which the clerk continued to address John, who was obviously incapable of making any sense, whilst she fumed and struggled. 'John,' she prompted, but John merely grinned blankly at her.

She fished in his inside jacket pocket for the necessary security. Tried his other pockets. Then his trouser pockets. He did not object, just stood there grinning at her in a lascivious manner meant to convey the sexual kick he was getting out of her probings.

'John, where is your driving licence?' she cried at last, stifling an impulse to walk away and leave him there, sexually aroused though she was.

Eventually she located the elusive licence inside his wallet and the clerk took the licence reluctantly, muttering about people who could not hold their liquor. Liz silenced him with a look. But as he called the porter and handed him their key, her excitement was intense.

It was all she could manage to keep herself upright and guide her errant husband safely to the lift and along the corridor. The porter kept glancing back nervously, as if he expected John to swoop upon his person at any moment and commit some unspeakable outrage.

'Be quiet,' muttered Liz, pushing him upright again as he lolled against her, murmuring his lustful intentions.

'Just wait till I get you alone,' announced John loudly. I'm going to show you. Man, am I going to show you!' The porter looked askance as if unsure as to whom John's intentions were addressed.

'Be quiet,' repeated Liz.

'I am. I am definitely going to show you.'

'I know, but do let's keep it to ourselves.'

'Thank you, sir. And *madam*,' said the porter, looking hard at Liz. She did not smile, rummaged in her bag for a tip. Deliberately, she under-tipped.

'Have a nice day,' the porter said affably, unconcerned.

'Cheeky bastard!' grunted John.

Their room, she was surprised to find, was quite homely in its décor, and florally co-ordinated. Pale blue Laura Ashley wallpaper, a chintzy bedspread and matching curtains. Unless you looked out of the window, you would never guess this was the ninth floor of a top London hotel.

She checked to see if the orchids in the blue porcelain vase were real. They were.

Before she could pursue her investigations any further, John was making his presence felt. He stood behind her as she inspected the flowers, cupped each full breast in a large hand, the hardness of his penis grumbling into the hardness of her coccyx. She could feel the heat of his breath on the back of her neck.

She groaned.

She had the feeling that if she moved away from him, he would fall over. 'Are you all right?' she inquired anxiously, more out of concern for her own imminent gratification than his personal welfare.

'Never been better.'

'Actions speak louder than words,' she informed him.

He managed with some difficulty to hook his fingers under the straps of her long black evening dress and peel it slowly down to her thighs.

'You dirty cow, you've got no drawers on,' he was slurring his words now. The 's' came out as a 'sssh'. He twisted her round, sank on to his knees and stuck his tongue in her navel.

The erotic shock made her recoil. She fell back against the

99

table and the porcelain vase crashed to the floor, shattering into a thousand pieces.

Somehow, they made it back to the bed, she almost tripping over the black silk garment trapping her ankles. The gold sandals dropped to the floor as she lay on her back and the evening dress crumpled into a black silken puddle on top of them.

Grunting, John struggled to his feet. Sweat stood out on his brow. A big bang of his tousled blond hair clung to the wetness of his forehead like a large ear of wheat flattened by the rain. He looked like a pirate, she thought, all he needed was a bandanna. Suddenly she was glad that this beautiful male animal was hers.

'Now I'm going to show you,' he announced, clumsily struggling with his jacket, then fiddling unsuccessfully with his belt.

'I know,' she gasped, wriggling herself into a more co-operative position for the impending violation. She held her breath. She waited. It seemed a long time coming. She opened her eyes.

'Let me help you with your belt,' she stretched out her hands, trying to sit up.

'This ish it. Here I come,' he was muttering hopefully, his eyes glazed, his breathing laboured. Then his jaw dropped as he swayed and a bewildered expression ghosted his features before he burped loudly and collapsed in an unconscious heap beside her on the bed.

She sat for a time, her head in her hands, then reluctantly showered to refresh herself and put her dress back on. Then she set about undoing the belt that had given him so much trouble and with a great deal of exertion, puffing and panting, she peeled off his trousers and underpants, shoving him this way and that to facilitate the process. Next came his shirt. When he was completely naked except for his wedding ring, she stood and stared down at him impassively.

His nudity no longer turned her on. It surprised her that it didn't. In fact, he did not appear at all glamorous now, his head lolling on one side, his mouth open, the sides of his nose retracting and releasing as he snored.

The golden skin was now deadpan, pale and sickly in the harsh light that shone directly on to him from the reading lamp. The cause of all the trouble, that vital yet unreliable piece of flesh he called his manhood, now lay apologetically, shrunken and white in the crease of his thigh, admidst the juices of his final, involuntary spasm. Like a dead thing. Beyond awakening.

She laughed. It pleased her to do so. She laughed again. It was a shrill laugh, not her normal throaty chuckle.

She gathered together all his clothes and climbed unsteadily on to a chair, released the louvre windows and slid each item, one by one, between the slats. She took a long time doing this. She needed to extract every ounce of satisfaction from this act of defiance. She needed to purge herself.

It was like the death of a bitter love affair she had endured as a teenager, when she had ritually destroyed, one by one, all the photographs of her lover that she had so caringly preserved during their one year of passion.

In the early hours of one winter's morning, she had burnt every shred of evidence of their affair in the empty grate, watching the happy images curl as she set light to them, one by one, just as she was savouring each moment now, peering through the slats as yet another item of John's apparel was seized by the wind and billowed downwards, outlined by lights from windows as it descended to the street below.

When she had finished, she closed the louvres, stepped down from the chair and replaced it at the vanity mirror. She carefully avoided glancing in the direction of John's prostrate form. Biting her lip in concentration, she renewed her mascara and eyeshadow, then slipped quietly out of the room to join the others.

No one seemed to have missed them. The ladies at the top table smiled at her uncertainly as she passed them, but did not speak. As for the other executives and their wives, they were all on the floor, bopping away with great abandon, good food, free-flowing drink and raucous music having cut them loose from normal inhibitions. She felt pretty relaxed herself now.

It was done. The end of an era. She knew she would never forgive him. She had always forgiven him before because he had been so fanciable, because he was her husband and a good father to Charlotte. But tonight she had seen him in a different light. He had lost her respect. It had been the proverbial last straw.

In that, there was a freedom of sorts. Finally, after a time of fluctuating emotions, she was free. It was like having a clamouring growth in your insides and when they took it away, the pain went, but so did your soul so that you stopped feeling altogether. Thus did Liz's purging and subsequent sense of alienation leave her unresistingly flat.

Why was she still here? God, she was bored with the whole set-up. She rose, flicking back her hair in a defiant gesture. Unsteadily she threaded her way back through the now haphazard confusion of chairs, people and personal belongings. The funny hats and the streamers had come out now. Any minute, the balloons would descend from the huge net hung about the ceiling. Just like the local Palais, where she had first met Eddie.

Funny how none of this seemed anything to do with her any more. All these strange, noisy people, managing to have a good time, being rude and flippant and silly and . . . just people.

She had left him there and taken a taxi home. She did not see him again until the following evening, by which time she had worked herself up into a state of ripe fury. She needed to feel furious with him if she was going to give him his marching orders.

She had *tried* to be a good wife, hadn't she? Tried to love him. Tried to be passionate and caring. But he had blown it. She could never feel the same way about him again.

She tried to analyse what had changed.

There had been no rapport between them for some time, except sexually. And he had made himself ridiculous in her eyes, physically ridiculous.

How flimsy were the threads of sexual attraction when unaccompanied by mutual regard and affection. That was all it had taken, the sight of her husband reduced to a pale, incompetent, snivelling apology for a man, to release her from her chains.

When he walked in, he was wearing new clothes, beige slacks

102

and a chunky green sweater she had never seen before. He was completely in control. Unconcerned. His hair was sleek, his golden skin had assumed its former natural glow. He poured himself a drink, ignoring her. She stared at the television unseeingly, waiting for a sudden verbal attack that did not come. It unnerved her. She felt as if she wasn't actually there. Nobody could be as cool as that!

Nobody except John.

John, who had planned his revenge in a way that only John could. He knew she needed his physical love. So he did not give it to her. He tried to take it from her.

She fought him like a cat as he suddenly grabbed her and forced her down on to the carpet, his hand pressing around the back of her neck. She struggled. Panted. Bit and beat him with her fists. Instinctively, she stifled her screams, aware of Charlotte, sleeping peacefully upstairs. Charlotte, whom she loved enough to endure his attack in painful silence.

He was tearing at her clothes. Violently she lashed out at him. Hit her head hard on the leg of the table and lay momentarily stunned. It was enough for him.

When she first cried out for Eddie, it was a cry from the heart. A cry of desperation. And it made him stop. She was mildly startled to see the pain, the horror in his eyes. Sensed it was only his ego that was injured rather than any sensibilities related to love and fidelity. It didn't matter. She had found a way to hurt him, to pay him back for hurting her.

Vengefully, deliberately, she repeated Eddie's name, over and over and over. Eddie. . . Eddie. . . Eddie. . . she chanted, never taking her eyes off him for a moment. Watching the dull, defeated expression on his face. He made a sort of choking sound, struggled to his feet, fumbling to adjust his clothes. Beaten, he stumbled from the room. Beaten and for once, vulnerable.

No, it hadn't been at all the way she had later explained to Patrick. She hadn't been consumed by passion, drunken or otherwise. Her mind was as clear as a bell.

Still, he had paid, hadn't he? Paid with his life. Poor John! She hadn't intended him to die so violently amidst the mangled wreckage of a lamp-post and a car. But when they dragged him from the muddle of twisted metal, his body, not surprisingly, was unrecognisable.

John Adams left his wife and child well-protected financially, if not exactly wealthy. Charlotte eventually went off to school and Liz had more leisure than she could manage.

Till she saw the card in the newsagent's window.

Part-time Typist Wanted.

Michael Carlton was a professor at Oxford University, and a Doctor of Philosophy in Chemistry. He wanted his thesis on the use of computers in drug research typed on a word-procesor, which he lent to Liz. She made a terrible mess of the typing, was so ashamed that she paid for a secretarial bureau to retype it.

Michael was *so* impressed, both by the typing and by Liz.

It took him two months to get her pregnant with Robbie, four months to be persuaded to leave his wife for her and, three months after Robbie's birth, they were married and went to live in Oxford, near his college.

Michael was fifteen years older than Liz and old for his age. it took her a week to discover that although she was tremendously fond of him, she didn't find him exciting any more. And his Oxford friends were a deplorable grind.

Michael died when Robbie was twenty-two months old.

He died of a heart attack. Just as she had told Robbie.

Well. . . almost. . .

But she didn't want to think about that right now.

12

'Patrick, you're so *huggable*.'

Charlotte was playing the coquette. She sat on Patrick's knee, chatting animatedly, her big dark eyes full of dancing lights. She resembled a cheerleader, in crisp, white, high-cut shorts and a red and white polka-dot vest, cut away from the shoulders. Her slender arm was coiled around his neck, her immature thighs flattened as they pressed into his lap, so that they seemed fuller.

He had telephoned from a call-box. In ten minutes he was on the doorstep, seeming larger than before, more eager, more intense. The children were delighted. Especially Charlotte.

Liz was feeling slightly uncomfortable, as if she, not Charlotte, were the intruder, the usurper. Robbie, disgusted with Charlotte's performance, sat cross-legged in front of the television, watching a children's Saturday morning magazine programme.

'Charlotte! Do give Patrick a break. You're nearly strangling him!' There was an edge to Liz's voice, but Charlotte merely giggled. 'Patrick doesn't mind, do you Patrick?' She regarded him through lowered lashes, teasing, twirling a tress of her silky black hair around her finger. 'Do you think I'd look more sophisticated with my hair up?' To demonstrate, she grasped the silky hank and coiled it on to the top of her head.

Aghast, Liz sat on the edge of her chair. What an act! She took in Charlotte's adolescent smoothness, the small dimpled pad of her chin, the way her under-chin lifted in profile, then swept downwards into the long clean line of her slender neck. The slight tilt of her adorable snub nose.

'I think it might look very nice when you're a couple of years older,' said Patrick diplomatically. 'Now come along, young lady, your mother has asked you three times to take your brother to his judo lesson.'

'He's old enough to go by himself,' pouted Charlotte.

'But I don't know where it is,' chirped Robbie.

'You're a Scout. Can't you follow a map?'

'Oh Charlotte,' reproved Liz, 'it *is* his first time. He just needs a little moral support.'

'You're his mother.'

Liz leapt out of her chair, but Patrick put up a restraining hand. 'If you speak to your mother like that once more,' he said, half-jesting, half-seriously, 'I'm going to have to deal with you very severely.'

But Charlotte only giggled again, still flirting at him with her eyes. He gave her a push and she got down from his lap, pulling a comic face at him.

After the children had gone, Liz apologised. 'She's just feeling her feet. It's such a difficult age.'

'That's OK. She's never had a father to practise her charms on. I am honoured that she has chosen me as a substitute.'

'That's all very well, so long as she doesn't pick the wrong guy, some day. She knows everything about flirtation and nothing whatsoever about men.'

'Would you like me to have a talk to her about it? She might believe it coming from a man.'

'It's true,' said Liz sadly. 'If I say anything to her, she's bound to think it's sour grapes.'

Patrick stood up, put his arms around her waist. 'What a whole lotta woman,' he rumbled. 'You know, Liz, you can't blame her. Most girls that age aren't in competition with their *mothers.*'

'Nonsense,' she said crossly, giving him a shove.

'Not nonsense,' he insisted, 'Don't you know your Freud? My lovely Liz, you look so sexy in jeans.' He began to fumble with her waist-button,at the same time running his other hand over the swell of her hips. She felt his tongue, moist and warm, on her earlobe.

'Hold it there!' she gave him a shove. 'Look here, I haven't heard from you for a whole week. What makes you think you can descend on me with ten minutes' notice? What do you expect, Patrick? A quick screw, then away to some other pressing engagement?'

Her stomach knotted as she saw she had aroused him to anger. A vein stood out on his forehead, his bright eyes narrowed and darkened. He stepped back from her. For one awful moment, she thought he might leave her, wanted to grab his arm and ask him to forgive her. Patrick once a week was better than no Patrick at all.

'I'll take your most important point first. I wasn't going to screw you, Liz, I was going to make love to you. Perhaps you don't know the difference, so I'll let that one pass. Secondly, I wasn't going to leave, I was going to ask you to have lunch with me. Thirdly, I have been very busy, working out the details about the new takeover with George Pascall. I haven't had a free moment all week. And lastly, you're hardly anybody's idea of a shy, old-fashioned maiden. What the hell was stopping *you* from contacting *me*? I could, at least, have put you in the picture.'

'All points taken,' she said quickly. He was unrelentingly immobile. Nervously she tugged at her hair. Then she started to chuckle; he looked so outraged. 'Come on, Patrick, let's screw. . . I mean, let's make love.'

Patrick remained unmoved, continued to appraise her sternly, distantly, like a cuckolded Victorian husband. To defuse his uptightness, she used her own eyes in much the same way as Charlotte had used hers, appealing for his indulgence. She ran her hands up and down his sinewy arms, savouring the hardness of him. Insinuated her hip against his body.

She knew exactly what was expected of her. She had to *work* at it. He demanded her submission. It was a game in which both of them were participants, and it had to be played out, each of them acting out a role. It was a game that she was winnning, if the sudden bulge in his jeans was anything to go by.

So she continued to eat her humble pie, triumphantly, with small conciliatory caresses and heatbroken moans, lowering her head against his chest so that he could smell the freshness of her hair. She slipped a finger between two buttons of his shirt, disturbing his shaggy body hair. As she sought his nipple, his shirt parted company with his jeans. Deftly she worked on his zip, flattened her other hand against his bare stomach, pushing down into his jeans waistband. She touched the flesh of his tip, flung back her head, let out an agonised groan.

He could stand it no longer.

Almost before she knew it, she was on the goatskin rug, with her cotton blouse pushed up to her armpits. He had unpinned her front-fastening bra and his face was between her breasts. Hungrily, he pushed the soft flesh around his cheeks and ears. He got angry with the button of her jeans, spat out a few choice curses when her zip refused to budge. Seething, he rolled off her, to allow her to assist him. She wriggled out of her jeans, panting in her haste. As she struggled, he was kneading her breasts so that the large, brown nipples stood erect and expectant for his mouth.

Then his face loomed over her as with one hand he pinned her wrists behind her unruly curls and, with the other, removed her panties. Grunting with animal urgency, he speared his erection into her moist and suppliant flesh.

He held her thus as he took her. No time for foreplay, for tender words, for gentle reassurance. This time it was for him. Yet, perversely, she reached her climax even before he did. She felt as if she had cheated him, by denying him what she owed him. So that when his spasms ceased and he remembered to ask if she had come, she instinctively denied it.

It didn't matter. He was still greedy for her anyhow. Almost immediately, she was able to coax him into readiness for her. But this time it was gentler, more caring, bodies writhing sinuously, now enjoying the visual aspect of their union, for he was propped up on his hands, his body taut, to permit her to watch him pumping her. She floated, transported on a cloud of ecstasy into heights of physical awareness so sublime that her orgasm, when it came, seemed incidental.

As he too shuddered, his passion spent, he fastened his

mouth upon her nipple. She stroked his head, her whole being flooding with an almost maternal tenderness for him. He lay beside her; she turned on to her side to face him. Their noses touched. That wayward lock of red hair that erupted from his cowlick lay flattened against the dampness of his forehead. She pushed it back, pressed her lips against the protruding eyebrows, ran her lips over his brow, tasting his sweat.

Nothing about him repelled her. Everything about him was sweet and clean and wholesome. They did not speak. It wasn't necessary. They lay there in each other's arms, replete, needing to be at one for a while before once again confronting themselves as separate beings. And there they remained till it was time to get dressed before the children came home.

13

Liz drove to work on Monday morning like an automaton. Her mind dwelt on thoughts of Patrick. She stopped at lights, changed gears, pulled away, as if she had been programmed to do so.

There was something so heady about the beginning of an affair, the excitement, the newness. The complete absence of hang-ups. A clean slate on which to create wonderful new images. A gaining of knowledge. The growing seeds of understanding, and learning precisely what made the other tick.

She shivered deliciously. She wanted all of those experiences with Patrick. She wanted to stroll across the fields with him, go out to dinner with him, disco dance with him, swap dirty jokes with him. She wanted to find every conceivable way to demonstrate the depth of her passion for him.

She thought about their lovemaking. Planned new exotic ways to keep him interested. And the fantasies she wove around this man knew no boundaries. . .

Once, in a snarl-up, the pictures in her mind became so erotic, so colourful, that her foot trembled violently on the accelerator. The car kangarooed forwards. Quickly, she stepped on the brake. The driver in front jabbed staccato blasts on his horn as Liz loomed up in his rearview mirror. The cars kissed bumpers. The driver turned, his face ugly, lips mouthing silent obscenities.

Liz leant back in her seat and smiled to herself.

When she arrived at Pascall House she parked quickly in her prescribed spot in the basement car park, hurried to her office, with perfunctory good-mornings to Johnny Morris and fellow-workers.

It was to be a heavy week. For some reason, there had been a mass exodus of staff from the central typing pool over the past two weeks. She was not surprised since, for some time, there had been dissent among the lower echelons of female staff within the building. You got a couple of bad apples and they turned the whole lot rotten. She had sussed out the original cause of the trouble: Cora of the ginger roots, and her cronies. But it had been too late to prevent the damage.

Since she was under severe pressure, she had decided to enlist the help of Dinah and Mrs Patton, supervisor of the central typing pool, to help sort out the wheat from the chaff among the new applicants.

She was sitting at her desk, dictating to Dinah and sipping a black coffee, when the message came through the intercom for her to go immediately to Sir George Pascall's office. She had been more irritated at the disturbance in her schedule than alarmed. In retrospect, she told herself later, she should have been prepared. Sir George was of the 'old school' and did almost all of his communicating via the internal memorandum. A sudden summons via the intercom was tantamount to a sign of impending doom.

She took the lift back down to the ground floor. Sir George's secretary, Julia, chic in a slim-fitting long-sleeved black dress and swinging, club-cut platinum hair, greeted her in her usual detached manner. She appraised Liz as if about to inquire what had taken her so long. 'Please go straight in, Mrs Carlton,' she cooed, 'Sir George is waiting for you.'

Irritated by her tone, Liz swept past her. As she entered Sir George's office, she could not help thinking how insignificant he looked, sitting behind that huge leather inlaid desk, in his high-back chair. She almost fancied he was nervous, for he was making full use of the swivel mechanism, showing her first his left profile, then his right, to and fro, back and forth.

Liz stood for a moment, suddenly a little unsure of herself. Sir George grabbed at his desk to stop himself face forward, mid-swivel. She was right. He had aged. The jowls which had once been so solid, a mark of power, had softened and collapsed, concealing his neck. His eyes were rheumy and, it seemed, took a while to register her standing there and subsequently recognise her. How was it she had not noticed before?

'Elizabeth,' he muttered gruffly. 'Sit down.'

She sat. Waited. He regarded her solemnly.

'You've been extremely busy, Elizabeth!'

Suddenly, she wondered why she had judged him nervous. There was still that certain something in his tone, that quality that brought competitors, adversaries and staff alike to their knees. Liz was no exception. Sensing the accusation in his tone, her mouth slackened and there was a fluttering in her insides.

The report was propelled across his desk, with an imperceptible flick of the wrist, to land across her lap. She stared down at it in abject horror.

'I'm waiting, Elizabeth.'

With difficulty, she found her tongue. Her eyes were still riveted on the report as she picked it up between her index finger and thumb, as if it were something rank and disgusting. She wished she could stop her hand trembling.

'Mr Jeremy commissioned me to produce this report,' she whispered, 'in confidence.'

'My son tells me he asked you to do a time and motion study on P & L. It seems to me you have seen fit to go far beyond the call of duty. In fact, I would go so far as to deduce that you have abused your position of rank and privilege within the Organisation.'

'Then you have been misinformed, Sir George.'

'Are you telling me that my son is a liar?'

She lifted her head, her jaw pushed aggressively forward, eyes blazing defiantly into his.

'Yes,' she said loudly and clearly.

Sir George was taken aback. A straight-talker himself, he encountered this quality so seldom in others that when it occurred he was both impressed and disarmed. Sensing she was on to a winning ticket, Liz attempted to consolidate her defences in this vein.

'I was reluctant to undertake this assignment. However,

since I agreed, in principle, that it was justified, I allowed Mr Jeremy to persuade me to do it.'

'Are you telling me that my eldest son asked you to compile an exposé on my youngest?'

'Yes, well . . .' she paused. She had to be careful here. Both she and Jeremy had known exactly what he was asking her to do. . . and yet. . . 'Not in so many words,' she concluded lamely, 'but you see . . .'

Even before he pounded his fist on the desktop, she knew she had lost ground. And ground lost to Sir George was notoriously difficult to regain. She stood up. So did he. Since his elderly bones took a little longer to respond, Liz momentarily had the advantage.

'Sir George,' she hissed, 'your son requested that I investigate the company under the pretext of doing a time and motion study. To find out why it wasn't paying. He told me it was under your instruction.'

'P & L not *paying*! What *are* you talking about, woman?'

'That was the information fed to me by your son.' She sat down again. This was going from bad to worse. She had to see it through. She would achieve nothing by backing down now. Was Sir George big enough to take the truth about his youngest son? It was a gamble, an all or nothing gamble!

'If you examine my findings, Sir George, you will see that the report was produced in good faith. For instance, the payments to Mr Trevor drawn under the code RB40.'

'You are mistaken, Elizabeth. I personally authorised that code for the use of Damien Lambert.'

'What!' Liz began to shake as the enormity of Jeremy Pascall's betrayal hit her squarely between the eyes. 'Sir George, forgive me for my bluntness, but can't you see that I am the one who has been set up? Your son has even gone to the trouble of priming the staff, no doubt without their knowledge, specifically to trap me. Don't you understand that all this has been engineered for the sole purpose of discrediting me?'

'Mrs Carlton,' his use of her formal title purposely indicated his coldness towards her, 'you flatter yourself if you assume

113

that my son would go to such lengths to discredit you. I would respectfully suggest that your imagination has run riot and done away with your common sense. Now please excuse me. I am tired.'

She tried to protest, but he had already pressed the buzzer for Julia to escort her from his office, thus rendering her helpless. As Julia took her arm, she stood, eyes riveted on the top of Sir George's head as his chin slumped on to his chest. Carefully combed but inadequte strands of silver hair fell forward, exposing red skin stretched taut and shining across his skull.

In that moment, she knew that she had shaken his equilibrium. He was a fair man. Perhaps all was not lost. She wished she could have had a little longer with him. He had been her mentor. He had always trusted her. At this moment, he too, was vulnerable.

But she had no choice but to follow Julia's affected, swaying gait to the external door, where she was dispatched, without ceremony, into the anonymity of the corridor beyond.

14

When Alexia telephoned, Gina was helping Jeremy to update the reference card system for his library. Or, to put it more succinctly, he was telling her what to do and she was following his instructions.

The library occupied three walls of Jeremy's study. It was not often that Gina was allowed into the dark domain of Jeremy's large den, except when he needed her assistance. That suited Gina. She found the study oppressive and gloomy, she hated its sombre colours, for however brightly the sun shone, that room closed in on her so that she felt she was an intruder.

Most of the telephone calls to their Pascall Lodge apartment were for Jeremy, although he never deigned to take them himself. When the maid wasn't around, it was Gina's job to answer, find out the identity of the caller and announce the name to Jeremy. Then to make the necessary excuses if Jeremy did not wish to talk.

She went to the phone, was delighted to discover that the call was for her and that it was Alexia. It was a welcome interruption.

'Gina,' Alexia's words tripped over one another. 'Gina, I've got a terrific idea. I'm driving to Oxford tomorrow to visit my twin brother before the start of the new term. He's bored out of his mind, poor darling, as all his friends went home for the holidays. I thought I'd go down and cheer him up. Why don't you come with me, Gina? We'll make a day of it. Do a spot of shopping, have a facial or whatever takes your fancy. Then we can meet James at Browns later.'

Gina's heart felt as if it would burst out of her chest. A day out with Alexia. Somewhere different. Different shops, different restaurants, different people. Just her and Alexia, giggling and comparing notes, catching up on the latest gossip, trying out crazy new clothes.

Gina pivoted in delight and the cord wound around her body, almost dislodging the phone.

As she came out of her spin, she caught her husband's eye. Just beneath its piercing black, a tiny tic, just visible, jumped.

'OK,' said Gina to Alexia, her tone much subdued.

'You'd really like to come? Are you sure? I don't want to put you in a corner, Gina. Honestly, if you'd rather not, please say.'

'Yes, that would be fine,' said Gina in modulated tones, painfully aware of Jeremy's gaze upon her.

'Well, if you're sure . . .' Alexia still sounded worried about Gina's apparent lack of enthusiasm. Yes, yes, yes, screamed Gina internally, yes, Alexia, yes.

'I'll call for you at ten, but if you change your mind let me know by nine-thirty.'

'OK. Right,' said Gina thankfully and carefully, quietly, she replaced the receiver, for Jeremy now seemed engrossed in the card index system. With forced nonchalance, she wandered over to the desk and began to shuffle some papers around.

'Was that Alexia?' said Jeremy softly.

'Yes. As a matter of fact, it was.'

'What did she want?'

'Oh nothing much,' said Gina airily, 'just girl-talk.'

'Humph,' grunted Jeremy in disdain, and Gina began to breathe a little more easily. She was certain that if he knew what she and Alexia were planning, he would find some way to prevent them from going. He wasn't happy about her and Alexia being alone together. Disliked the way they had become such good pals.

And they were. She and Alexia were confidantes, who never betrayed each other's trust, who helped each other whenever they could. It was good to have a friend. Someone to boost your morale when you were down. Someone to tell about your period giving you cramps, about your soufflé that didn't rise, about the crowsfeet that had begun to appear around your eyes.

116

'They really don't show at all,' Alexia would tell her loyally. 'But if you're worried, there's a new cream on the market that I'm told is very good . . .'

If she told Alexia about a *faux pas* she made at dinner yesterday, then Alexia would dream up a worse one that she had made so that Gina would feel better. And Gina would do the same for Alexia.

Gina had never had a proper girlfriend before. Had felt, despite her classes, isolated at Pascall Lodge. Jeremy had always been adamant that she should not bring anyone back from the village, and as for the studios in Floral Street, where she did her jazz dancing, it seemed impossible to make any long-term friendships there. People came and people went. That was how it was in the big city.

But Alexia would one day be her sister-in-law. Gina longed for the day when Alexia would join Martin in his apartment at the Lodge. They would have such fun, she and Alexia.

Little wonder Jeremy was so uptight. Jeremy was worried that she might tell Alexia his secret. And then, Alexia would tell Martin.

And Martin must never know.

She was damned if she was going to give up the best friend she had ever had, just to put Jeremy's mind at rest.

'If it's as crowded as this during the holidays, whatever can it be like during term-time,' commented Gina, tucking in to her steak.

'I expect a lot of students return early to sort themselves out for the new term,' replied Alexia. She had never before been presented with a salad she felt she could not finish. She kept finding new exciting tastes. Strawberries, prawns, *croûtons*, olives, bananas, some melon. 'Since you can't spear *croûtons* on your fork,' she inquired, 'should you pick them up with your fingers, or shovel them up with your fork?'

'Debrett says it's OK now to shovel peas,' replied Gina knowingly, 'so I suppose it's OK to do the same with *croûtons*.'

'Does it really matter?' groaned James.

'Misery!' muttered Alexia.

117

The evening had started well enough. Alexia had introduced Gina to her twin. 'He's older than me by twenty minutes, so the selfish little beast grabbed all the brains. Which is why he's now at university and I'm only an assistant librarian.'

James had visibly preened, enjoying their admiration of his cleverness.

He was ash-blond and big like his sister. Since she had coiled her long hair into a tight knot on top of her head, revealing the shape of her face and ears, they looked stunningly alike.

Except Alexia, as always, was happy and bright. But gradually, as the evening wore on, James became more and more morose.

'What's the matter, James?' Alexia asked him, with sisterly concern. 'Aren't you looking forward to the beginning of your second year?'

'Yes.'

'Do you like the course?'

'My tutor's a pain. Too old. But he's only a year from retirement, so they're not going to sack him now.'

'That's a shame, but what's really the matter?' said Alexia perceptively.

Gina marvelled at the rapport between these two, felt a sudden stab of homesickness, a need for her own siblings. The banter, the rivalry, the fights, the togetherness. Alexia was peering hard at her twin, willing him to be honest with her, letting him know he could not evade her questions with weak half-truths.

'My friend just bought a flat for fifty thousand pounds. And he's a year younger than me. And he hasn't got even an O-level to his name.'

'So that's it! You idiot! With all you've got going for you, you jolly well ought to know better. I always thought I knew you as well as I know myself, but I see I don't.'

'It's not just materialism. By the time I've finished my course, I'll be so far behind financially. And anyway, I don't know for sure that I'll get a decent position at the end of it all.'

' 'Course you will. Anyway, maybe Daddy will help you.'

'I want to do it on my own.'

'And deprive the world of your talents?'

'It's not just that. There's Deborah . . .'

'Oh James, you dark horse! You never breathed a word . . .'

'I don't tell you everything.'

'So I see.'

Suddenly Gina felt distanced from them, excluded by their closeness, the incredible one-ness they exuded even in the midst of their bickering. Her eyes began to wander over the throng of people waiting for their tables. They alighted on a familiar figure and Gina started.

'I don't believe it! It can't be! It *is* . . .'

'Who?' cried the other two in unison.

'It's Elizabeth Carlton. Here, of all places . . .' Gina forgot her manners and pointed. 'Over there, that rather statuesque woman with the big, black hairdo.'

Three pairs of eyes bore into Liz as she booked her table, collected her ticket, then wandered over to the bar.

As Liz walked back towards the partition separating the bar from the restaurant, she caught sight of Gina excitedly flapping both hands at her. Looked surprised, then pleased, raised her hand in acknowledgement. Gina gestured for Liz to join them.

'It's so nice to see you, Liz,' said Gina as Liz approached their table. She quickly introduced Alexia and her brother. 'Martin's fiancée?' said Liz, and Alexia nodded. 'Liz is the Pascall overnight success,' gushed Gina, 'she's cracked the last bastion of male chauvinism at Pascall House.'

'Hardly,' objected Liz, for once looking embarrassed. Overnight success indeed! It had taken a lot of hard work and more than a few traumas for her to get where she was. What would Gina Pascall know about that?

'Are you eating alone?' said Gina.

'I'm meeting my stepson, Robbie's half-brother. He's following his father's footsteps and doing chemistry, although he wants to go into teaching rather than research.'

Alexia's fascination for this formidable woman, in her dark-navy coat-dress and pale blue silk scarf, overcame her discretion, her sudden reluctance to draw attention to herself.

119

'Would that be your step-son by your last husband's first marriage?' she inquired.

Alexia winced as James kicked her under the table, but Liz just looked amused. 'That's right,' she said easily. She appraised the younger woman with her huge, sand-coloured eyes, knowing eyes that registered, understood and forgave Alexia for her gaucheness. Alexia could not meet her gaze.

'At least sit down and have a drink with us,' said Gina quickly. 'James, go find another chair.'

'More easily said than done,' said James with more truth than lack of gallantry.

'I'd love to but I can't,' said Liz. 'I can see my stepson now. Please excuse me. It was so nice to see you.'

'She's nice, isn't she?' said Gina as Liz departed to meet her stepson. 'So attractive.'

'Depends on your taste,' muttered Alexia.

They finished their meal in silence. Gina, who had so looked forward to this day, tried to jolly the other two out of their black mood, but to no avail. Eventually, James excused himself to go to the Gents.

'What's the matter, Alexia?'

'Oh nothing.'

'You know,' said Gina, needing to confide in her friend, 'I feel terribly badly about her.' In answer to the question in Alexia's eyes she continued, 'About Liz. Elizabeth Carlton.' She paused. 'Jeremy's after her blood, you know.'

'For goodness' sake, why? I thought she had done very well for herself.'

'Maybe that's why. My husband's a terrible chauvinist. But I don't know for sure why he hates her so much.'

'Then how do you know he hates her?'

'Things I've overheard. He was on the telephone last week. "I'll soon take care of Mrs Clever Carlton," he said. "She's not going to make a monkey out of me." ' Gina lowered her tone. 'Then he said, "Goodbye darling" to the person he was talking to.'

'Oh Gina!' cried Alexia in shocked sympathy.

'It's all right, Alex. I don't kid myself my marriage is all it

120

should be. But I do feel sorry for Liz. I almost feel I ought to warn her. Or have a word with my father-in-law about my suspicions.'

Alexia considered. 'She's not a close friend of yours, is she?'

'Not exactly.'

'Then why should you stick your neck out?'

'Because it's not fair.'

'Oh come on, Gina! Nobody's that altruistic. In any case, from what I've heard, Elizabeth Carlton is quite capable of taking care of herself.'

'I'm not so sure. In business, Jeremy is a ruthless adversary. I haven't been married to him for twelve years without knowing that.'

'But why should you interfere, Gina,' said Alexia worriedly, 'and bring trouble on yourself? Jeremy would be furious, would never forgive you. Or is your relationship with him so bad that you're just looking for a chance to stir things up?'

'Not at all. Oh Alexia, how can you say such a thing!' Abstractedly Gina fiddled with the peppermill, her small face sad and drawn. Alexia waited for her to compose herself. 'She's got two gorgeous kids. Has to bring them up all by herself. It can't be easy. I met them once at the Lodge when Sir George brought them over one weekend. She adores those kids, you can see it in her eyes. The girl was crazy about horses. She has one of her own and he's her life. And the young boy. He's an absolute poppet. . . I just can't bear to think that their security is under threat.'

'A lot of kids manage on a lot less,' commented Alexia.

'That's not the point,' insisted Gina. 'A lot of kinds don't have what her kids have, so they find their security in other ways. Poor kids have. . . whatever poor kids have. But what Liz's family has is what's important to them now. Their friends, their lifestyle, their home.'

'I'll tell you what poor kids have,' said Alexia, 'street corners and poor friends.' Suddenly she looked a little shamefaced. 'I'm sorry, Gina, I don't mean to be facetious. I know what you mean. But I really don't think you should interfere.'

'I suppose you're right.'

121

'You really are an idealist, aren't you. So incisive. Even though you're so terribly vain, I can forgive you that because you're so kind.'

Gina had to smile. Alexia, lovely as she was, had never been applauded for her diplomacy. Alexia believed in the truth, the whole truth and nothing but the truth – however brutal. But at least she was loyal. She would tell Gina she thought her vain, but she would never say such a thing to anyone else.

'I suppose it's true,' admitted Gina, with an honesty that was nothing whatever to do with vanity. 'I do spend too much time on myself, at the hairdresser's and the beauty salon and the fitness classes. But until you came along, I was so lonely. Imagine me, stuck in the Lodge with only old Ma Pascall to ask in for coffee?'

'Yuk,' said Alexia, 'she terrifies me. Every time she looks at me, it feels as if she's looking right through me. I want to shrink right into the ground. She's got such an incredibly long neck. She always seems to be craning it, to see what I'm up to. As if she wants to catch me out. She reminds me of a vulture!'

'Do you know why vultures have bald heads?' said James, who had just returned to the table. 'It's so that they can wriggle their heads right into the entrails of their victims without getting caked in blood.'

'Come to think of it,' said Alexia conversationally, 'Old Ma Pascall is beginning to lose her hair.'

Simultaneously the three young people clutched at their sides and rocked with mirth. Their laughter filled the restaurant. It was so good to be able to joke about things that intimidated you. It put them back into perspective. And their laughter made other people happy too. conversations ceased, heads turned, eyes were drawn sidelong towards them and everywhere faces crumpled into indulgent smiles that echoed the infectious laughter.

15

The following day, Patrick buzzed Dinah to request an appointment to see Liz. 'I can spare him a few minutes if he'd like to come up right away,' she told Dinah. As Dinah went back to her office, Liz strained her ears, heard Dinah's affirmative murmur indicating Patrick's acquiescence. She brightened up at the thought of his ambling into her office, with his infectious, easy smile, settling himself gingerly into her visitor's chair as if nervous that it might break beneath his weight.

While she waited, she quickly checked her make-up in her compact mirror. Two bright spots of anticipation burned in her cheeks. She thrust forward her rounded chin and dabbed on some rouge to balance the cheeks, rendering them less obvious against her naturally translucent skin.

Before Patrick arrived, the intercom buzzed again. 'There's a call for you on line two,' said Dinah. 'It's a Mrs Doughty, but she said it was personal so I don't know what it's in connection with.'

'Oh yes, Benedict's mother. Put her on, Dinah,' Liz picked up her phone, pressed button two. 'Hello, Mrs Doughty.'

'I'm so dreadfully sorry, Mrs Carlton,' the other woman gushed, 'but I'm afraid I can't collect Robbie this afternoon. Benedict has an abscess behind his tooth and his poor little face is swollen beyond recognition. I have to take him to the dental hospital and God knows how long that will take.'

'I understand, Mrs Doughty. I'll make arrangements to collect Robbie myself.'

She put the receiver down, her face glum. That was all she needed. Why did everything happen at once. Quickly she dialled Mrs Oakes's number. But by the time she had finished

123

with Mrs Oakes, she felt as if the whole world had conspired to thwart her.

'Mr Evans has arrived, Mrs Carlton,' said Dinah from the outer office.

'Whatever's the matter, Liz?' inquired Patrick in alarm as he entered her office, taking in the way her elbow rested on her desk, her chin supported in her palm, her woebegone expression suggesting her world had fallen apart.

'Oh, it's just that the woman who collects Robbie from school can't make it today. I'll have to go myself.'

'Aren't you being a little over-protective?' ventured Patrick. 'Surely Robbie is old enough to see himself home from school.'

'There are special circumstances,' she replied evasively. He gave her a questioning look but did not press her to expound. 'I had two afternoons off last week to meet him.'

'Then I'm afraid you aren't going to be pleased with what I have to say, Liz. You see, I have instructions from Sir George for you. No doubt you are aware of the negotiations for the takeover of Robinson's Surgical Instruments?' He paused, his chest visibly swelling with pride. Indulgently, she half-smiled.

He looked so proud. His simian eyebrows seemed more assertively protruding than ever. He was in charge, in control.

'Your baby,' she acknowledged.

'My baby,' he agreed. 'Well, the crux of the matter is that Sir George wants you to take a ride down to the factory to check things out, let him know what you think. It's arranged that Martin Pascall will accompany you '

Her feelings were mixed as she listened to Patrick's news. What on earth was she to do about Robbie? She must find a way. After all, wasn't Sir George offering her an olive branch? Wasn't it his way of saying that, in essence, he still trusted her? That despite her fall from grace, if only due to her own *naïveté* in allowing herself to be fooled by Jeremy Pascall, he still had faith in her abilities? Christ, if she blew this one. . .

She checked her Rolex. Nine twenty-five. 'It's early yet,' she told Patrick, 'I could leave now and get back in time for Robbie.'

124

'Afraid not. Martin Pascall is in a meeting at the moment and plans to depart after an early lunch. And the factory is, in any case, on the ᴗther side of Birmingham. It's an overnight job, Liz. You won't be back till tomorrow.'

Her heart sank. 'I can't go. I can't risk it.'

'Liz, you have to.'

'Close the door, Patrick,' she whispered, pausing as he complied. 'Look, you don't understand. I don't understand it myself, but I am being harassed. And now Robbie has been involved. I *have* to meet him from school. I've asked Mrs Oakes but she won't break her routine. It's her club night.'

'Surely she could make an exception just this once?'

'I begged her, but she won't. I think it's something special. She says she has to be there by five o'clock.'

'I thought she really cared about you and the kids.'

'There's naught so strange as folks,' she quoted bleakly.

'By whom are you being harassed? No, don't tell me! That little jerk with the Adam's apple!'

'Yes, that's right. Eddie. Eddie Smith.'

'Why don't you call the police?' spluttered Patrick. 'Why don't you, Liz? Answer me?' His eyes bored into hers, searching for clues. They both knew that she was not being entirely honest with him. 'I have reported the incident to the school head,' she said eventually, 'but I'm not one hundred per cent sure it's him, so I can't name names.'

'I believe the police are discreet in these matters.'

'I wish I had your confidence,' she replied.

If there's a man hanging around outside the school gates for Robbie, then I don't see that you have much choice in the matter. It's up to the police to find out who it is and it's up to you to give them any help you can. Oh, all right, calm down, Liz. Don't worry. I'll collect Robbie for you this afternoon. Then we'll pick up Charlotte and I 'll take them both for a McDonalds. I'll stay with them till Mrs Oakes arrives for them tomorrow morning. Then we can talk. Or even better, why don't you take an early lunch and I'll meet you in the bistro next to the wine bar at twelve-fifteen?'

He was moved by the deep gratitude that flooded into her

eyes. She fumbled into her handbag, handed him her door key. 'In case I forget later.' He slipped it into his inside pocket.

'See you in a couple of hours. You look as if you need to relax a little before you go tearing off down the motorway with the effusive Martin Pascall.'

His light sarcasm about Martin Pascall's lack of verbosity was lost on her. He noticed she had a slight twitch under her left eye. She was nervous, preoccupied.

There was more, much more, to this than even he had suspected. He would have to find out, wouldn't he? If he was going to be of any help to her at all, he needed to know exactly what was going on in that crazy head of hers.

He marvelled at the barrier of icy reserve she was able to erect around herself, belying her natural warmth and vibrant sensuality. Certainly, she was no retiring violet sexually, but had any guy, ever, got close to her spiritually? Could *he*? He was beginning to have his doubts.

The bistro was normally crowded, but fortunately Patrick and Liz were early enough to secure a corner table, which afforded them a little privacy to talk. After their order was taken they sat silently for a few moments, each reluctant to be the first to broach the subject uppermost in their minds. To break the silence, she asked him about Robinson's Surgical Instruments.

'It's a medium-sized factory,' said Patrick, 'involving about fifty technicians. Everything is handled on site, administration, distribution, etc. Obviously, we would extend the factory and move the administration into Pascall House. Therefore, your trip will not be a popular one for the white-collar workers. Those not prepared to move back this way will have to be made redundant.'

'I see. How wide is their product range?'

'It's very extensive and we think that might be one of the major problems. They have been too ambitious for their size. they make just about everything, the tools used in the operating theatre, prostheses of every description, you know the sort of thing, hip replacements and so forth. In my opinion they have diversified too soon, spending a fortune on research before they have managed to capitalise on the existing range. They just don't have the wherewithal to do it. The creditors are after them and the bank, I believe, is about to foreclose.'

'It's sad,' she admitted, 'but an excellent opportunity for you.'

'Yes it is. I'll be in charge of the new administration, directly under Sir George. I made it plain I didn't wish to work in double harness with one of the Pascall sons and Sir George has sufficient confidence in me to agree. Not, of course, that I put it to him quite as bluntly as that, but he understood my meaning.' He flashed her an impish grin.

Once again, Liz felt the unwelcome twinge of jealousy she had experienced once before, in the foyer of Pascall House. Sir George had a new prodigy, and she could not help but see him as a threat, especially now that her own standing in the old man's eyes had been somewhat diminished. Patrick's panache, his self-satisfaction, the manner in which he was so 'all together' irritated her beyond reason. As her full mouth turned down at the corners he misread her thoughts, leaned across the table and put his hand on hers. 'Don't worry,' he said.

At that moment their food arrived, green lasagne for her, spaghetti for him. Hungrily, he rolled the pasta around his fork, but several strands escaped en route to his mouth. With an apologetic grimace, he glanced around to ensure he wasn't observed, then helped them along with his fingers. In spite of herself, she relaxed slightly, grinned at him. He seized the moment.

'Tell me about Eddie,' he said, resting his fork on his plate.

'I don't know where to start.'

'Try the beginning.'

The beginning. Where was the beginning? The two incidents had become confused in her mind, images of girls with nipped-in waists and stand-out skirts. Paper nylon petticoats that flashed beneath the flared cotton as they walked. Youth clubs and country hikes and boys in thick-soled trainers and DA hairstyles. And Eddie, who had managed to transcend the years, ageless and intact. Yet not *quite*, something *missing*. . .

The smooth, clean-cut image of the club spanned time in her mind and was tainted with the gloom of that singles bar. And Eddie! One coin, but two sides. That brief meeting. She had recognised him immediately, kept her eye on him till he spotted her there. Slim, almost mystical in his gauntness, his intensity. With easy confidence he had approached her, his knowing eyes running the length of her body, taking in the well-shaped calves, the obvious swell of her breasts. He had undressed her with his eyes. It was like a scene from an old film, a 'B' rated film, a film where men were men and women liked it that way.

He'd licked his lips suggestively as he had peered boldly into her cleavage. She hadn't minded. It was his right. It was all part of the game. People who worked hard needed to play hard. The brief drive through town to his spartan Chelsea flat. The even briefer session of so-called lovemaking. At that stage in her mind-play the two Eddies ceased to be interchangeable.

'Liz, are you all right? You haven't touched your food.'

'I'm not hungry.'

'Tell me about Eddie,' he repeated.

She didn't tell him about the singles bar or the drive or the lovemaking. She didn't tell him because she did not consider it relevant, or, for that matter, any of his business. She told him of Eddie's harassment of her by telephone and by his occasional physical presence. And that she suspected he might be the man who had accosted and so frightened young Robbie.

'You're not being completely honest, are you Liz? If Eddie was already harassing Robbie last school term, that was back in late June or early July. I remember precisely the date he arrived with the flowers because it was the day I first asked you out after my successful meeting with Sir George. It was the fifteenth of August.' Patrick paused, studied her minutely. 'Don't you see?'

'What you are saying is that he had planned it all, before he had even met me. Planned to find out all about me. There must be a reason. Why? I wonder why?' She moved her fork in her lasagne abstractedly till it was a brown splodge of liquidised pasta and meat. 'Maybe he's just a crank. Maybe

128

he's observed me from a distance and become obsessed with me. I just don't know!'

'Did you ever sleep with him, Liz? Either before or after the end of summer term?' inquired Patrick, his voice loaded with tension.

Her hesitation in replying condemned her in his eyes and she could not fail to sense his disappointment in her. Yet, egotistically, she was more indignant that he should dare to ask than embarrassed at her presumed fall from grace. After all, it had happened before she had become involved with him and was, in her opinion, nothing whatever to do with him.

'Liz, it's unfair of you to ask for my help and then only give me half a story.'

'I did not ask for your help. You proffered it,' she pointed out.

'Please yourself.' Furiously he attacked his meal, lowering his chin closer to his plate and shovelling in the pasta as if his life depended on it. Icily, she watched him. Then she remembered Robbie. As if reading her mind, he said, 'Don't worry, Liz, I'll collect the boy anyway. For his sake, if not for yours.'

'Thank you Patrick,' she replied and only now, in the light of his concern, did she feel a sudden stab of shame.

'Eddie and I met in a bar,' she began haltingly, 'and although I don't wish to use this as an excuse, since I *was* feeling sexually receptive that night,' she shot him a sharp, defiant stare, 'he did remind me uncannily of my first husband, his namesake. We had sex that night in his flat, but it was an unqualified disaster.

'He has not left me in peace since that night. But I'll tell you this for certain. That meeting took place three weeks after the end of the school term, when Robbie was accosted. So if it *was* Eddie who was trying to find out about me through my son, he must have planned our meeting. Must have planned everything . . .'

'What evidence do you have that they are one and the same?'

'Nothing concrete. Except that I showed Robbie a photograph of my husband, Eddie, and he recognised the

129

likeness. I don't understand, but . . .' she paused, needing to voice her bewilderment, to get her half-formed suspicions into focus, 'but it's so weird. I almost find myself wondering if there is some supernatural force at work. Maybe Eddie is my husband's reincarnation. Oh, I don't know!'

'Why would Eddie, your husband, Eddie, want to hurt you in this way?' asked Patrick, cunningly humouring her in the interests of further possible revelations. 'Is there any reason why he would want revenge?'

He saw he had gone too far. She had clammed up. He knew from the set line of her jaw, the way its small muscles worked behind her skin. As far as Liz was concerned, the matter was closed.

'I am sure there's a perfectly logical explanation for all this,' he said comfortingly, 'even if it's only that one guy has a very sick mind. Don't start thinking about malevolent spirits, Liz.' He almost choked on the word 'spirits'. Irishman though he was, he had never believed in the 'little people' or any of their cronies. Patrick's world was far too ordered to make space for such nonsense.

'I'm sure you're right. Look, Patrick, I have to go. Martin is expecting us to leave in about ten minutes. You have my key?'

He nodded and she rose, her jacket over her arm. As she made her way, half-dazed to the street, he hurriedly settled the bill before escorting her in silence back to the office.

16

'She's not in this afternoon,' said Johnny Morris. 'I mean she's *really* not in. She's off down the M1 with Mr Martin to do a hatchet job on some poor buggers in Birmingham.'

'That's OK,' said Eddie. 'I didn't come to see her. I came to give you these.' He placed a brown carrier bag on Johnny's desk. Johnny peeped in, glanced up at Eddie showing his uneven teeth in a wide grin.

'Are these the Continental ones?' he asked. Eddie grinned lewdly.

'They're from Sweden actually. Hot stuff. All in colour, just the way you like them.'

'Thanks mate,' said Johnny gratefully. Then, recalling Eddie's remark about not wishing to see Liz, he asked, 'You gone off her then?'

'Weeeell,' Eddie stuck his hands in his pockets, appeared to ponder, pushing out his lower lip in concentration. 'It's hard to say, exactly. Let's put it this way. She's not a bad fuck but she's not really my type.'

'She's not?' Johnny's mouth gaped in amazement. 'Why not?'

'Well, she's into all the heavy stuff. Not my scene, whips and leather gear and blood-red lips. She even rouges her nipples, you know, and wears a black bra with peep-holes in the cups.'

'Never,' gasped Johnny. 'Who would have thought it?'

'Oh, yeah, she's a right little raver. Needs to grovel, to be somebody's slave. Give her a right-hander and she's all over you, slavering at the mouth.'

'Wow,' croaked Johnny. 'Well, all I can say, mate, is I wish it was me!'

'Don't let me stand in your way, Johnny. I've found other interests now, got myself a cute little blonde of seventeen going on twenty-eight.'

'She wouldn't look at me.'

'That's up to you, isn't it, Johnny. Haven't you ever read *Lady Chatterley's Lover*? Old Lawrence knew all about women. These high-powered birds all love a bit of rough. I'll tell you this, Johnny old chap. whether you're good enough for her is entirely up to you. Anyway, have a look at those magazines I've brought you. There are a couple there should give you some ideas.'

'Right, thanks a lot,' called Johnny to Eddie's retreating back. Eddie's hand lifted in a light-hearted wave. Johnny fumbled in his bottom desk-drawer, brought out his copy of *Country Life*, licking his lips in anticipation.

For the first part of her journey, Liz went over the previous three years' balance sheets for Robinson's Surgical Instruments. When she had finished, she slipped them back in her briefcase and pressed the recliner button on her seat. She glanced at Martin Pascall. Taciturn he was, but not due to any inadequacy of intellect or ability. He was never prone to gossip or conjecture. He only spoke when he had something meaningful to say. This made him hard going, but Liz felt he was worth the effort. Of the three Pascall sons, she liked him the best. She hoped he had not been involved in the distasteful P & L affair.

'Patrick Evans said you would explain exactly what Sir George expects from me with regard to this trip,' she said, studying his rather attractive profile.

Even in repose, Martin Pascall's features were intimidating. His upper lip curved gradually in a widely spaced bow, so that the tramlines running from its blunt arrowtips were indistinct. It gave him a rather cruel expression, almost Arabic, which suited his swarthy complexion. Women were both attracted to and frightened by him. He had a handsome, narrow nose and a well-defined bone structure. Liz, being Liz, was neither frightened nor intimidated by him, saw beyond the off-putting exterior into the uncomplicated, orderly mind of the man.

132

'He wants you to assess the administrative staff, check their work records and their duties. He believes there's a lot of dead wood there, jobs for the boys, that sort of thing.'

'The usual hatchet job,' said Liz wryly.

'Someone has to do it,' said Martin, 'and you *are* very good at your job, Liz.'

'Thanks.' She gave him a grateful smile.

'It takes courage to do what you do.'

She raised her eyebrows in surprise. He was actually making an effort to have a casual, personal conversation with her. Idiotically she felt proud and flattered. But his next words shook her out of her complacency.

'Nevertheless, you should continue to be on your guard.'

'What do you mean, Mr Martin?'

'It's difficult for me to be specific, you must understand that, Liz. As you know, my father thinks a great deal of you. But you are an attractive and accomplished woman and as such, you are bound to make enemies. Be careful, Liz, don't leave yourself exposed in any way.'

'What do you mean?'

'That's all I can tell you,' said Martin Pascall, 'and I've already said more than I intended to.'

'Thank you,' she whispered tremulously, studying her fingernails, aware that there was no point in pursuing that line of questioning, yet grateful for the warning. Indeed, it had been quite a speech for Martin Pascall, who was never one to exaggerate or over-react.

The following Sunday Liz took a trip to the small Kent village where her first husband Eddie's parents still lived. She did not visit. She drove to the parish church, St Mary the Virgin, where Eddie was buried. So much had happened. She needed to tell him about it. Reassure herself that Eddie was still on her side. She would know. Just by standing by his grave, she would know.

She opened the boot of the Scirocco and took out the flowers. Red roses for love, a huge bouquet, just coming out of bud. Red roses for Eddie's birthday.

She entered the churchyard through the lychgate, which was smothered in ivy. A blackbird beat its hasty retreat from somewhere by her feet, with its shrill raucous cry of warning. She knew all the tombstone inscriptions off by heart, the loving messages, the names, the dates, the small verses. They intrigued her. A huge stone angel gazed down upon her with mournful, iris-less eyes. She glanced up at the stone church's Gothic spire, wondering if Eddie's parents had visited today, felt a few drops of rain on her face and was glad of it. It was time the thirsty ground was replenished. It had been so close, lately, so sticky. The rain would clear the air.

She slipped across the grass, taking care not to step on the graves, till she came to Eddie's small plot. Edward William, said the small headstone, Beloved Son of Edna and Wilbur, Taken Suddenly and Tragically, The Fourth Day of July, Nineteen Sixty-Eight.

She fell to her knees beside the grave, held the roses out in front of her to deposit in the large stone urn. It was then that she saw them.

The creamy florets. Out of season cow parsley, well past its best, the tops beginning to turn green and brown. There was a small message attached to one of the stalks. Relectantly, she put out her hand, pinched it between her thumb and forefinger. Didn't want to look, but had to.

On one side of the card there was an illustration, a line drawing of a motor-bike and rider, swirls of the charcoal pencil indicating the dust under the wheels as they turned at speed. She quickly reversed the card. It showed a drawing of the front of a train. It was an engine, like a child's toy, and it had a sad face, a turned-down mouth and mournful cartoon eyes, with a tear about to slide over the rim of one eye. There were no words, just a small inked-in RIP.

Her hand shook as she replaced the card. She backed away, dropping the roses on the grassy hump between the headstone and the urn. Stumbling, weeping, she ran from the graveyard, not stopping till she was safely in her car where she clung on to the steering-wheel, her forehead on her hands, her heart juddering against her ribcage like a trapped bird trying to escape from a dark, confined space. The bird beat its wings, futilely, pumping, throbbing, bursting, exploding into a mess of anguish, a red haze of terror.

Suddenly Liz threw back her head and screamed. She could not hear herself, but she screamed and screamed and screamed.

When her screaming was done, she sat for a long long time before she was able to compose herself sufficiently to start her journey home.

17

As Patrick paced the room, his hands in his pockets, Charlotte lounged meditatively on a Habitat beanbag, her dark head still, but her cat's eyes following his movements as if he were prey. He wished she would stop it. He wished Liz would get back soon. And where was Robbie?

'Where's Robbie, Charlotte?' he said.

'Staying with his friend for two days,' replied Charlotte. A hank of hair had fallen across her eye and she brushed it away with the back of her hand. So feline was her movement that he almost waited for her to lick the small knuckles and rub them around her face.

They had started off so well, he and Charlotte. A beautiful budding friendship between an impressionable young girl and a solid mature man. A touch of humour, a touch of flirtation, but safe. Now her precocity alarmed him. So ladylike, Liz had told him, always so perfectly behaved, her Charlotte. Demure and correct. And now look at her. She was wearing very sheer tights and had allowed her skirt to ruck up as she lolled, to permit the maximum view of her coltish legs up to the triangle of her pants, shaded darker by her pubic hair.

'I'll pop back in half an hour,' said Patrick defensively and started for the door.

In a trice, she was on her feet and blocking his way. 'Don't go, Patrick,' she implored, 'I'll make you some coffee and a sandwich. Oh Patrick, you do look sexy in your black pinstripe suit.' Her sleek white fingers coiled around his sleeve. 'Do stay. Mummy won't be long.'

'I'll be back,' he insisted.

'But I'm frightened here on my own.' Desperately she clung to him. He wrenched his arm free. 'Stop it, Charlotte, stop it!'

He grabbed her by her fragile shoulders and shook her soundly. Alarm ghosted her delicate features.

'Oh Patrick!' she cried, excitement in her tone.

As he released her, she stumbled a bit and sat down hard on her beanbag, her lower lip protruding petulantly, accusation flashing in her huge dark eyes. 'So what's the matter with me?' she yelled at him.

He glowered. She stuck out her chin, looked down her nose at him.

'You don't need to worry about Mummy, Patrick,' she told him slyly, 'she's only just telephoned and she isn't leaving the office till nine.' She raised her spider-leg eyebrows. 'We've got plenty of time.'

'Charlotte!'

'I'm all right, aren't I? I've got all the necessary bits and pieces. they just haven't been around so long, that's all. Doesn't mean I don't know what to do with them. What's stopping you, Patrick? Anything wrong with the goods?'

'There's nothing wrong with you, Charlotte,' he hissed, 'that can't be put right very easily indeed.' As he advanced on her, looming over her, gigantic, dark and murderous, she drew up her knees to her chest with a startled gasp, half excitement, half fear. Suddenly she was over his shoulder, like a sack of potatoes. His strong angry fingers bit into her calves. She screamed as he bore her to the bathroom. Without hesitaton, he deposited her in the pink shower basin and turned the cold water on her.

She screamed and kicked out at him, gaping like a child that had lost its lollipop. He turned the jets on harder. Her hair dripped wet and spikily onto her bare shoulders, her halter top clung to her like a second skin and her tight skirt was bunched around her undeveloped thighs.

He did not let up till he had reduced her to a shivering, blue-tinged wretch who wept and begged for mercy.

'Now get dressed,' he said shortly, as he clipped back the shower head, 'in something decent and becoming to a young lady of your station. Then we'll have a little talk while we wait for your mother. I think it's about time, don't you?'

He grasped her wrist and hauled her to her feet, than gave her a none-too-gentle shove in the back to propel her into the hallway. As she stumbled, weeping, towards her bedroom, he helped her on her way with a hefty, stinging slap across her pert wet bottom.

'And that was just a taster,' he bawled after her, 'if you ever try anything like that again, I'm warning you, it'll be the whole works.'

Humiliated, she scampered away and Patrick scratched his head, perplexed, hoping that, in his cruelty, he had done her some good.

By all the saints, the women in this family took some understanding and a lot of handling. He smiled sadly to himself. Poor little cow, saddled with a combination of beauty and feelings she didn't know how to deal with. Her youth, her mother's stunning looks and vitality and sensuality. No father to guide her, to teach her about men, to put his foot down when she went too far.

Eventually she re-emerged, woebegone, contrite, her hair combed, and clad in a sensible T-shirt and baggy three-quarter trousers. She stood in front of him, biting her lip, hanging her head, not looking at him.

'I'm sorry Patrick. I know I deserved that. I hope you can forgive me and that we can still be friends.'

He pulled her down beside him and put his arm around her, gently stroked her long damp hair.

'I'm glad you get cross when I'm bad,' she whispered.

Patrick was worried about Liz. She had not been the same for the past week, ever since she had visited her Eddie's grave last Sunday. She had left home at four o'clock to drive down and he had waited for her at the house, with the children, but when she had returned, she had been morose and withdrawn.

He had tried to comfort her, but she would not let him get close to her.

For a week she had made excuses not to see him.

'I'm too busy, Patrick, I'm so sorry . . .'

'I have to go to Oxford tomorrow to see my stepson.'

138

'I'm working late.'

'I'm taking the children to see their grandparents . . .'

'I have a headache.'

On the evening of her alleged trip to Oxford, he hired a car and followed her. It wasn't difficult, as because of the long journey she left straight after work. Only when he had assured himself she was bound for the appropriate motorway did he give up and return home.

He even tried to persuade her to allow him to accompany her to visit the grandparents.

'How could they possibly object?' he had pleaded, 'It's years since John died.'

'It would be awkward,' she had stated firmly and put the phone down on him.

Maybe he could have accepted all of that. But the headache! Woman's eternal excuse for everything! Only it didn't work for Liz. Liz, who would never permit anything so mundane as a headache to interfere with her normal routine.

Anything, anything, to keep him away.

At first, he had put it down to the strain of visiting the cemetery, and although they had agreed to treat each other as workmates while on Pascall territory, he had been anxious enough to accost her in the corridor one day. She had pooh-poohed his gentle concern. He asked her if Eddie Smith had bothered her again and she had denied it so emphatically that he was compelled to believe her.

Overwork? Stress? Her period?

'I'm all right,' she had finally yelled at him, 'I'm perfectly all right.' A head poked out of a nearby office and some young girls turned and stared. 'Go away. People are looking,' her accusation was both abrupt and unfair, for it had been she who had made all the fuss.

She wasn't all right. She was a closed book with so much between the covers that at some time it would all burst out of its binding.

She didn't want to see *Cats* with him. She didn't want an Indian curry. No, she didn't want to see *that* film, she hated political movies. And comedies and love stories and thrillers.

139

And no, she didn't want to see any blue movies either and would Patrick kindly stop being so bloody sarcastic.

Patrick sighed, buried his face in his hands. He wasn't *supposed* to be here now. Surely she was missing him! Would she be surprised to see him? It seemed a year since last Sunday.

'Here's your tea, Patrick,' said a small voice.

'Thanks, love,' he sipped and smiled at her. 'You make a lovely cup of tea, Charlotte.'

'I might take domestic science for one of my options,' replied Charlotte.

She went to the television and turned it on. It was another soap. Charlotte sat on the floor and watched the beautiful, plastic people flit across the screen. She was enthralled. She dipped her biscuit in her tea because her mother was not there to stop her.

Patrick stared unseeingly at the screen. The soap ended and the ten o'clock news came on. Another air crash. No survivors. The famine in Angola. And the Greenham women were getting bolshy again.

It all made Patrick very sad. But no toothache hurts quite like your own. He glanced at his watch.

Where *was* Liz?

18

Johnny Morris did his round of the building, checked each floor from fourteen to basement.

Not a soul around. Except for *her*.

Johnny couldn't believe his good luck. This was it. Now or never. There might not be another opportunity like this for fifteen years.

He licked his lips lasciviously, put his dirty magazines back in their brown carrier bag and stowed them away in his bottom drawer, which he then carefully locked.

But the fantasy layouts were still imprinted on his mind. He had particularly liked one set, entitled 'Business After Hours'. It even looked like her office. But the model wasn't a patch on her. Oh no!

She was such a lovely big woman, wasn't she!

Johnny Morris stood up. Took off his hat, slicked down his thinning, greasy hair and put his hat back on again.

That type loved a uniform.

He straightened his tie and tugged his jacket from the hem. His pants were too tight. And his balls were throbbing as if they had a life all of their own.

He locked the big glass foyer doors and then went to the side of the building and padlocked the double doors which led to Goods In. He bolted all remaining secondary doors.

He did all of it carefully, methodically, out of habit. As he had been doing for twenty-two years.

Then he rode the lift to Level 8.

The ante-room was closed. Gently, Johnny turned the handle, crept in surreptitiously, his eyes darting around Dinah's tidy office. Ran his hand over the cold metal surface of the filing cabinet. Three drawers. Just the right height. There was a picture in the 'Business After Hours' layout. A girl bending over a three-drawer filing cabinet. Mini-skirt, no drawers, a red suspender belt, black stockings.

Johnny released his waistband button, tugged again at his crotch. Gained no relief. Relief! That's what he was here for, wasn't it? She had got him like this, hadn't she? It was up to her to give him relief, wasn't it? That was only right.

He peeked round her door. She was still working at her desk, her dark head down. He couldn't see her legs because of the courtesy panel and her breasts were shielded by her arms, which lay across the papers as she wrote. But he could imagine!

Boldly, he entered her office. Stood right in front of her, drawing himself up to his full five feet ten. She looked up at him, mildly alarmed to sense someone standing there, visibly relaxed as she saw it was only him.

'Johnny!' she exclaimed, 'You gave me quite a start!' She carried on writing, as if he wasn't there. He continued to stand there, thrown by her physical presence, her matter-of-factness. He cleared his throat. Scuffed her carpet with his foot. Eventually she spoke: 'I won't be a moment, Johnny. Why don't you get us both a cup of coffee? I believe Dinah left it perking on the tray in her office. It might be a little strong, but it should be warm.'

Johnny remembered his new macho image.

'Look here, Mrs Carlton,' he began falteringly, 'Don't you tell me what to do.' She immediately glanced up at him, a crease of puzzlement in her brow. Gratified, Johnny warmed to his theme. 'You stuck-up cow!' he said. It sounded good. Positive. 'You stuck-up cow!' he repeated proudly.

Her full mouth was a small O of amazement. Johnny grinned. That had taken her by surprise all right. he could feel the excitement welling up inside him. Eddie had been right. Some women just needed telling.

'Have you been drinking, Johnny?'

He walked around her desk till he stood beside her. Leered down at her. He could just make out the shiny swell of her cleavage through the light cotton of her white shirt. Was

142

vaguely disappointed that she was only wearing an ordinary white bra.

'Get up,' he barked.

'Oh no,' she whispered. Her astonishment at his extraordinary behaviour had been so great that it had overshadowed any other emotion. Now a spark of fear made her hand fly, involuntarily, to her throat.

'Get up,' he repeated.

She stood.

'Undo your blouse.'

'Johnny, what's happened to you? Why are you doing this?'

'Never you mind. Just do as you're bleeding told. Get your blouse undone before you feel the back of my hand acrost your face.'

He felt the victory, the heady power, flooding through him as she complied, starting at the neck, undoing each button, one by one, pulling her shirt out of her waistband so that it gaped, exposing pale smooth shoulders and midriff and an expensive white lace bra.

'I'm very disappointed in you,' said Johnny insultingly. She did not reply. 'Ask me *why* I'm disappointed in you. Show a little interest in my feelings.'

'Why are you disappointed?'

'Because you're not wearing your black lace bra with the holes in the cups.'

'I don't have a bra like that.'

He leaned forward, grabbed a bunch of her black curls, pulled her face towards him. 'Don't lie, bitch!' he hissed. She gave a gasp of fear, but she didn't scream. Suddenly he wanted to make her scream. He shook her by her hair.

'It's all right, it's all right,' her voice was high and urgent. 'I've got some scissors. I'll make some holes.'

He released her with a flourish. She extracted a pair of scissors from her desk tidy. He slavered as she carefully removed one full, brown-nippled breast from her cup, pulled the cup to one side and snipped off its centre. Then she replaced the breast and repeated the exercise with the remaining cup. Finally she stood there, the white lace

143

surrounding each brown nipple inside its circle of smooth white flesh.

He pinched her left nipple between his thumb and forefinger. She winced. He led her thus around the desk and into the centre of the office.

'Please, you're hurting me,' she implored him.

'But you like being hurt, don't you! I know all about you, sweet Lizzie.' He grinned and tweaked the nipple hard before releasing her. She stood before him, trembling violently. Her fear was an aphrodisiac. He began to fumble with his trouser buttons.

'Don't do that Johnny,' her voice was wheedling now, as if she wasn't frightened of him any more. 'It'll spoil it if you get undressed yet, Johnny,' she continued. 'You have to keep your uniform on till the very last minute.'

As he hesitated, Liz held her breath. She had his number all right. And he thought he had hers, but he was wrong. Delay. Give herself time to think. All the while he still had his trousers on, she stood a chance of thwarting him. Distraction and confusion and then, maybe, a chance to cut and run. . .

He bent, licking his lips, lifted the hem of her grey knife-pleated skirt. Insidiously he ran his fingers up the inside of her thigh. She knew there was a steel paperknife on her desk. She could just make it out from the corner of her eye. Leaned slightly to one side. It was too far, too damned far. Her movement was sufficient to startle him. 'What are you doing?' he hissed accusingly as he stood up, his gnarled hand pinching viciously into the soft flesh of her upper arm.

'It's all right, Johnny. I'm sorry. I just lost my balance for a moment.'

Johnny smiled. The excitement, quite obviously, was too much for her, that was the trouble. He was glad she was wearing stiletto heels. Just like the girl in the picture, the one kneeling on all fours on the desk. *She* had a rather scraggy bum though, not like Liz, full-bodied beautiful Liz. Johnny liked his women to *look* like women.

He grabbed her by the shoulders, spun her round, pushing her up against the desk. Some papers and a stapler fell to the floor. She began to scream. Her screams sounded more like fear than arousal. He had wanted her to scream but now it just got on his nerves.

'Shut up, you silly cow! It's no good yelling. No one can hear you.' He stepped back, surveyed her with satisfaction as her cries slowly subsided. Her breath came in short, sharp gasps, as she stood there, in her prissy skirt and shoes and her sexy peep-through bra.

Johnny was panting now in his excitement. Could hardly contain himself. She would be his slave by the time he had finished with her. He drank in the sight of the large nipples poking through the holes in her bra. He leaned forward, hooked his fingers, like a claw, into the waistband of her skirt. With a jerk he broke the waist-fastening and the zip separated.

He was so close now, she could see the red veins in his broad nose, the dark hairs that erupted from his nostrils. Could smell the drink on his breath, the odour of his armpits, she felt her skirt falling from her hips, gasped as his ungentle hands grabbed at her lace slip.

'Johnny,' her tone was high and insistent, 'Johnny, let's go into Dinah's office. It'll be better in Dinah's office.'

'The view looks fine right here,' said Johnny pleasantly, tugging down her slip. 'He told me you wore suspenders,' he growled, suddenly dangerous.

'Who told you that?' she whispered, yet afraid to know the truth.

'Bloody Eddie Smith,' muttered Johnny disparagingly.

She could feel his fingers in the waistband of her tights as he started to draw them down. Could sense his hot breath against her flesh. Couldn't believe that this was happening to her. Never in her life had she felt so helpless. Wanted to bring up her knee, but he was already too close for that and as she was pinned against the desk, her movements were hampered.

She forced a tremor of titillation into her voice.

'I do wear suspenders, Johnny,' she told him. 'I keep them in the filing cabinet in Dinah's office.' Her tights were now around her knees, but she still had her panties on. Amazement at her words momentarily halted him.

145

'I absolutely *love* wearing my suspenders, Johnny,' she continued. 'There are lots of lovely things in Dinah's filing cabinet. Please Johnny, come and see.'

'You mean that primped-up secretary of yours knows what you get up to?'

'Dinah and I are very good friends,' replied Liz suggestively, 'you know what I mean, Johnny?'

All manner of new and exiting images raced through Johnny's brain. Oh boy, this was even better than he had expected! Desperately, Liz improvised. 'Why don't you come up and watch sometime,' she suggested invitingly. 'But right now, there's just you and me, so we might as well have a good time. Come on, Johnny, there's a whole lot of really exciting stuff in that filing cabinet. Suspenders and stockings and a black bra with holes in. There's even a birch if you want to beat me first.'

He groaned. Spittle ran down from the corners of his thin mouth. He raced into the outer office and she heard him pulling out the filing cabinet drawers, raking furiously around. heard his muttered curses, heard him yanking out the files and thowing them to the foor in his haste. Quickly, she kicked off her shoes and tights, ready for flight. Wanted to grab her shirt. Didn't dare.

As she crept into Dinah's office, he had his back to her, bending over, still desperately scrabbling through the filing cabinet. She watched him for a moment, clad only in her bikini panties and improvised peep-through bra. 'Not that drawer, Johnny,' she said craftily, 'the bottom one, right at the back. Please hurry, Johnny, I can't wait much longer . . .'

Now he was on his knees, but the anti-tilt mechanism would not allow the bottom drawer to open as the top one had not been pushed back properly. He swore obscenely, tugging at the bottom drawer, but to no avail. She edged nearer to the outer door, as he continued to struggle, oblivious to the cause of the problem. Next moment, she was through the door and running along the corridor, her hands cupping her heavy breasts to support them in her flight. Fear and revulsion lent wings to her heels. Somewhere behind her, she could hear his

146

heavy boots clomping in pursuit, which spurred her on to even greater exertions.

She did not risk waiting for a lift. She tore down the emergency stairs to the third floor, then raced along the corridor.

There was a fire escape outside the main office of P & L Maritime. She had noticed it when she was doing Jeremy Pascall's time and motion study. Which door? They all looked the same. She couldn't remember. In her panic, she ran first into a broom cupboard, then into the Ladies' Cloakroom. Resisted the urge to lock herself in one of the toilets. couldn't bear to remain in the same building as that evil man. Eventually she found the way. It stretched down below her, a spiral of silver metal that led to final, blessed release, her Nirvana.

Soon she was climbing out into the crisp autumn night, half naked, sobbing with terror and humiliation, needing her home and her children and Patrick. The city streets were almost empty at this time of night, but she spotted a group of people disgorging from a building opposite. There was no room for false modesty. She screamed at them to help her. As she stumbled to the bottom of the fire escape and fell into a huddle on to the concrete surface of the goods yard, she glanced up towards the street. She could see a couple of men climbing over the huge iron gates. Someone placed a coat over her. Someone else muttered something about calling the police.

She came to in the police station. She was lying on a bunk with a blanket over her. Beside her sat a very young woman PC. Gently the policewoman began to question her, but she wept unrestrainedly throughout the interview, her replies muddled and almost incoherent. They brought her a cup of tea. Then she saw the doctor.

Just after midnight, Patrick arrived to collect her. His face was a mask, concealing his pain. But his arms were strong and warm and comforting.

19

Whilst Liz desperately bargained with Johnny Morris for what was left of her dignity, the atmosphere at Pascall Lodge was strained. It was customary for the family to eat together on Friday evenings and Sunday lunch-times. This particular Friday evening Gina sat, with a faraway look in her eyes, idly picking at her food, while her husband, seated beside her, hunched possessively over his, as if afraid someone might whisk it away from him.

Sir George did not speak except to complain that the wine was not properly chilled, sending Smitherson, the butler, scuttling away in a panic. Martin, the taciturn one, conveyed his own unrest by staring fixedly at his plate as he ate. Even Alexia and Trevor, who normally had plenty to say for themselves, were intimidated by the general air of foreboding.

Only Lillian Pascall was untouched by this palpable tension. Lillian was unbudgeable. She was the original immovable object. She had all the confidence which came from never having had to worry about her personal security. Sir George had already been well embarked on his climb to the top when they had met, and Lillian had floated dreamily from the safe custody of her merchant banker daddy and socialite mummy, to that of the talented city newcomer, George Pascall.

The transition from old money to new had been smooth, easy, unmarred by troubles, for Sir George was well thought of and held his own among all classes.

'Hasn't anyone got anything to say for themselves?' scoffed Lillian, raising her hand to attract the maid's attention. 'More Duchesse potatoes,' she commanded imperiously, as if she thought she was the next stage down from God. She never addressed the female staff by their names and the male staff only by their surnames. Lillian did not believe in familiarity with the servants. It had taken her a long time to learn to use Gina's Christian name, and even now, she sometimes stumbled over it, as if it were a dirty word.

The dining-room was a long, narrow room, sombrely furnished, the walls covered in old paintings. The dining table was large and oblong, made of solid oak. It was actually a boardroom table. Sir George had purchased it through his company from their executive furniture suppliers, thus saving the tax.

But Lillian had never forgiven him for this. 'No one would ever know,' he had pointed out truthfully, but Lillian would always know. She felt quite resentful when she set out the silver, the pretty damask napkins, the crystal glasses. She did not trust the maid to lay the table. Or Smitherson for that matter. Lillian liked everything 'just so'.

'Cheapskate,' she would mutter to herself, although she knew, deep down, she was being a little unkind to her husband. Sir George would do anything for her, or for their family. He just couldn't help being thrifty.

His father had founded the business. His father was a pioneer. And Sir George had watched his father, pinching and scraping in order to keep his business solvent during the worldwide economic depression of the Thirties.

Also, despite his vast wealth, Sir George liked to think he had got something for nothing. So if he could get one over on the Inland Revenue or Customs & Excise, he would gloat like a kid with a toffee-apple. Yet he gave willingly and generously to charity. Children's homes, hospitals, educational institutions and the starving in Africa were all on Sir George's list of beneficiaries.

He remained convinced that his taxes only paid for beer for the 'layabouts' and for peculiar sculptures, masquerading as art, in the middle of town squares. Sir George had no time for the abstract. He liked all his t's crossed and his i's dotted. He was interested in logic, not dreams. He preferred the efficiency of design to the fanciful machinations of artistic interpretation.

Hearty debate was valid, music and reading an escape and therefore a weakness.

149

He glanced at his son, Martin. He was glad Martin had finally seen sense and abandoned his musical career. In Sir George's opinion there was something almost effeminate about having a son who played the piano for a living. Of course, Martin still dabbled, but at least it was in the privacy of his own apartment.

Sir George had refused to help him to finance his tuition. Deliberately, he had trimmed down Martin's allowance to the barest minimum. Had told himself that if music was Martin's true vocation, then Martin would find a way to sustain himself. Martin's subsequent failure had merely proved Sir George's point.

Suddenly Smitherson hurried in, interrupting Sir George's reverie. 'There's a telephone call for you, sir,' he said, then lowered his voice. His whisper was clearly audible to everyone present. 'It's the police.'

The women looked alarmed. Jeremy straightened his back and swallowed the last morsel of Maryland chicken.

'Don't worry, Pop,' he said quickly to his father, 'I'll go.'

'Shall I bring the phone to you, sir?' inquired Smitherson helpfully.

'I'll take the call in my father's study.'

Jeremy rose. Gina and Alexia exchanged glances. Martin continued to study his plate. Lillian Pascall flapped. How dared the police ring at such a time when most civilised people were at dinner!

Sir George, who took most things in his stride, merely hoped that whatever it was, it wouldn't take up too much of his valuable time.

'Wonder what that's all about,' ventured Alexia.

'Nothing serious, I hope,' replied Gina. 'I hardly see anything of Jeremy as it is. I hope he hasn't got to go rushing off again.'

Alexia smiled gently at her friend. Marvelled at her devotion to Jeremy, and at the same time, pitied her for it. Somehow, Gina looked so vulnerable this evening. She had dragged back her fluffy honey-coloured hair into a low ponytail, so that her face, in relief, seemed smaller, more elfin and deeply wistful.

Her cheeks were sunken and her delicate cheekbones stood out, the bone almost seeming to shine through the transparent skin.

Alexia wondered why everyone was so miserable this evening. Was it that the tension between Jeremy and Gina had somehow inhibited them all? Or was it something else? She leaned sideways, extending her hand below the table towards Martin, needing to feel the warmth of his strong fingers around hers. But Martin was still preoccupied with his thoughts and did not respond. Lillian coughed loudly and Alexia caught her stern gaze of disapproval. 'Can't you wait till you're on your own?' her expression seemed to say.

Lillian had no time for young lovers.

Quickly, Alexia snatched back her hand as if it had been burned and returned it, safely, to her lap.

At that moment, Jeremy returned. He hovered just inside the doorway. Gina eyed him anxiously, and Alexia thought how formal he managed to look, even when dressed in casual fawn slacks and a light cashmere pullover. He was the sort of guy they put on the covers of knitting patterns.

'I have to go,' he announced briefly, a look of long-suffering boredom on his aquiline features.

'Oh no!' groaned Gina, and she in turn was subjected to Lillian's stiff, beady-eyed attention.

'What's the problem?' abruptly Sir George turned to face his son.

'It's alleged that a female employee has been assaulted at the offices,' Jeremy replied pompously, choosing his words with caution.

'You sound like a ruddy lawyer,' commented Trevor with typical bluntness. Jeremy ignored him.

Gina glanced at her father-in-law. She could see he was intensely shocked and upset, for he had always taken his employees' welfare very much to heart, considered himself responsible for their wellbeing, mental and physical. He expected a lot from anyone who worked for him, but he was prepared to give a great deal back.

'Who was it?' he inquired eventually. 'Do I know her?'

151

'Elizabeth Carlton, as a matter of fact,' said Jeremy coolly. 'I'll keep you informed. I don't know how long I'll be. I suggest you go to bed, Gina, and don't wait up for me.'

Stunned, Gina could only stare at her husband, as Jeremy departed, yelling for Smitherson to arrange for his car to be brought around to the front of the house.

Usually, after dinner, the men retired to the library and the women to the lounge. Sir George's was an old-fashioned household. Alexia found this outmoded practice an insult, for her family was close and valued its women highly. But Gina accepted it as a normal English custom. From the time she had first arrived at this house, it had never been any different. In any case, even if she had objected to it, she would have understood.

Poor Sir George! He would only have to listen to Lillian whingeing on about the meat being undercooked, the vegetables not being fresh, the fact that Smitherson had spilled a drop of hock on her crisp, white tablecloth.

Sir George treasured a little time with his sons, without the intervention of Lillian's nagging and sudden sharp gibes. Good, solid, masculine banter and not having to worry about talking shop in front of the ladies. And if any of them wanted to have a good cuss, get some bug out of their system, then they were free to do so.

But tonight it was different. Tonight they remained seated around the table. They drank their coffee, then ordered more. They conversed in low, anxious whispers.

'I wonder how serious it was,' commented Gina. 'She couldn't have been. . . *raped*, could she?'

'My God! I hope not!' breathed Alexia.

'There's no point in conjecture,' said Sir George, for ever practical. 'We just have to hope for the best.'

'But who could have done such a thing?' Gina looked as if she were about to burst into tears. Kindly, Sir George reached over, squeezed her arm reassuringly.

'Get Mrs Pascall a brandy,' he said to Smitherson. Gratefully, Gina clutched at his hand.

Sir George's hand was trembling.

'Could be she asked for it,' commented Trevor. But he shifted uncomfortably in his seat, for although no one contradicted him, five pairs of eyes were fixed on him, and he didn't like what he saw in them.

'I guess I spoke out of turn,' he retracted weakly.

'Yes, Trevor, I think you did,' retorted his brother Martin.

Smitherson offered the brandy around and they ordered yet more coffee and sat there, drinking and thinking and waiting for Jeremy to contact them.

20

'I think you should go away for a few day's rest,' said Patrick. 'I have a small cottage in the heart of the Cotswolds. I used to go there for weekends. That is, before I met you and started coming here instead.'

He wished she would say something. Or even better, cry or shout or throw something. Just one small normal human reaction that he could handle. But she just sat. She had her legs drawn up beside her on the sofa making a space between them, keeping him at a distance.

'I'm all right,' she said.

'I'm sure they'll catch him,' said Patrick, but without much conviction. 'They'll catch him and get him to confess.'

'He's not important. He was just a pawn.'

'What are you saying?'

'Nothing,' she told him obstinately. He glared at her.

'There's no proof,' she said flatly. 'It's just his word against mine.'

Patrick's silence confirmed the truth in her statement. He had had a long chat at the station with the officers involved in the case, and the final analysis was that there did not appear to be a case.

Incredibly, there was nothing in the building to substantiate her story. Not a shred of evidence. The police had methodically checked out her office and everything was intact despite her insistence that the filing cabinet had been emptied, and the desk, by which the attempted assault had taken place, voided of its usual office paraphernalia. Indeed, there had not been the slightest indication of a struggle of any description. Her memo pad had been lying on her blotter, with her pen beside it just as if she'd just finished writing. No debris on the floor.

'What about fingerprints?' she asked him.

'I don't know,' he'd replied largely, doubtful that the police would have attempted to isolate Johnny's fingerprints amid the hundreds to be found in her busy office. Especially since they were entitled legitimately to be there. He was the building's caretaker.

As for Liz herself, she had not been bruised or marked. There was no sign of sexual assault on her body. She had pointed out the redness around her nipple where she had been manhandled. The police doctor had not been impressed, for the mark had virtually faded by the time she was examined.

'Someone must have put everything straight,' she had told the doctor, 'and in any case, I told you what happened. I was degraded and defiled in every way except by actual sexual intercourse.'

She had seen the look in the police medic's eye. *Who* put it all straight, it seemed to say. Your attacker? or are you suggesting there was an *accomplice*? No disturbance, no blood, no semen stains anywhere. *Of course, he kept his trousers on through the whole procedure!* Pull the other one, missus.

They had thought she was a frustrated attention-seeker, an exhibitionist, acting out her sexual fantasies for a cheap thrill.

'I talked him out of it, just for the moment. I got him to believe that there was exotic lingerie and sex toys in the filing cabinet, so I could get away while he was looking for them.'

The officer had looked up from his report, a quizzical glint in his eye.

'So this guy, all steamed up looking at you in a compromising position by your desk, suddenly stops in his tracks, at your bidding, to look for *exotic lingerie?*'

'That's the type of guy he is. A voyeur.'

'You should know, lady!'

She had been too weak to argue. Too tired. Too humiliated. Of course, they had taken a different tack with Patrick. They would, wouldn't they. A man-to-man talk. 'Don't worry, sir, we'll see what we can find out. Get her home now, get her to bed.' Then later, after they had left, 'Poor sod, tied up with a fruitcake like her!'

155

'You'll know the truth tomorrow, Patrick,' she said listlessly, 'because I'll bet Johnny Morris will ring in sick. He won't disappear, because that would confirm his guilt. He'll ring in sick and wait for it all to blow over. The police might go and question him, but he'll deny it all. Either he, or someone else, has convered his tracks. It's just his word against mine,' she repeated, 'and you have to admit, my side doesn't sound terribly convincing, does it?'

He marvelled at her cool and factual assessment of her predicament, without anger or recrimination, so soon after such a profoundly traumatic experience. But what was she saying about 'someone else'? And about Johnny Morris being 'just a pawn'?

'Liz, you appear to be of the opinion that someone put Johnny up to it.'

Liz sighed deeply. Couldn't muster the energy to evade his questions. Had already said too much to back out now. 'Something Johnny said. About Eddie telling him I was a masochist of some description.'

Patrick closed his eyes in pain, couldn't blot out the blinding sea of red that threatened to consume him. 'Eddie should know,' he growled, wanting to lash out at her, yet regretting his words immediately he had uttered them. She did not react, just continued to stare dully ahead of her.

'Let me stay with you tonight. Just to hold and comfort you,' he pleaded.

'What about Charlotte?'

'I hardly think that my staying for the night is likely to damage your daughter for life. I trust I'm little more than a passing fancy.' He paused, could not resist adding, 'Unlike your friend, Eddie.'

Why did he keep trying to hurt her? She was hurt enough already. She regarded him witheringly, a semblance of her old spirit returning to her. 'It's not necessary for you to do this to me, Patrick. Don't you think I haven't regretted my mistake a thousand times over?'

'I know, Liz, I know. I'm sorry. I just can't help myself. I can't help feeling angry with you. Can't understand how you

156

could have slept with that despicable excuse for a man. What do you think that does to me?'

Suddenly she sat up, put her stockinged feet squarely on the floor in front of her, turned her face towards him, her sandy eyes red-rimmed, her cheeks dark hollows. Piercingly, her eyes held his, direct and unafraid. He was instantaneously both relieved and disconcerted by her aggressive glare.

'Patrick,' she told him, her voice clear and unwavering, 'I am a woman of an age that is usually described as "uncertain". I am a woman of normal sexual appetites. I have had three husbands, all of whom I have cared for, and a number of lovers that I remember with affection. I live a life that is meaningful, at least to me, and I have no wish for that meaning to be clouded by the doubtful consequences of sexual frustration.

'I admit that this time I made a mistake. I did something I now regret. I picked the wrong guy. Haven't you ever made a mistake, Patrick?'

Once again, he could feel the blood rush to his face. His face was burning. Just like a woman! She always turned the tables. Made it seem as if he was being unreasonable. Always justified herself, yet without seeming to do so. She should be contrite, feel guilt that she had precipitated a situation that had put herself and her son at risk. But she would not be demeaned. Not even a little.

She had made a mistake. Hard cheese, Patrick! I got it wrong, Patrick. So what! Don't hassle me, you have no right to hassle me! Put your own house in order, Patrick!

Suddenly she softened. Put her hand tremulously over his. 'Patrick, you must understand. It's different for me. It would have been all right if Eddie had survived. I'd be a happily married, middle-aged matron now. I'm not trying to make you feel sorry for me, but until I met you, I was reluctant to become deeply involved with another man. My track record isn't exactly encouraging, is it?'

'What happened to Robbie's father?'

'One day maybe I'll tell you. But not right now.'

And he had to be content with that.

'Look, Liz, Mrs Oakes will be here in the morning. I'll

157

arrange for her to stay over with the kids, make it worth her while to stay for a week or so. Then I'll drive you down to my cottage so you can get right away from it all. I have a sister living near by who would be happy to keep an eye on you.'

'I'd rather be alone.'

'Okay, if you're sure you'll be all right. But you wouldn't mind if I joined you at the weekend?'

'What about the office?'

'Leave that to me. Jeremy Pascall was called out to the building, so I should think by now it's common knowledge in the Pascall clan. Nobody will be surprised if you take a few days off. And Liz, I think it's high time this Eddie Smith saga was brought out into the open. If you won't tell the police about him, then I will.'

'If you had been a fly on the wall when those policemen were questioning me,' she told him, 'you wouldn't waste your time.'

That night, the first night Patrick had stayed over, they lay incongruously back to back, together yet apart. The barrier between them became a monster, feeding off their mutual resentment until it became an entity that was self-perpetuating. She would not bridge it, and he, fearing her rejection of him, dared not try.

Eventually, sheer fatigue enabled Liz to fall into a restless, disturbed slumber. But Patrick lay awake, not regretting that he had stayed because he needed to be close to her, but wishing he could find release for the turmoil of confused images that crowded into his mind.

At first light, he sat up, listening to the dawn chorus, watching her as she lay on her side, her breathing fast and shallow, her hand in front of her face clutching the pillow, making a fist.

He was overwhelmed with tenderness for her, loving her exactly as she was, with all her faults, wanting, yet not wanting, to change her.

Wished he could make love to her. Not for the usual reasons of lust and physical attraction, for these had been diminished by the events of the previous night. Not diminished in any lasting way, he knew that, just temporarily overshadowed by pain and uncertainty.

158

Only by making love to her could he drive away the demons, be close to her again, be at one with her. Only when she could remember her last sexual experience as being with him would the damage perpetrated by Eddie and Johnny finally begin to abate.

At nine-thirty in the morning, after Charlotte had left for school and while Liz was in the shower, Patrick sneaked down to the telephone in the kitchen, dialled Pascall House.

'Can I speak to Johnny Morris?'

'Oh, I'm sorry,' said the switchboard operator, 'he's not in today. Would you like to speak to his stand-in?'

'No, that's OK. Hey don't hang up. What's up with Johnny, do you know?'

'Hold on one moment, I'll find out, sir.'

The line went dead for a few long seconds. Clicked back into life again.

'Hello, sir. I'm afraid he won't be back for several weeks. He's got shingles.'

'Thanks,' said Patrick weakly, replacing the receiver. A glint of determination in his eye, he chewed thoughtfully on his thumbnail. Now what?

There was only one thing for it. He would just have to find out. Turn detective. Starting with Eddie Smith and his perverted wonderland of sexual fantasy.

'I'm not going,' said Liz flatly. She sat on a high stool at the breakfast bar, which ran the entire length of one wall of her spacious, streamlined kitchen. Considering her ordeal of the previous night, Patrick thought, she had coped very well.

She was still in her silky red housecoat, but her hair had been shampooed and dried and her jet-black curls shone in the morning sun that filtered through the blinds. She wore light makeup, grey eyeshadow, coral lipstick and a touch of rouge. Seemed composed in a strangely detached way.

'I wish you wouldn't be so stubborn about staying in the cottage. It's in a very beautiful spot, especially at this time of the year when the leaves are just beginning to turn. It's quiet

159

too, no neighbours so you don't need to talk to anyone unless you care to walk down to the village, which is just a mile or so away.' Patrick was disappointed. He had hoped she would go, as much as for her own sake as for his. He was looking forward to joining her at the weekend. Just the two of them. Bliss. Complete isolation, maybe a chance to get their act together. Bury a few ghosts!

Liz sipped thoughfully on her black coffee. He was so kind. She owed him some sort of an explanation. 'It isn't that I'm ungrateful, Patrick. I love the countryside and I couldn't bear to live in the heart of town. Just the same, I don't think that right now is a good time for me to bury myself in sheep and birdsong.'

'You need the rest.'

'That's the last thing I need. Alone with my thoughts and nothing to occupy me. I will have a few days off, Patrick. And I shall plan to hold an "at home" next weekend.'

Patrick's first reaction to her words was one of total astonishment that she could think of such a thing at such a time. He stared at her, his mouth gaping, crouched forward on his stool, his hands on his knees, taking in the lines of her neat, tight profile. His next reaction was admiration for her willpower, her lack of self-pity, her innate ability to recover. Lastly he felt mild amusement. So Liz was thinking of holding an "at home". Most other people simply had parties. Professional socialites – and Liz – held an "at home".

'You're crazy!'

'Not so crazy. It's the best thing I could do. For myself, for the children, for my image. I don't know how much of what happened last night is going to filter through to the troops, but no one's going to accuse Liz Carlton of cracking up under the strain. Not over a little jerk like Johnny Morris.'

Grudgingly, he had to concede that she was on target in her line of reasoning. 'Who will you ask?'

'I'll make it a combination of business and pleasure,' she decided. 'I'll ask everyone I like and everyone who matters, even if I don't particularly like them.'

'Which of those categories do I come into? Or not, as the case may be.'

'I like you very much Patrick and you matter to me a great deal. Yours is a very special category indeed!' She laughed. 'I say all the right things, don't I.'

'I wouldn't entirely agree with that,' he gibed.

'By the way, I haven't seen Charlotte this morning. How much, if anything, does she know about last night?'

'She knows nothing. She was sleeping when I left to collect you, so I left a small note by her pillow to reassure her if she woke and got frightened. It was still there when we got back, so I removed it. This morning I made her some breakfast, and I told her you had a hangover. She went off to school quite happily.

'Thanks,' she said drily.

'Look, Liz, I don't believe she could have handled the truth. And since you're so invincible and refuse to catch anything even so mundane as a cold, I couldn't say you were ill. She wouldn't have believed me.'

'I'm sure she believed you about the hangover.'

'Didn't bat an eyelid.'

'You're a beast!'

He stood up behind her, slipped his arms very gently around her waist, being careful not to touch her breasts. Pushed his face up into her neck, under the corkscrew twists of her nape hair, pressed his lips into her warm skin.

'It's all right, Patrick,' she said softly, 'I'm not that delicate. What happened last night hasn't changed anything to do with you and me. I still want you to throw me across the bed and ravish me to pieces.'

'Dearest Liz,' he muttered, 'you are truly a most remarkable woman.'

161

21

As Patrick prepared to leave for the office around mid-morning, Liz was settled, in a shocking pink tracksuit, in the centre of her lounge carpet. She was surrounded by cookery books. A scattering of recipes she had saved from magazines also littered the floor. There was a large memo pad at the ready on her lap.

She prepared for her party as a general would plan a strategic military manoeuvre, every scrap of information at her finger-tips, step by step, with calculating precision. A game of chess.

It was exactly as she planned everything that was important in her life, several moves ahead. With the notable exception of the one area of her being that meant most to him, that related to her sexual behaviour. Could he hope to persuade her that she had a vested interest in being faithful to him, when she had known so many men? He did not doubt the warmth of her feelings towards him, only their constancy, their permanency. Was she inherently a sexual butterfly or had she merely been unfortunate?

A fastidious man, Patrick felt uncomfortable wearing yesterday's shirt and underclothes, but there was insufficient time for him to return to his flat to change. He had to get back to Pascall House, into the thick of it, assess what damage, if any, had been done to her standing within its sober confines.

Surely the directors would be discreet! And what of the outsiders, those who had become involved when she screamed for their help from the fire escape? No reason to suppose they might have any links with the employees of Pascall House.

Fervently, Patrick prayed they did not, that the whole matter could be kept low-key in the interests of Liz's morale and future success. God help her if any newsmen got wind of it.

If she had been a less extrovert woman, less successful, less colourful, less confident, it would not have mattered so much. All that her predicament would have evoked among the masses would have been a deep-felt and genuine sympathy. But her wide sexual experience, now common knowledge at Pascall House, spread by wild rumours among the lower echelons, inaccurate yet with an inkling of truth, did not help her now.

He wondered how it could have happened. Liz could hardly be accused of being indiscreet about her personal life, was far too professional to gossip at work. Of course, Eddie Smith's sudden appearance had added fuel to the flames, already fanned by her marital history.

Sadly he had to admit to himself that her past would only lessen the enormity of Johnny's offence in most people's eyes. Yet there was a world of difference between consenting sexual interaction, however indiscriminate, however impulsive and unwise, and the kind of sexual abuse and degradation Liz had suffered so bravely, at Johnny Morris's hands. Despite her coolness, her humiliation was as painful as that of any sixteen-year-old virgin. Her saving grace was her tremendous reserve of strength and determination which she now drew upon.

For that Patrick was grateful.

'Patrick,' she spoke up, her tone clear and modulated, brisk and businesslike, 'before you leave, could you make a couple of mental notes for me? I'd be grateful if you could have a word with Dinah. Tell her I've left a tape for her to transcribe in my top right-hand drawer. Also could she organise the redecorating of my office while I'm away. It's all been cleared with the powers that be. I've left a list of my instructions in the tray.'

'Yes, Ma'am,' said Patrick, wryly tipping an imaginary cap. 'Anything else, Ma'am?'

Playfully she aimed a Sainsbury cookery paperback at his head so that he had to duck.

'Go on,' she told him, 'do that for me and then I shall spend the rest of the day making Beef Stroganoff for your dinner tonight.

'I hope you're not expecting me to make me sing for my supper,' he jested, as he picked up his briefcase.

163

'I shall expect a whole opera,' she replied, with all of her old verve and vivacity.

He left her, with a brief kiss, feeling much better about himself.

But as he walked out of the door, the tears fell unchecked down her cheeks.

It had been worse, much worse, than he had thought. Patrick had gone straight up to Level 8, made directly for Liz's prestige corner office. To reach it, he had to traverse the typing pool area. There were three workmen in green overalls bustling around, shifting desks up to one end of the large office. Incensed by the changes being forced upon them, the typists congregated in clusters, low indignation in their chatter. A couple of large perspex screens stood in one corner, surrounded by brown corrugated packing material. They had obviously only just been delivered and unpacked.

For a moment, he stood outside Dinah's office. The first thing he noticed was the letterbox-shaped oblong of dark shiny wood on the door, just below the spy-hole, wood that had not been exposed to light as the remainder of the door had been. He creased his brow in puzzlement, then realisation dawned. Liz's nameplate had gone.

Perhaps they were going to replace the door when they decorated? Or perhaps her job title had been upgraded? The door did not seem warped or damaged. She had no doubt been promoted. She deserved it.

As he raised his finger to the buzzer, something made him halt in mid-action. Dinah was talking to someone. Her voice was naturally clear and bell-like in tone and carried easily, so he had no difficulty in making out her words.

'What can you expect,' she was saying in a querulous tone, 'the way she throws herself about, dispensing her favours to all and sundry. It's surprising it didn't happen a long time ago.'

There followed the deeper drone of a male voice and Patrick continued to eavesdrop, but the tone was indistinct. At one point, he half-fancied he heard the expression, 'silly bitch'. He frowned.

'She always did set herself up above her station,' continued Dinah patronisingly. 'Thought she was a cut above the rest of us. But I reckon she's had it now. She might consider herself Sir George's blue-eyed girl, but by now even he must be losing patience.'

A terrible fury consumed Patrick. He did something he had never done before in all of his life. He burst into an office unannounced.

Dinah sat on the desk, facing him, her feet propped up on her visitor's chair, her well-turned knees slightly parted as they poked out of her plum-coloured skirt. As Patrick stormed like a tornado through the door, it was only the intervention of the doorstop that prevented the man leaning against the wall from being flattened by the intrusion. Dinah gasped and instinctively closed her legs. The man for whose benefit they had been parted in the first place let out a growl of fury.

'Who do you think you are? Bursting in like this?'

Patrick, his hazel eyes afire, faced Jeremy Pascall's furious black buttons.

'You crazy fool,' fumed Jeremy. 'I'll have you thrown out on your ear for this.'

Jeremy Pascall, being a cold, detached man who prided himself on never losing control in any circumstances, suddenly thought better of awaiting explanations, turned and, slamming the door behind him, left the office. Dinah stood down from her desk, straightened her skirt. 'I do have a buzzer, Mr Evans,' she said reprovingly. 'It is there for your use.'

'Sit down,' growled Patrick. Dinah was startled at his mood, obviously unaware that he had overheard her words of betrayal.

'Sit *down*,' Patrick repeated. 'I want to know just what's going on.'

Dinah complied, assuming her haughty, 'I don't know what you mean but I'm sure I wouldn't like it anyhow' expression. Once she was safely ensconced behind her desk, he picked up her visitor's chair, set it dead centre in front of her, then he too sat down, his elbows on her desk top, his large body inclined agressively forwards. Defensively, in response, she leaned back in her own chair, wary, trapped.

'I thought that the first duty of any decent secretary was loyalty to her boss,' he began, hoping to appeal to her better nature, if she had one. 'Mrs Carlton trusts you implicitly, and if she heard what I have just heard, I don't think she would believe her own ears.'

'I'm no longer assigned to Mrs Carlton,' Dinah informed him coldly, thereby completely taking the wind out of his sails.

'Why? Are you leaving?' he asked feebly.

'No, but I believe she is.'

'What! Then to whom are you being assigned? Or have you suddenly been promoted on account of your little understanding with Mr Jeremy?'

'How dare you!' she shrilled.

'I want to know,' he yelled back, his eyes wild and angry beneath the ferocious eyebrows.

'I'm being assigned to you, Mr Evans.'

Suddenly Patrick felt he could take no more. His hands were cold and clammy, he pressed them over his ears as if to shut her out. His defensive gesture gave her courage.

'Look, Mr Evans, I'm sorry we've got off to such a bad start,' she faltered. 'I was looking forward to working for you. I realise that you must have overheard my conversation with Jeremy, but truly, you must understand that my integrity is normally above suspicion. It's just that, with all due respect to Mrs Carlton . . .'

His eyes dared her to continue. She thought better of her intended character assassination of Liz, tapered into defeated silence.

'All I can say is you must be feeling extremely confident about your position here, because I can assure you, young lady, you won't be working for me. Now, I want to *know*. Why all the changes outside? Why the upheaval in the typing pool? Why has Mrs Cartlon's nameplate been removed?' His tone was stark, severe, his words exploding like bullets from his taut lips.

'They're making space for the Robinson's Surgical Instruments people. The typing pool is being moved up and the screens will divide the main office into two. Mrs Carlton's office will be your office from now on. And Mr Jeremy expects me to be working for you,' she shot him a defiant glance. 'You should have heard from Mr Jeremy this morning. It's not that you've been deliberately kept in the dark. It's just that it was all a sudden decision, but nobody could find you to inform you.'

Patrick groaned.

'What's so terrible, Mr Evans? This is a very good office. Plenty of people have been after it. I would have thought you would have been delighted.'

Patrick stood up. He did not speak. He did not need to, for he conveyed exactly what he thought of her most succinctly by the withereing scorn in his eyes.

Like Mr Jeremy, he too slammed the door behind him, but with such force that the chattering typists were reduced to stunned silence and the two workmen dropped, with a resounding crash, a desk that they were moving.

Patrick marched the length of the new-style main office, eyes forward, head erect, completely oblivious of the dozens of pairs of eyes riveted on the departing figure of Pascall's newest and angriest executive.

Patrick took the lift to the ground floor, turned left towards George Pascall's offices.

Julia was not surprised to see him. Greeted him with a smile. Patrick had now been taken into the fold of the élite, so it was OK for her to smile sweetly at him.

'Good morning, Mr Evans.'

' 'Morning Julia. I want to see Sir George.'

Julia smiled again. It didn't take long, did it? She could remember, not so long ago, Patrick nervously requesting an interview with her boss. Wanted to tell him about the potential of Robinson's Surgical. He hadn't been so cocky then. 'Please would you ask him if he could spare me a moment,' he'd asked, with all the obligatory subservience of a minion. Now it was a brusque, 'I want to see Sir George.'

Not that Julia minded. Positive men turned her on. Especially red-haired positive Irishmen. Still, for the moment

167

she had her eye on Mr Martin. You couldn't do better than a son, could you? However attractive this young Irish prodigy of Sir George, he could never measure up to family.

Pity Mr Martin was engaged to that horsy Amazon, Alexia Potts. A frown spoilt Julia's smooth white brow.

'I hope it's not invonvenient,' said Patrick, misunderstanding the vertical creases that had appeared just above Julia's perfect *retroussé* nose. She flashed him a disarming smile.

It wasn't inconvenient. Sir George granted him an immediate audience.

After the obligatory greeting and handshake, Patrick launched straight into the attack.

'I'm not at all happy with my office arrangements,' said Patrick. Sir George raised his eyebrows.

'I had never intended for my promotion to precipitate the removal of Mrs Cartlon from her offices.'

'Mrs Carlton's being moved, is she,' said Sir George as if it was news to him, but from the guarded glint in his moist eyes, Patrick disbelieved his assumed ignorance.

'Yes. To make way for me and Robinson's Surgical.'

'Don't worry about that, my boy. I am sure Jeremy will find her a cosy little spot elsewhere.'

'That's not the point, Sir George,' insisted Patrick.

'Sit down, my boy, you're making me nervous.'

Reluctantly, Patrick sat.

'Now Patrick,' began Sir George, as if he were talking to a mentally retarded four-year-old, 'if you are unhappy about the arrangements, you must have a word with Mr Jeremy. He is in charge of Robinson's installation in the building.'

'But Sir George . . .'

'There's not much point in my employing dogs and barking myself,' said Sir George dramatically, trotting out his old favourite. It had always succeeded in getting him out of difficult situations before. But not this time.

'Sir George, I beg you to listen to me. Liz has been treated most unfairly . . .'

'I'll give you a word of well-meant advice, young man. If you want to move upwards, you can't help treading on a few toes on the way. That's business. Mrs Carlton knows that. She's trodden on quite a few herself, I can assure you.'

'But she doesn't deserve this. Liz is first-class at her job. Everyone knows that. She's earned her position in this group. At the moment, through no fault of her own, she is operating at less than her usual high standard. But she's a fighter.' Patrick paused. 'Sir George, you are obviously aware of the Johnny Morris saga?' Sir George remained poker-faced, so Patrick assumed his silence to mean affirmation.

'Sir George, the last thing Liz needs now is something like this. It's so desperately unfair. I appeal to you to intervene . . .'

Sir George slowly lifted the lid to his cigar case, extracted a short, fat cigar and lit it, puffing, trying to conceal that his hands were trembling, his moist lips making sharp sucking noises against the tobacco leaf casing. Patrick waited, not sure if he had already said far too much.

'I see it's Liz now, not Mrs Carlton. You are becoming too personally involved with the delectable Mrs Carlton, young man. You are no more than the latest of many who have fallen into her clutches. Still, you'll not listen to an old man, will you? All you young men are the same, think you know it all. Going to reform her, are you? Going to be the one to tame her? You'll be in for a hard time, young man. Shakespeare wrote a play about it, you know. *The Taming of the Shrew.* I wish you luck, you will need it.'

The sound of Sir George's buzzer seemed incongruous in the light of his rhetoric. And Julia materialised at his side like a genie out of a bottle.

Spluttering helplessly, a subdued Patrick had to permit himself to be speedily dispatched, as had a thousand others, including a victimised Liz, before him.

22

When Patrick got back to Liz's flat that evening, a wonderful aroma of frying steak assailed his nostrils even as he stood, hesitant and dejected, on her doorstep. He heard her run to the door. She had made a tremendous effort to look nice for him She wore a Chinese-style blouse with a mandarin collar and matching trousers in a shiny silky scarlet material with gold Paisley embroidery. A pair of large red and gold painted ethnic-style hoops dangled cheerfully from her lobes. Her face was attractively flushed from the cooking and she had Afro-combed her hair into its full gorgeous glistening glory.

In her rush, she had slightly smudged her lipstick at the corner of her mouth. Affectionately he removed the imperfection with his forefinger.

'It's all ready, Patrick. And Mrs Oakes has taken the children back to her place for the evening to show them her new kittens.'

Never before had he seen her so radiant, so eager to please him. And never before had he carried such distressing news for her.

As he followed her through into the lounge, he could see the table set out in the dining-room annexe. The delicious sounds of Vivaldi's 'Autumn Concerto' erupted from her compact disc player. He felt a lump in his throat that she had even bothered to obtain a disc of his favourite piece to make the evening perfect.

The table was a set piece that took his breath away. Resplendent in pristine white lace, tall crystal glasses, the wine nestling gently in its basket. Red napkins, beautifully folded, delicate white china with a red rose motif. The seafood platter was carefully arranged in large scallop shells, awaiting their pleasure.

His stomach sank. How could he knock her down again, after all this?

'Let me take your jacket, love,' she said. 'Sit yourself down and relax. Is the music loud enough? Too loud? Would you like an aperitif first?'

'Everything's perfect. I'll just have a glass of wine,' he croaked.

He ate, not tasting. He drank, but the excellent Bordeaux might have been cheap Spanish plonk. He responded automatically to her conversation. Forced his mouth into a smile. Wondered why she could not see that something was badly wrong.

She piled his plate high with Beef Stroganoff, sauté potatoes, broccoli, asparagus, carrots and salad. He wanted to decline the meringue, strawberry and ice cream dessert. He managed half, then pleaded repletion.

'Don't make yourself uncomfortable. So long as you have had sufficient,' she sparkled, removing his plate. She brought him coffee and zambuki floating with coffee beans. They flamed like a small victory, died out like a defeat. just like life. She flapped a bit lest he put the glass to his lips too soon and burned himself.

'You didn't tell me you were a Cordon Bleu cook,' he said at last. He wished he did not feel so sick.

'Just because I have a high-powered job doesn't make me a washout as a woman,' she told him teasingly.

'Oh, Liz!'

She stood and leaned towards him. He could smell her perfume. Her warm lips pressed against his ear, her wet pointed tongue played around and behind his lobes. 'I'm going to give you the time of your life tonight,' she murmured, 'because you are the sweetest and best baby in the whole world.

Her affectionate baby-talk, ironically, jerked him into the resolution he had hitherto found so elusive.

'Liz,' he forced himself to say, 'Liz, I have to talk to you. And I'm afraid you're not going to like it.'

* * *

171

'You mean you've pinched my office and my secretary and you expect me to understand?' screamed Liz.

Patrick sat very still, his bright head bowed. There seemed little point in disputing her wild accusations. Liz was beside herself. Fury had murdered logic and fathered vindictiveness. The soft flush of her skin had flooded crimson, making her face appear lumpy, weathered. In that instant, Liz looked every bit her age.

She drew breath as if to prepare herself for a further onslaught of abuse. Stood up, began crashing plates and dishes together as if they were made of tin and not the finest bone china. Stamped into the kitchen, still muttering vehemently, throwing the fine china into the dishwasher with utter abandon.

Patrick remained, immobile, at the dining table. He was in an agony of indecision, as he listened to the crashes and curses emanating from the kitchen, the smash of a dish that had slipped through her uncaring fingers. The explosive string of four-letter words because she couldn't find the dustpan and brush.

And in between, the ongoing tirade, her fury with life, with men, with their treachery and their low cunning and the way they always had to be on top of women, both literally and emotionally.

Patrick's Irish temper began to gnaw in the pit of his stomach.

Mrs Oakes was getting it in the neck now! It seemed she had hidden the dustpan for the express purpose of frustrating her much maligned employer. Patrick groaned, debated whether to help her search, decided discretion was the order of the day. Keep a low profile. He was dynamite to her in her present mood.

Eventually, from the unmistakeable sounds of her sweeping up broken china, he knew she had found the dustpan and he breathed a sigh of relief.

Suddenly she stood framed in the doorway, between the dining-room annexe and the kitchen. In her fury she looked wildly magnificent if, ironically, faintly ridiculous, portraying all the unchecked frustration of a child's temper tantrum with the venom and articulate intensity of a mature woman. In spite of his increased irritation towards her, he felt himself becoming aroused.

'Well, what have you got to say for yourself?' she growled at him finally, challenging him.

'Not a lot,' said Patrick insolently, 'it seems that you, in your infinite wisdom, have said it all.'

'You bastard,' she shrieked, her face distorted and ugly.

'If they could only see the real Liz now,' taunted Patrick. 'All those misguided employees at Pascall House who think you're so laid back, those impressionable little girls in the typing pool. Not to mention the directors and the managers.'

Next moment, she had grabbed the wine bottle from its basket and it was poised threateningly over his head in a downward motion. By all the saints! The crazy bitch was going to bash his brains out! Patrick's hand shot up, seized her wrist in its vice-like grip. The neck of the bottle tipped ominously downwards.

Maybe he could have prevented what happened next had her right breast not brushed distractingly against his face, had he not caught her faint, musky, arousing odour as she lifted her arm. As it was, the bottle's contents emptied in a steady crimson stream directly into his crotch. The wetness seeping through his flies startled him into releasing her and she dropped the bottle.

Even then, it might have been all right. Even then maybe he would have forgiven her, would have attempted to placate her. Made her feel ashamed when she perceived the futility of her juvenile behaviour. But it was not to be.

As he clutched at his flies, his mouth gaping with abject surprise and horror, she laughed. She doubled up, clutching her arms around her, chortling mercilessly at his discomfort.

Unbearably humiliated, he rose, gave her an angry shove against her shoulder so that she half-toppled. As she struggled to regain her balance, still spluttering with unrestrained mirth, he, panting with rage, clenched his fists into balls so that the knuckles showed white.

A man doesn't hit a woman – ever. Whatever the provocation. He clung to his father's words and for several moments his upbringing fought a battle with his baser urge to wipe the grin off her face.

The conflict was too much for him. He left the room, grabbed his jacket from where he had left it draped across her beautifully inviting sofa. He had half hoped, that in spite of everything they might have ended up together on that sofa, he comforting her in her distress and reassuring her that somehow he meant to find a way to make it all come right for her.

She had ruined it all now! Thought she was the bloody Queen Bee, didn't she? Used to getting all her own way, that was the trouble. Because of her vivid beauty, she had been spoilt by men. Well, he was blowed if he was going to help her any more, putting his job and his future on the line for her.

As he stepped from the lift and walked to his car, it suddenly occurred to him how little she knew about him. She had never asked to see his flat. Never admired his bowling trophies. Never expressed any interest in his parents, his upbringing, his childhood in Ireland. Nor how he had come to be at Pascall House in the first place.

She didn't know he could read music, play the guitar and sing a little.

They shared nothing that was not directly relative to Liz herself. Sex, Pascall House and Eddie Smith. That was the beginning and the end of it.

Christ! He was better off without her!

After Patrick left she could hardly remember which day it was, had to consult her watch calendar.

Friday tomorrow. The last day of the working week and the first day of the rest of her life. She would get in an early night and tomorrow Pascall House was going to wonder what had hit it!

Power! For power she had suffered and gone through hell. The power to have some say in her own destiny, to give her children the freedom to choose.

There was no power in being short of money. No power in

being answerable for your every action. No power in being under some man's thumb.

Funny how there was always someone around to kick the bucket out from under you. People just couldn't stand it if someone else got more than they did.

Especially if that someone was a woman who never made excuses for herself.

The ticking clock in the centre of the mantelpiece made an eerie, hollow heartbeat in the silence. It was strange that she had never noticed it before, but now she was afraid of the ticking clock, afraid of the terrible silence it broke with its relentless tick, tick, tick . . . It seemed to mock her for her own mortality, her helplessness as she mentally battled with the unknown, her insides aflame with feelings that amounted to nothing but total confusion.

She was hurt and that hurt went even deeper than anything Johnny Morris could have done to her. It went deeper than ego, deeper than pride, deeper than dignity.

In the first place, Sir George had not bothered to contact her after her terrifying ordeal with Johnny Morris. She had expected him to care, to inquire after her welfare, to commiserate and strengthen her spirtis with words of comfort and empathy. She was mortified beyond even her own under-standing at his apparent lack of concern.

And now this. Had Sir George really stood by and allowed her to be thrown out of her own office?

Scream internally as she might, she now had to re-harness the control she had relied upon before, a control on a level that was almost superhuman. She had to present to the world a calm, collected exterior, submerging her destructive feelings till she became once again the Liz Carlton who believed in herself, in the validity of her being, the rightness of her direction.

She slept badly that night, her mind a turmoil of confused thoughts and emotions. She did not blame herself for any of it, nor did she indulge in futile self-pity. It was something that had to be dealt with one way or another. She would see Sir George. She would see Martin Pascall. She would even see Jeremy.

175

So she hatched schemes and counter-schemes, most of which would have seemed either impractical or impossible to anyone with less moral courage than she.

Three times that night she crept into Robbie's room, needing to draw succour from his nearness. Felt instant maternal guilt because Charlotte, of the rebellious and independent spirit, failed to evoke a corresponding need in her.

By dawn her throat was prickling so badly she envied the birds the clarity of their song. Her nose streamed and she dosed herself with Lemsip and Vick. At seven, she went to Charlotte's room to awaken her.

'Oh Mummy!' exclaimed Charlotte, who always woke instantly, wide-eyed and alert. 'Oh, Mummy, you look terrible!'

It was true. Her mascara was smudged around her red-rimmed eyes, where she had not bothered to remove it the night before. Her nose was red and swollen to twice its normal size. She resembled a sick clown.

She had actually caught a cold. And Liz never caught colds. She had always believed in mind over matter, had assured herself she didn't have the time to catch colds, and now she had caught one.

'You silly cow!' she told her reflection in the bathroom cabinet mirror. Puffed up sandy pinpoints, that used to be eyes, stared back at her in angry accusation.

'It'll have to wait till Monday,' she told herself gloomily.

It would not promote her cause to arrive at the office in such a pathetic state. The last thing she needed was for her adversaries to start feeling sorry for her. Pity was too close a companion to contempt for Liz's liking.

No, she had to sock it to them good and hard! Work up a little aggression. Give them some grief so that they would wonder why any of it had been allowed to happen in the first place.

Uninterestedly, she prepared breakfast for the children before Mrs Oakes arrived to whisk them off the school. Needing some time to herself, she gave Mrs Oakes the rest of the day off. But couldn't she just this once, please collect Robbie from school? Benedict, unfortunately, was having his teeth fixed so Mrs Doughty couldn't go.

Mrs Oakes went off happily enough, rambling on about a 'mooch round the shops', to fill in her unexpected free day.

Liz spent the day trying out all her well-tested pick-me-ups. She read some of her favourite lines from Walt Whitman, the famous American peasant poet, lines which normally uplifted her, made her feel good about herself and life in general.

She still didn't feel good.

She played Gilbert and Sullivan's 'Mikado', sang along to the 'Pirates of Penzance'. She even gave her favourite musical, 'Joseph and the Amazing Technicolor Dreamcoat', a whirl. That did not help at all. She identified so totally with Joseph and his suffering at the hands of his jealous brothers, due to his winsome personality and intrepid love for his beautiful coat, that she felt more depressed than ever. Switched off the tape half-way through, quite forgetting that Joseph had actually won the day in the end.

She had a facial sauna for her cold and her morale. Watched a Laurel and Hardy matinée on the TV. But even her highly developed sense of the ridiculous failed to come to her rescue, for by the time Robbie came home, she was half-heartedly polishing the silver without even the minimal concentration needed for such a task.

'This one's still dirty at the bottom, Mummy,' said Robbie reprovingly, but Liz continued to stare apathetically into space.

'What's the matter, Mummy?' he inquired anxiously, planting a kiss on the back of her head.'

'Nothing, darling.'

'Mummy,' said Robbie earnestly, 'it's very difficult for me to have to worry about you, when I don't know what's wrong with you. If you don't confide in me, how can I tell you what to do?'

Liz put down her cloth, stared at him in amazement. He sounded like a little old man as he echoed her own words of just a few short weeks ago, when she had been similarly anxious about his wellbeing. Obviously the incident of Eddie Smith's unwelcome attentions was still on his mind.

'Has that man been bovvering you Mummy?'

'Bothering,' she said automatically.

'Bovvering,' said Robbie, with a great effort.

'Oh Robbie,' she turned and hugged him. 'It's not him, darling, don't worry. I suppose I'm a little upset because I've fallen out with Patrick.'

'Oh no!' Robbie's face dropped. 'Won't he come to see us any more?'

'I don't know,' she said resignedly.

'Why don't you say you're sorry?'

'What makes you so sure it's my fault?' she countered sharply.

'Patrick's so easy-going and nice,' said Robbie with a child's total disregard for diplomacy.

'Well, really!' she didn't know whether to laugh at him or scold him soundly.

'I didn't mean that you're not nice,' said Robbie quickly, 'but sometimes you're a handful.'

'Who said I was a handful? come on, Robbie, you never dreamed that one up. Did Patrick tell you I was a handful?'

'No. It's just that you always say Charlotte's a handful, and really, Charlotte is just like you. So that makes you a handful too.'

She grinned. 'You're probably right. And I suppose it was partly my fault,' she conceded.

'Then telephone Patrick and say you're sorry.'

'Not on your life. Don't forget it was partly Patrick's fault too.'

Robbie's knowing look told her he didn't believe one word of it. She sighed, placed the last candlestick back into its gargoyle holder.

'I think that's called stalemate,' Robbie informed her, with the heavily fatalistic air of one who has no option but to give up on a bad job.

At least Charlotte was happy. What was she playing on the

178

tape recorder in her bedroom? Johnny Mathis singing 'Feelings'. Whatever had happened to Dire Straits and Prince and Michael Jackson?

'Charlotte, you dinner's ready,' yelled Liz, trying to make herself heard above the mellow strains of Johnny's velvety warbling.

Charlotte wandered into the dining-room, a faraway look in her eyes. Liz waited for her to stop and expostulate 'Not salad and vegetarian pie, again!' But Charlotte did not say a word. She sat down, began to eat as if she was performing a duty but didn't really mind one way or the other.

'Charlotte's in love,' Robbie informed Liz as he sat opposite Charlotte. 'Mummy, why can't I have burgers and chips?'

'Because I want you to live a long and healthy life,' Liz informed him, her eyes still on Charlotte, registering her dreamy expression.

'I'd rather die young and have a good time,' grumbled Robbie, but he began to eat, if somewhat reluctantly.

Liz could not bear the suspense any longer.

'Is there something you want to tell me, Charlotte?'

'No, Mummy,' said Charlotte, all innocence.

'Are you sure?'

'Well, not really. Except I have a date, tomorrow. Nothing too heavy of course,' she added reassuringly, almost as an afterthought.

'I should hope not,' said Liz wryly. 'But I shall want to know who he is, where he lives and exactly where he intends to take you. Only then will I give my permission.'

'Of course, Mummy,' agreed Charlotte with unexpected sweetness.

23

Gina Pascall had a special place, all of her own, where she liked to go to do her thinking. It was down the drive a short way, across the east-wing lawns and into the woods, veering slightly to the left. There was a clearing, where there were badger setts and a low wall overgrown with ivy, the remnants of a labourer's cottage when the Lodge had been a farm. The old chimney-stack was still there, its crumbling red brick overgrown with creepers. She liked to sit on the wall, listening to small mammals scurrying about, watching the nut-hatches, like flies on a wall, jerkily running up and down the tree trunks and busily pecking for food.

She did not usually go to the special place on a Sunday morning, because Jeremy was home. But this morning he had risen early, abruptly informing her that the had urgent matters to deal with at the office. Then Lillian Pascall had telephoned. It had always amused Gina that Lillian used the telephone rather than walk the short distance from her own quarters to their apartment, but in a way, she was rather glad she did. At least Gina was never caught by surprise.

Lillian had put on her pained voice. The one that meant either the new maid hadn't polished the silver properly, or her account with Harrods did not agree with her books, or she had been given two months to live, or she had fallen out with her beautician, or her brother Dermot had been run over by a lorry.

'I'll call in for a coffee and a talk later,' she had informed Gina in her usual royal manner, as if bestowing some great favour upon her daughter-in-law.

Gina had sighed. She really wasn't up to Lillian at the moment. So Gina had fled. Fled to her secret place where no one could find her. She would pay for it later, but later was not as important as now.

She thought about last night. Last night Jeremy had made love to her. That in itself was not unusual, for occasionally Jeremy did indulge, though not as often as Gina would have liked. Jeremy made love in the same way that he conducted himself in every other area of his life. Efficiently. Without wasting energy. Dutifully. Only last night, it had been different.

It wasn't that he'd been particularly caring or particularly adventurous. He had not even succeeded in bringing her to orgasm. The difference was in his demeanour. There had been something almost mystical about him. As if he was on a high. A sort of controlled high. But his eyes had an unnatural gleam, and he had bared all his teeth, tightly clenched, as he came. She was so used to his face, tight-lipped and guarded, even when in the throes of sexual release, that it had almost frightened her. He had looked like the devil!

Afterwards she had tried to hug and kiss him. Had wriggled her tongue in his navel, a small attention he had once found pleasing, but he had irritably pushed her away.

She wondered who was performing that small service for him now.

Not that she felt the other woman to be a threat to her position. She was an adequate wife. She was an excellent hostess when they entertained and she had, over the years. learned to mix easily and naturally with his business contacts and their spouses. She never made waves for him, seldom nagged and for the most part had learned to check her quick temper, her natural impetuosity.

And she knew Jeremy liked a well-ordered life. And that his affair was probably one of many.

Only Gina wanted more. Gina wanted love and passion and warmth and the wonderful feeling of his approval. Not just the approval of her abilities, but his approval of her as a woman.

What did Sir George always say when an employee failed to make the grade, failed to come up to his exacting standards? A rather strange English expression. Oh yes. . . 'It's like flogging a dead horse', he'd say in his deep, positive voice.

181

That's what she was doing, wasn't it? Flogging a dead horse, Trying to make Jeremy love her. Trying to make Jeremy into something he was not. Something he couldn't be.

If only she had a child, perhaps it wouldn't be so bad. Perhaps her life would not feel so empty. Something to love. Something small and fragile and dependent upon her. Something to *be* something for.

Tears of self-pity began to course down Gina's delicate cheeks.

Sir George was meandering around the shrubbery, admiring the host of butterflies alighting on the deep purple, cone-shaped clusters of the butterfly bushes. He was impressed by the beauty of the flowers and of the butterflies, the depth of their colours, the delicacy of bloom and wings. Not that he was here for aesthetic reasons. On the contrary, the garden served mainly as a means of escape from Lillian.

He had other escapes of course. Apart from his business affairs, there were his occasional sorties to one of the village pubs, his games of chess with his old friend, Dr McTavish, and his hunting expeditions.

He was not surprised when he spotted Gina emerging from the woods, waif-like in her skinny jeans and T-shirt. He shivered, for there was a chill in the air, but Gina did not seem concerned about the cold. She wandered, dream-like, across the lawns, unaware that she was not alone.

Sir George smiled to himself. He had known where she was all along, had known about her little hideaway from when she had first arrived, a shy, frightened teenager, all legs and arms and tremulously lowered lashes. She was the reason he was in the garden in the first place.

'She was expecting me to drop in on her,' Lillian had complained to him, 'and now she's disappeared. What are young people coming to, that's what I'd like to know? No respect. No respect at all. Where *is* that girl?'

'I'll see if I can find her,' said Sir George agreeably, humouring her. He had found that was the best way to deal with his wife. He could not change her. Nobody could. So he had come into the garden, but made sure he stayed well clear of Gina's woodland retreat. If Gina wanted privacy to think, then he was the last person to intrude upon her thoughts.

Suddenly she caught sight of him and waved, started to run towards him, her fair hair billowing out around her face.

'Pop, what are you doing?' she greeted him affectionately, slipping her arm through his. He did not say anything, just raised his arm and pointed his middle and index finger at the side of his head. Gina raised her eyes heavenwards, for she knew exactly what he meant. *She* was at it again.

'I'm in trouble too, I think,' said Gina.

'I know. But she always takes it out on me first. Now is that fair, young lady?'

'Sorry, Pop,' laughed Gina, 'but I know your shoulders are broad.'

Together they explored the shrubbery. He told her the names of his favourite specimen trees. The Paperback Maple with its patches of red-orange bark, the Japanese Angelica with its huge, decorative leaves. Gina listened, taking it all in. She loved to learn, absorbed information easily and permanently. Sir George felt sad for her. Her talents, her bright personality, were being squandered by his eldest son. He had always been reluctant to interfere in the private affairs of his offspring and their partners, but maybe he was wrong. Maybe, sometimes, one was justified in poking one's nose in. Maybe some things just had to be said, regardless of a man's finer feelings.

'Gina,' he said gently, 'I know this is a personal matter, but . . .'

'Yes,' she said, stopping in her tracks, her trusting grey eyes on his, waiting for him to continue.

'Gina, you and Jeremy have been married for twelve years now, and I wondered, I just wondered . . .'

'Why we haven't made you a grandfather yet?' Gina's voice was flat as she put into words what he had been chewing over and over in his mind for a long, long time. 'Oh, Pop, I'm sorry. It's what I want too. I would have talked to you about it before, but Jeremy always got so uptight if I even suggested it.'

'Are you unable to conceive, Gina,' Sir George's voice was barely a whisper, 'are you infertile?'

183

'No, Pop. Jeremy is.'

Solicitously, Gina clutched at her father-in-law's arm as he swayed, as if winded by a sudden blow to the stomach. 'Pop,' she squeaked. He had gone so pale. His eyes were moist as if he were about to weep. 'Pop, I'm sorry. I should have broken it to you more gently. it's just that I have lived with this knowledge for over five years and I didn't realise it would be such a shock.'

With a superhuman effort, Sir George recovered, steeled himself to face the agony in her expression. 'It's all right, Gina. But I'm sure Jeremy could be helped. With the right medical care. There is so much they can do these days, so many new techniques . . .'

'I've already been through all that. He won't have it. Won't accept it.'

'Then I'll have to have a word with him.'

He was further shocked by the sudden fear in her eyes. 'Oh no! You mustn't tell him I've told you. Please, Pop, he'd kill me.'

'Really, Gina, don't exaggerate. What are you saying? That my son is some sort of monster?'

She began to weep, softly, heartbrokenly, her head drooping to hide her face from him. But her shoulders juddered, scrawny shoulders in her flimsy T-shirt, arms that looked as if they might snap if you touched them. He hadn't realised she had become so thin. Didn't know what to do with her. He followed his instinct and grabbed at her, pulling her to him, encircling her fragile body in his strong arms.

'Gina,' he coaxed desperately, 'Gina, Jeremy is your husband. He loves you. He's not a monster.'

'Yes he is. He's a monster. That's exactly what he is. You don't know, Pop, you just don't know.'

Sir George, for once, was silenced by the vehemence of her words, stood silently, still holding her. She buried her face into his chest, gaining temporary comfort from his warmth and the innate strength he exuded.

She could not know how weak he was now, how empty, how helpless. To want desperately to do something, something to help two people you loved, yet be thwarted by the stupidity of false pride. Sir George had money, power, influence. And money, power and influence got you just about anything you wanted in this world. But it couldn't make everything right. The frustration that suddenly raged through Sir George, consuming him in its intensity, made him crush Gina to him like a vice.

'Oh Pop,' she gasped, 'please don't. You're hurting me.' As he released her, again their eyes met.

'You won't tell him, Pop, will you?' she pleaded. 'You won't tell him I told you. Please promise. I should never have told you.'

'Your confidence is quite safe with me, my dear,' he told her and was horrified at the depth of her gratitude and obvious relief. For the first time, he perceived how in awe of her husband she was and how deeply she feared his wrath.

And from that moment on, sir George began to see his son in an entirely different light.

24

During that evening and for most of the following day Charlotte kept a low profile, playing records in her room and avidly devouring romantic novelettes. Liz, preoccupied with her own problems, was taken by surprise when Charlotte suddenly appeared, fresh and beautiful, in a skimpy, deep blue mini-dress, matching low-heeled pumps and with a bright blue butterfly comb pinned high over each ear, prettily anchoring her long, dark hair.

Liz had forgotten about The Date.

'It's all right, Mummy,' said Charlotte quickly, 'he's calling for me.'

'Good,' said Liz.

Charlotte began to fiddle and fuss in the antique, heavily gilt-framed mirror over the Adam fireplace. Liz watched her daughter's reflection in the oval expanse, adjusting and readjusting the blue combs, arranging the wisps of fringe across her forehead. Grimacing because it wasn't quite right, combing this way, that way. Then putting it back the way it was in the first place.

Liz sighed deeply, more in empathy than in irritation. Hadn't she been exactly the same at around Charlotte's age? Especially when she had been courting Eddie. Endlessly primping and teasing. Would he prefer it this way? Would he prefer it that way? Did men actually ever notice such minor details?

Robbie, in typical small-brother devilment, lurked at his sister's elbow, doing a comic imitation of her titivations. Even his facial expressions were cleverly, girlishly petulant. Liz smothered a smile as with concentrated disdain, Charlotte ignored his mimicry.

When the door chime sounded, Robbie bounded away to answer it before either Liz or Charlotte could prevent him. Sympathetically, Liz glanced at Charlotte's small apprehensive face. Abandoning her ritual of self-worship, Charlotte spun around.

'Little prick!' she muttered, at Robbie's departing back.

'Charlotte!' cried Liz, shocked at the first truly vulgar expression she had ever heard from her daughter's angelic lips.

A howl of anguish distracted them both and, alarmed, their eyes met. Only in such moments of pain or uncertainty were mother and daughter truly united. Robbie burst into the room and threw himself, full pelt, into his mother's arms. He was sobbing loudly and frantically. His small skinny body shook violently inside Liz's embrace.

'What is it, soldier?' she soothed.

Robbie was unable to articulate, but by now it was not necessary. Her answer stood framed in the doorway.

Six feet of gangly youth, in big black Doc Martens, skinny jeans and a leather jacket. He wore sunglasses so large and owlish that his face seemed even narrower than usual. His hair was cut shorter, almost a crew-cut. Eddie had had a crew-cut too, on the day he had died on his motor-bike.

Unable to speak, Liz stared at him aghast.

'Mummy,' said Charlotte, her sense of etiquette surfacing despite the dreadful atmosphere in the room, 'Mummy, I'd like to introduce you to Eddie.'

In normal circumstances, Liz would have put her right. It should have been the other way around. In the first instance, Eddie should have been introduced to her. But there was a mist in front of Liz's eyes and through the mist it seemed that the room was going around and around, the walls vibrating inwards. Everything was swimming, swimming, a whirlpool, a nightmare too awful to be real.

'You!' she spat out finally. 'You *dare* to show your face here!' Then she hissed, 'Charlotte, go to your room.'

'But Mummy!' objected Charlotte. Her mother was staring at Eddie as if he were the devil incarnate. Charlotte's stomach churned, felt as if it had a hole in its pit. She knew, of course, that he was a little old for her, but in her immature and idealistic mind, love overcame all obstacles. Her mother should know that. Had told her often enough. 'Mummy,' she repeated, her voice an octave higher.

'You despicable animal! What do you think you're doing? She's just a child.'

Eddie gyrated insolently into the room, settled himself in the Parker Knoll. Put his feet up on the matching footstool.

'You said I should look around for something I could handle. Nearer my own age. You must admit Charlotte's a lot nearer my age than you are,' he told her softly. Then he added, his tone nastier, 'I thought that under the circumstances, it would be all right with you. A sweet young virgin, untouched, unsullied. Just the ticket, don't you think?'

Liz stepped forward, releasing and instantly forgetting Robbie, who crumpled to the floor in a ball of misery. Dangerously she advanced on Eddie. 'You creeping paedophile!' she snarled. 'You touch my child and I'll kill you. I promise you I'll kill you!'

Eddie's slender hands clutched at the arms of the chair and he involuntarily stiffened. Charlotte could see that he was afraid of her. Charlotte half wanted to run to him, but hesitated, confused, hating the awful things he was saying to Mummy. Robbie still lay inert on the carpet, trying to make himself into a tight, insignificant ball.

Liz halted her tiger-like advance and a glow of triumph lit up her eyes. Pushing Charlotte roughly behind her, she backed up to the table, her hand clutching wildly at space behind her. He was sufficiently alarmed to leap defensively to his feet.

Suddenly she had the breadknife in front of her. Its cruel serrated edge glinted with a menace equalled only by that in her eyes. She clutched it tightly with both hands, her knuckles showing white as she gripped, wielding it with all the ferocity of a madwoman, between her breasts, point forwards.

A second time she advanced. This time more purposefully, more terrifyingly, and her breasts rose and fell furiously beneath her light sweater. Her crimson skirt billowed around her full thighs, a flame of wrath.

Six feet from him she paused. 'If you don't leave this minute,' she growled, 'I'll cut off your balls.'

Involuntarily Eddie's hand flew to his crotch as he backed away. Then he was out of the door and they heard his feet pounding the hallway to the front door.

'Remember I love you, Charlotte,' he had the gall to yell just before the door slammed behind him.

'Eddie!' breathed Charlotte.

Liz could feel Charlotte's hot breath on the back of her neck. A terrible rage consumed her. She flung the breadknife at the door and it stuck and quivered in one of the upper panels. Charlotte began to shake uncontrollably. Liz grabbed for her daughter, but missed as Charlotte sprang aside.

'Leave me alone,' screamed Charlotte.

Helplessly, Liz stared at her daughter. There was more, much more than mere teenage rebellion and natural fear in her eyes. Hatred? Contempt? Alienation?

Suddenly Charlotte's body slumped.

'How could you, Mummy?' she whispered heartbrokenly, all the fight gone from her now.

'Because I had to,' replied Liz. There was little more she could say. How could she hope to explain to a fourteen-year-old in Charlotte's lovesick condition the complications spawned by the tragedies of the past. The reasons. The causes. The sins. Of the fathers.

And of the mothers.

Several times Liz attempted to talk to Charlotte, but Charlotte was morose and withdrawn. She threw away all her romantic novelettes, including those she had not read, but continued to play Johnny Mathis at full blast, over and over till Liz felt she would go mad if she heard that song one more time.

Liz prepared a light tea for Charlotte. Charlotte lay face down on her bed, her face buried in her pillow, did not speak as Liz set the tray down on her bedside table.

'Try to eat something, darling,' implored Liz.

Charlotte did not flinch, or flicker so much as an eyelid. 'Trying to forget those feeling of love . . .' crooned Johnny Mathis. A tear formed in the corner of Liz's eye.

'Charlotte,' she persisted.

Defeatedly, with a last glance at the uncompromisingly prostrate form on the bed, Liz left the room.

Downstairs Robbie was seated on the sofa, leafing uninterestedly through a football magazine.

'You all right, soldier?'

'I think you ought to telephone Patrick, Mummy,' said Robbie. 'Patrick will know what to do.'

'All right, darling, I will. How are you feeling now?'

'I *was* going to fight him for you,' said Robbie with spirit, 'if he hadn't gone away when you told him, I'd have fought him to the death.' He looked a little abashed as he said it. Liz gave him a hug. The heart was willing, but heroics did not come easily when you were only ten and in the midst of a highly charged, adult situation you could not hope to understand.

'That's why I wasn't afraid,' said Liz gently, 'because I knew that if the going really got tough, I could rely on you.'

Robbie visibly perked up. Put down his magazine.

'Would you like me to make you a cup of tea?'

'Lovely,' said Liz.

'And afterwards you can ring Patrick,' bargained Robbie.

Before she telephoned Patrick, she decided to check once more on Charlotte. Consumed with dread at the thought of Charlotte's probable chilly reception, she climbed the stairs with heavy tread, like a prisoner en route to the condemned cell.

But Charlotte was gone.

Her heart pounding, Liz raced to the bathroom, almost expecting to find her daughter prostrate on the floor amid a collection of empty pill bottles. But the bathroom was empty. So was the shower. Liz yelled Charlotte's name. 'She's not in here, Mummy,' called Robbie from the lounge.

Liz wondered if she was going completely mad. She rushed back into Charlotte's bedroom, crazily looking in cupboards and under the bed. The tape had finished but the recorder was

190

still switched on. Her food lay untouched on the tray, just as Liz had left it.

But there was something on the pillow. It was a note. It had slipped down, so that it was partly concealed by the quilt.

There was no opening phrase, no softening 'Dear Mummy'. 'I am going for ever,' said the biro'd note in Charlotte's spidery scrawl. 'And I am never coming back. You will never find me, so don't try. You will never see me again. NEVER.'

The note was merely initialled with an impersonal 'C'.

Liz's legs could no longer support her weight and as they trembled at the knees, she sank heavily on to the bed, ran her hand over the hollow imprint of where Charlotte's body had lain. Buried her face in the gentle valley of the pillow, seeking to imbibe the sweet and comforting odour of her daughter's skin.

She was trapped in some painful eternal nightmare. Some other world's hell. Would it *never* end? Sometime, surely, she would awaken and everything would be all right.

Somehow she mustered her failing resources, forced herself to go into her bedroom and dial 999.

'Don't worry, Madam,' said the officer with long-suffering resignation, 'girls that age are always leaving home and are usually found safe and well. Let me have her description and we'll circularise the information.'

'I'll bring a photgraph down,' said Liz.

'Not necessary, at this stage,' said the policeman.

Distraught and frustrated, she screamed abuse at the policeman for what she saw as his apathy, his lack of concern. This was her *daughter*. The officer reacted with neither anger nor embarrassment. Just as he was used to young women leaving home for a couple of hours, or even a couple of nights, so was he accustomed to dealing with their mothers, overly protective, uncompromising, shrilly convinced of rape, murder and worse.

'Leave it to us, Madam,' he said, trying to reassure her. 'If nothing comes up in the next few hours, we'll send someone round to see you.'

'It'll probably be too late then,' wept Liz.

'In the meantime, if she turns up, do let us know,' said the policeman, and the line went dead.

When she finally got through to Patrick his manner was offhand, which was no more than she had anticipated. However, she was sufficiently confident of her hold over him, of the bonding that had been established between him, herself and the children, to call his bluff.

'It's only that Charlotte's left home, and I have reason to believe she's with Eddie Smith, but obviously I should not have bothered you about that,' she told him with cruel and false detachment. Then hated herself for being blasé about something so important.

'Hold on, Liz, no so fast. I'll be over. It's difficult talking on the phone,' he said worriedly, as she had known he would.

She put down the receiver, in the sure knowledge that he was already racing to his car and dragging his jacket around his shoulders, Charlotte's safety uppermost in his mind.

'I don't know the address of Eddie's flat,' said Liz, 'but I could take you there.'

'I'll go alone. I don't want you to leave Robbie. He's had quite enough to contend with lately, poor little chap! Show me on the map approximately where you went and give me a description of the block.'

'It's not a block. It's the top floor of a private terrace. One of hundreds, in rows, all exactly the same.'

'What's the matter with you, Liz? You were driven there and you found your way back yourself. Surely you have some idea of how to direct me.'

She felt stupid, ineffectual. 'I had other things on my mind at the time,' she snapped.

'Stone the crows!' Patrick glared at her as if he could cheerfully strangle her. She shifted awkwardly in her chair. 'I'd feel a lot better going alone and knowing that you were here safe with Robbie. OK, Liz, get Robbie ready and pop him into the back of your car. I'll follow you there. Then I want you to drive straight back with him and start doing your duty as a mother.

192

Spend a little time with him. Read him a story, or something.'

She was shattered, silenced momentarily, because of his unfairness. 'Are you accusing me of failing my duty as a mother, Patrick?'

'Of course not. But you don't realise how disorientated you've become lately. Haven't you seen the state of him? He is even beginning to develop nervous habits. He blinks his eyes all the time. He's so screwed up about you and Eddie Smith, he hardly knows what day it is. You've got to reassure him, Liz, encourage him to be a kid again.

While she drove, Robbie curled up in the back of the car, finding refuge in sleep, but spasmodically stirring and muttering to himself. She made straight for Chelsea Bridge and then took a couple of wrong turns. Once she lost sight of Patrick's red Granada in her rearview mirror and anxiously pulled into the kerb. Peering round, was relieved to see him looming up behind her, flashing his lights for her to continue.

Once she had found, almost by accident, the general area, familiar landmarks came back to her. She remembered it was just off a square. Eventually she pulled up outside the three-storey terrace, recognising the brass horseshoe knocker and the green plastic window boxes, now bereft of blooms. She pointed her finger towards the house, saw Patrick's affirmative nod in the rearview mirror.

On the way home, she picked up a takeaway deep pan pizza for Robbie and a large bottle of Tizer and dreamed up an exciting new story about the Wobblyglucks to recount to him before he went to sleep.

25

The night air was especially crisp, caught in Patrick's throat as he got out of his car. He had tucked the Granada in tight to hoardings that concealed a building site, and well out of view of the flat. He wasn't sure quite why he was behaving in such a cloak-and-dagger fashion, but some deep-rooted instinct, or perhaps his Irish intuition, told him to exercise caution.

There was a dim light on in the top flat and a door was slightly ajar, leading on to the balcony. Patrick strolled up to the street door, peered at the residents' identification tabs. There was one for each of the ground and first floor, a second floor front, a second floor back. The third floor tab was blank, however, which struck Patrick as odd since it was the only flat with a light on.

All of which was very convenient. Rather than alert Eddie directly to his presence, he could, if he played his cards right, fall back on the element of surprise. And the omission of identification for the top flat occupant would render his inquiries more plausible.

Gambling on the likelihood of the ground floor being occupied by the landlord or landlady, he pressed the bell.

After some time the door was answered by a middle-aged woman who looked as if she had just emerged from a kitchen-sink TV play. She sported, with considerable panache, threadbare carpet slippers, a crimplene housecoat and a thatch of wispy bleached hair. Half a cigarette dangled from the corner of her orange mouth.

'Yeah?'

'I'm most dreadfully sorry to disturb you,' began Patrick, allowing his shoulders to stoop a little in a posture meant to convey ingratiating subservience, 'but I understand a Mr Eddie Smith lives here.'

She dragged on her cigarette and wordlessly pointed to the identification tabs.

'I know,' said Patrick. 'I saw them. But I can't see Mr Smith's name there. I'm sure he lives in this house. Could it be that he occupies the top flat? There's no name displayed beside the top flat bell.'

'The top apartment's rented by a company,' said the woman snootily. Then, her voice thick with disapproval, 'All sorts of odd bods come and go.'

'I'm sure that would be it,' said Patrick, making as if to step inside.

'Not so fast, young man, not so fast,' said the woman, barring his way. 'I can't let you go barging up there without checking your authority. Nothing personal. Rules, you know.' Patrick nodded sadly in agreement. You just couldn't trust anybody, these days! The woman decided she liked the look of him. Polite, he was. Respectable. You could tell.

'Have you got a card or something?' she inquired helpfully.

Patrick fished in his inside pocket, handed her one of his business cards, hoping that the prestige of Pascall's might encourage her to grant him entry. If she had ever heard of Pascall's.

'Pascall! That's it. Why on earth didn't you say you were from Pascall's in the first place?'

Patrick stared at her amazed. Eddie's flat registered in the name of *Pascall*!

'There's people up there already, so give them a bang on the door to let them know you're coming. One just never knows what folks get up to inside four walls!' She raised her black-pencilled eyebrows in a suggestive leer and Patrick smiled awkwardly, began to climb the steep, uncarpeted stairs.

At the top, there was a narrow corridor. The sounds he could hear came from the back of the house. Accordingly he turned left, went down a couple of steps. The door, which he presumed led to a bedroom, was half-way open. The whole of the facing wall of the room was covered in floor to ceiling

195

mirror tiles. The two people on the bed were obviously having an absorbing time and he was able to observe them with no fear of being discovered.

His first emotion was relief that it wasn't Charlotte. This girl had long, light wavy hair.

The man lay back on the bed and Patrick could not see him properly, only the soles of his feet and the outline of his chest. But the girl was crouched on her knees, her back to the mirror tiles. She was slender and fragile-looking.

'You needn't worry about all that old stuff.' He could almost visualise her pouting from the tone in her voice. 'You know I *like* being penetrated.'

The man abandoned his frantic manipulation of her clitoris with an audible sigh of resignation. Tried to reason with her.

'Darling,' he replied patiently, 'you've made it abundantly clear that you don't suffer from penis-envy and I'm sure that if Freud was screwing you, he'd be convinced too. But for heaven's sake, I'm not a bloody machine. What is more I have an important business function to attend tomorrow.'

Patrick almost cried out as he recognised those smooth, hated tones. Jeremy Pascall. And the girl? Of course!

The girl was Dinah.

'Never mind, Superstud,' trilled Dinah. 'I know what will get you going.'

The man gasped loudly as the girl's head obliterated the sorry sight of his limp organ, her crafty tongue making little teasing stabs at his flesh. Patrick was fascinated; could hardly tear his eyes away. Felt a vague sense of shame at his voyeurism.

Jeremy writhed, trying to push Dinah away. She unbalanced slightly and her teeth must have caught the flesh of his tip, for he let out a yelp of pain.

'Jerry, stop whingeing,' she complained.

'I'll go into the kitchen and get a candle,' he retorted.

Instinctively Patrick backed away from the door. But his sudden anxiety was misplaced, for Dinah began to laugh, joyous peals of mirth that drew Patrick back, intrigued. Her whole body shook. She had a boyish body, strong and straight and lean. It must have been the way she moved that made her so divinely sexy. She had turned slightly so that the mirror showed her body in profile. By peering through the crack in the door he could see her full frontal. The erotic sight of her small round nuts of breasts, jiggling about like a striptease dancer's, must have stirred Jeremy's imagination. Even Patrick could imagine a shiny red tassel affixed to each pink nipple. But whatever was in Jeremy's mind, it was strangely more erotic than the thought of the intended blowjob.

'You little bitch,' he hissed, sitting up and bearing her down, pinning her wrists each side of her head.

As he mounted her, Patrick decided he could risk a ten-minute search of the flat. It was obviously not the first time that day, so they ought to be busy for at least as long as that.

He spent some time searching the flat but found nothing.

Found nothing, for he was already aware of Jeremy and Dinah's betrayal of Liz, and their affair did not particularly surprise him. Yet the one piece of information that he had discovered was the most unexpected and riveting piece of news imaginable.

That Pascall's were the lessees of the flat where Eddie Smith had taken Elizabeth Carlton.

The door opened before he put his finger to Liz's bell.

You must have been waiting on the doormat.' He took in her radiance, the way that the hollows had filled out in her cheeks.

'She's back.'

'Is she all right?'

'Not good. But at least she's back.'

Patrick followed Liz into the lounge where Charlotte sat, her face as white and smooth as marble, her dark eyes shockingly old and beaten. Patrick sat down beside her, took her hand in his.

'The police have only just left,' said Liz, falling into the armchair opposite. 'They found her wandering around outside Pascall House, believe it or not.'

'Did you find him, Charlotte?' asked Patrick gently. She nodded, not looking at him. It worried him that she had *known*

197

where to find Eddie. Was the whole affair much deeper than he had formerly thought? Exactly what was the hold Eddie had over Charlotte? A teenage infatuation. . . or something else?

'He didn't touch you, did he?' He hated asking her that, so afraid was he that she might answer in the affirmative. Charlotte said nothing, hung her head, picked abstractedly at the hem of her blue mini-dress.

Suddenly, Charlotte burst into tears.

'No, no, no,' she yelled, 'he didn't touch me.'

'Are you sure?'

'Of course I'm sure. He didn't want to. Laughed at me. He said what did he want with a useless, skinny kid like me when he'd had my mother.'

Liz gasped. If Patrick had glanced at her then, he would have thought she was about to be sick. And suddenly there was murder in Patrick's heart.

'I hope you're not stupid enough to believe any of that. That guy is sick, really sick. Your mother knows that and that is why she wanted to protect you from him. Good grief, child, do your really believe *everything* you're told? Because if you do, your life is going to be pretty damn tough.'

'I suppose not,' whispered Charlotte, 'but how did Mummy know him?'

Patrick lifted her chin, forcing her to look him straight in the eyes. 'We don't know for sure where he comes from or who he is. All we know is that he is infatuated with your mother, obsessed with her.'

'He *must* be sick then,' said Charlotte bitterly.

The change in Patrick's mood brought Liz to her feet, both hands held out in supplication. 'It's all right, Patrick, she's just upset,' cried Liz. But Patrick ignored her, yanked Charlotte to her feet by the neckline of her dress.

Whereupon, in all his terrifying, fiery Irish magnificence, he castigated Charlotte soundly for all of her sins. Liz trembled to witness the splendour of his rage. Even his red hair seemed to stand out like a crown of flames each time his head gave that peculiar little jerk, as if he was trying to control an emotion so intense as to be almost overpowering. Charlotte cowered and hung her impudent head.

If Liz had been in Charlotte's shoes, she knew that never again would she dare to cheek her mother, dare to take off after some strange man without a word to anyone, carry on as if she were some modern-day Lolita. Knew that she would go straight up to her room and take that muck off her face and concentrate on her 'O' levels.

'And while you're at it, you can take off that ridiculous dress and put on something suitable for your age. How dare you walk around the streets in a bloody fanny pelmet.'

Charlotte shrank and Patrick jerked up her face, again, his knuckles hard under her chin, forcing her to look at him. Terror shone in her eyes as he towered over her. Yes, she was sorry. Yes, she would apologise to her mother. Yes, she had behaved like a spoilt unruly child. Yes, she knew what he would do to her if she ever again *dared*, or even *thought*, about contacting Eddie Smith.

Eventually he allowed her to go to her bedroom to compose herself, turned to Liz, who was still white and trembling.

'That was a bit strong, Patrick,' she gasped. 'It was not your place to talk to her like that.'

'Maybe not,' said Patrick, 'but she needed it Liz, a bit of straight talking.'

'She's been through such a terrible ordeal.' Liz began to cry quietly, wiping her tears with her sleeve.

'Then it was just the right time to catch her,' said Patrick easily, 'at her most receptive.' He ambled over to Liz's drinks bar and helped himself uninvited to a whisky mac. He didn't offer Liz anything, seemed impervious to her tears.

'I'll tell you one thing. Charlotte feels a lot more secure now than she ever did before. And she won't be sitting on her bed hatching romantic teenage plots about how to get back at *you* and the system in general. I guarantee you'll see a different Charlotte from now on.'

She felt angry again, at his self-righteousness, his confidence. He really took too much upon himself. How dared he usurp her position as a parent! How dared he use her flat as if he owned it!

199

'Regular little Doctor Spock, aren't you!' her voice was heavy with sarcasm.

'If you had ever read one word of Doctor Spock, you wouldn't make such a statement. Doctor Spock went out with the Ark.'

'You should know! You seem to know everything, don't you?'

'No, I do not,' he drained his glass, poured himself another. 'What do I do about you, Liz? I only wish a good telling-off would sort you out.'

She softened. What would she have done without him, after all? 'You could try sending me to bed,' she murmured suggestively, moistening her bottom lip with her wet, pink tongue.

'At a time like this, after all we've been through, you're feeling *horny*?'

'It's at a time like this, one needs it most,' she replied lightly. 'How else does one forget one's troubles?'

Just once in a while she revealed another small piece of herself, so that he could fit her together slowly, painfully, like a jigsaw and learn to understand her a little better. Maybe one day he would have the total picture. But then, pigs might fly . . .

It was incredible, and a blessing, how the smallest demands could push aside other greater issues, making themselves felt amidst the chaos. She smiled at him. He saw behind the smile the courage that belied her apparent coolness, the determination never to be crushed, the wanting to make him feel better.

'I'll not object to that,' said Patrick.

She stroked him admiringly as he lay naked on his back on top of the quilt. He had his eyes closed, his face a study in ecstasy.

'A man's body is so beautiful,' she whispered, 'So brave and positive.' She giggled. 'And so upstanding. So much more *together* than a woman's body, with that little pink knot of twisted flesh.'

'Do you say things like that for the specific purpose of winding me up?' growled Patrick, enveloping her.

But she spoilt it all.

She forgot herself and cried out once again for Eddie. Fortunately, he forgave her, had more or less expected it to happen again sometime.

'I can only guess at what deep-rooted guilty secret makes you do it,' he said, 'but I hope at some time you will help me to find out so we can conquer it together. Don't be upset, Liz. It's all right, darling.'

She sat up, rubbing her eyes. There were dark shadows beneath them that were not entirely due to smudged mascara.

'I'm sorry,' she whispered. The apology sounded strange, coming from her. It was the first time she had ever asked for his forgiveness and he was moved by her contrition. Gave her a quick hug.

'Talking of Eddie,' he said, as if her *faux pas* had been no more than a chance remark in an ordinary conversation, 'I think you ought to see this.

With a startled cry, she grabbed at the perspex-covered document. Eddie Smith's crafty eyes seemed to leap out of the document at her, but they were not part of it. He had wedged three passport photographs into the corner of the perspex. And the document was a driving licence.

Only he wasn't Eddie Smith.

He was one William John Fraser. Aged 24. An address in South London. Flat 3, Tower Buildings, Cob Street, Lewisham.

She sat for several moments, her quilt wrapped around her shoulders, trying to absorb this startling new information. The ghost from her turbulent past was not a ghost at all. He was an impostor, a trickster, a conman!

'Did you find this in the flat?' asked Liz.

'Not exactly. When I left I found it lying by the skirting-board in the hall, just beneath the wall pay-phone. He must have been making a call and dropped it out of his jacket. It was an incredible stroke of luck that I looked.'

'What can it mean?' mused Liz, wrinkling her nose in puzzlement.

'That's not quite all I discovered,' continued Patrick grimly.

'Dinah and Jeremy were there. It's OK, Liz, they didn't see me. And what is more, I learned from the landlady that the flat is registered to the Pascalls.'

'I don't believe it,' said Liz, incredulous.

'It's true. I think this puts quite a different light on the whole sorry situation. I don't believe any of the traumas you have experienced have been directly inspired by Eddie Smith, or William John Fraser, as we now know him. I think the whole affair is a set-up, engineered by Jeremy and possibly others in league with him.'

'My God!' breathed Liz. 'You're saying that Jeremy Pascall masterminded everything, including my first meeting with Eddie in that singles bar? And that Eddie only pretended to find my business card and trace me to Pascall House? That all the time, he knew everything about me?'

'That's exactly what I'm saying. It all seems to fit.'

'So even Eddie's, I mean, William Fraser's manipulation of Johnny Morris was part of a plan?'

'That's right. I think that Jeremy has investigated your past, proceeded to attack you on every front, in your business life and emotionally. Anything to discredit you and drive you into a state of mental ineptitude which would eventually destroy you.'

'But why?'

Thoughtfully, Patrick appraised her. 'I've given myself a headache trying to figure that one out. I thought at first that perhaps you had become too powerful for Jeremy's comfort. But even that, even *that* does not seem sufficient grounds for him to have gone to such lengths.'

'How could he hate me that much?'

'He doesn't hate you but I think he must be afraid of you. I don't believe someone as cold as Jeremy either loves or hates. He just operates. Liz, tell me, has Martin Pascall ever made any overtures towards you? Now, come on, be honest, no false modesty please.' Then he added, with a grim half-smile, 'Not that false modesty appears to be one of your major faults.'

'Well,' Liz pretended to consider, so that he should think her neither falsely modest nor conceited. 'I must admit he has never approached me directly, but I do believe he is attracted to me. A woman knows these things,' she concluded mysteriously.

'Could it be that he fears Martin's attraction towards you? Jeremy is a very perceptive man and if he has sensed the depth of Martin's feelings towards you, then I should imagine he might feel threatened by your abilities and your unquestionable rapport with his father. If your status were increased by marriage to one of his brothers . . .'

'Marriage!' she squeaked. 'Marriage, to Martin Pascall!'

'Maybe not,' conceded Patrick. 'Martin is engaged, after all. It does seem a little far-fetched. But Jeremy is an ambitious man and he is playing a dangerous game. What do you know about Jeremy, from a strictly personal point of view?'

'Not very much,' said Liz. 'But I know he can't have children.'

'Why not?'

'He has a low sperm count or something like that. His wife Gina told me when I visited the Lodge with the kids last spring. She loves kids. Kept calling Robbie her bambino, much to Robbie's embarrassment. It's a dreadful shame for her. But, Patrick,' she gave him a sudden, direct stare, 'you mustn't repeat what I've told you. Gina told me in strictest confidence. She was most upset at the time, and I think a little regretful that she had blurted it out to me. She said Jeremy would be very angry if he found out.'

'Hmmm,' mused Patrick. 'I wonder if Sir George knows this. Come to think of it, I rather doubt it. Sir George is a traditionalist. He was the eldest of four sons and he inherited his father's business. Now, if Sir George is running true to form, then Jeremy would be his main beneficiary. It might not be to Jeremy's advantage if he was known to be sterile and then Martin got married and produced sons.'

'So?'

'You, Liz, scare the pants off Jeremy Pascall. And that's a very dangerous piece of information you have just imparted.'

'Jeremy doesn't know that I know.'

'And Gina doesn't know that *I* know,' countered Patrick ominously.

203

'Whatever am I going to do?' Liz lay back on her pillow, staring defeatedly at the ceiling.

'What are *we* to do?' corrected Patrick. 'The first thing I intend to do is to put a private dick on Eddie, correction, William Fraser's, tail. Next week you stay right here in this flat, Liz. I insist. It won't help your cause to turn up at Pascall House before this thing is settled for once and for all.'

She grimaced. She was becoming increasingly irritated at the manner in which he kept telling her what to do, without asking her opinion. Ordering her around, as if she were his responsibility. Only her gratitude for his protection and the knowledge that he had her best interests at heart prevented her from rebelling.

She didn't really mind that he was probably right. Only wished she could shake him out of his annoying complacency.

'Sir George has suggested that I spend a weekend at Pascall Lodge,' said Patrick, 'to go over a few things with him in peace and quiet. What I intend to do is to try to engineer the invitation for next weekend. And I shall take you with me.'

'What?' she sat up, staring at him as if he was mad.

'The element of surprise. I don't know why exactly, Liz, but I have a feeling that's the right thing to do. They will be completely thrown by your presence. If necessary, you can distract them while I take a look around. Come on, Liz. I know I'm right. Call it intuition if you like.'

She didn't call it intuition. She called it bloody stupid and said so.

'Aren't you up to it?' he countered scathingly.

'Don't use psychological blackmail on me, Patrick. I wasn't born yesterday, you know. Whether I'm up to it or not is irrelevant. Personally, I think the whole idea is crazy.'

'At least it's positive. It could bring things to a head. Come on, Liz. We've got to take some risks or we might as well give up and let Jeremy do his worst.'

She had had enough of the conversation. She coiled her body around him, enveloping him in her warmth till he groaned for her yet again. She concentrated very hard. Patrick, Patrick, Patrick.

204

She said his name over and over to herself, chanting it in her mind, like a mantra, as he caressed her and then mounted her. So that finally, when she climaxed, she got it right.

26

On Monday, Patrick went straight to his old office and dictated all his correspondence on to tape, then left it in the general typing pool's in-tray. He was anxious not to compromise himself by using his new offices and his new secretary, the devious Dinah.

After he had finished dictating, he made a series of telephone calls to say that he would be out for the remainder of the week. While he did not wish to appear to condone what had happened, his instinct told him it would be detrimental to his cause to make any more waves at the moment. He would keep a low profile while he was gathering information, preparing his strategy and getting his defences together. He was determined to attack from strength, not weakness.

It never occurred to him for one moment that he would not, somehow, find an answer. Part of Patrick's charm was his incurable optimism, an optimism that even suppressed his natural logic and common sense.

As the new incumbent of his old office entered, throwing his briefcase on to a chair and giving Patrick an affronted stare, Patrick quickly rose to his feet.

'Sorry old chap. Forgot to clear out my desk. Won't be a moment.' He stuffed a few items from the bottom drawer into his briefcase, and with a quick nod, departed.

He was a displaced person now. Ejected from his old office and barred by his own sense of morality from his new office, he had nowhere to go in Pascall House. His office now was in the back seat of his car. It was ludicrous. Patrick snorted.

As he rode the lift back down to the ground floor, he thought about his conversation with Liz. About Jeremy's infertility and Gina's innate fear of Jeremy. The more he thought about it, the more convinced he became that Gina would never have admitted to Jeremy that she had told Liz of his inability to become a father. He felt sorry for Gina and wondered what she was like. Wondered if he would like her. He would soon find out, if he could manage to get this weekend organised.

It was weird how so many pieces of the puzzle seemed to fit, yet in total, they did not make a picture.

Somehow, everything he had said went against the grain. His was a logical mind, a scientific mind. With a different background, a better education, a more relevant upbringing, he might have been a chemist or a physicist. And now the very basis of his thinking had been rocked. Sometimes it seemed the entire structure of his world had crumbled. His clear mind had become a vortex of confused thoughts as he fought the irrationality he had witnessed, balanced it against the logic that had been the mainstay of his live.

When he was puzzled he sometimes tried to turn the entire argument upside-down. He tried now. Tried to look at it from different angles, upside-down, inside-out, back to front. Only succeeded in giving himself a headache.

Maybe it was all very simple.

Maybe Jeremy was mad!

For the remainder of Monday morning, Patrick skived. He automatically drove straight home, but as he approached his turning, he saw the cut-in to the bird sanctuary car park. On impulse he drove in. He walked through the woods and across the fields. It was a fine morning, warm for the time of year, but he hardly noticed. He did not notice the lovely autumn bronzes and golds, or the dogs gambolling on the grass or a pair of young lovers strolling, teasing each other with their eyes. The kinds of things that normally made him smile and feel glad he had been born.

He sat on a grassy knoll, an incongruous sight in his city pinstripes. He sat and thought.

When it came to him, it seemed so incredibly simple he wondered why he had not thought of it before.

Which of the three brothers was the most outspoken, the most indiscreet, the most careless?

Trevor Pascall!

And who, in Pascall House, apart from his father and brothers, knew Trevor Pascall the longest, had worked with him closely, was virtually his guardian?

Why, Damien Lambert, of course!

Instantly, Patrick knew what he had to do. He had to cultivate Damien Lambert. He resolved to ask Damien out to lunch as soon as possible, the next day if he was free.

He glanced at his watch, frowned, felt a sudden stab of guilt for his truancy. He had to *move*. He'd be no help to Liz if he got himself the sack.

Chin thrust aggressively forward, he hurried back to his car.

Liz was bored and restless, stuck in the flat. She complied with Patrick's wishes up to a point and did not contact Pascall House, but she felt claustrophobic hemmed in by four walls. So she slipped out once or twice to shop at the local small parade. Explored a little of the surrounding woodlands and fields.

She gained great comfort from the peace and tranquillity and space. Lay down on her stomach in the sweet-smelling grass, her arms outstrtched, embracing the world, feeling as if she was throbbing in counterpoint to the heartbeat of the universe, a part of it. Pascall House and its politics for once faded into insignificance.

On Wednesday, she received a call from Martin Pascall.

'Liz,' he said, 'I'm off to Birmingham for a further look around Robinson's factory. I know you're off this week, but I'd greatly appreciate your help. And your company! Do you mind?'

'I'm flattered,' said Liz, 'and I'd be delighted.'

'I'll pick you up at ten,' said Martin, and hung up. Precise and to the point. No words wasted. As always.

She welcomed the opportunity to get back into gear business-wise. Got ready carefully, happy to put on a business suit and feel part of it again.

'Liz,' said Martin, as they pulled away from her block, 'Liz, I don't want to harp on unpleasant matters, but I'm so sorry. About your ordeal.'

'I'm glad that someone allows me some credibility,' said Liz wryly. 'I thought the whole thing had been pooh-poohed and hushed up.'

'That's another thing I'm not too happy about,' said Martin. 'I would talk to my father about it, but he has not been well, lately. He seems too feeble to take any more pressure. You are aware, I suppose, that he has been suffering quite debilitating bouts of angina?'

'I wasn't. I'm sorry.'

'And as for my brother,' said Martin, obviously alluding to Jeremy, 'I am afraid we do not always see eye to eye, and although he is an excellent businessman and negotiator, unfortunately he lacks sensitivity in other areas.'

She gave him a searching look. Was convinced he had nothing to do with the Pascall dirty tricks department. There was something almost childlike about him, one could almost describe him as naive. He felt her questioning gaze on him, quickly put his hand over hers as it rested upon her knee. Snatched it away lest she misunderstand this small intimacy.

'I know what you're thinking. Why can't I intervene for you? Why can't I get you back into your office, in your rightful place? Liz, there is a limit to what I can do for you under the circumstances. My brother is senior to me both in years and in length of service. I'm afraid I broke my father's heart by rejecting his offer and spending the best part of my youth following my romantic ideals.'

'What were they?' asked Liz, intrigued.

'I wanted to become a concert pianist. But I wasn't good enough,' said Martin flatly. 'But if I hadn't tried, I would always have wondered. I wouldn't have missed it for anything, though. I still play as much as I can, however ineptly.'

'It's easy not to fail if you never try.'

'Thank you,' said Martin simply.

'I think your father's attitude is a little unfair.'

'That is a matter of opinion, I suppose, but I'm glad we agree.' He turned, flashed her one of his rare smiles. 'Liz, I could offer you a measure of protection.'

'How?'

'You could marry me.' He looked straight ahead as he said it. Someone hooted loudly as they tried to overtake and Martin quickly straightened his wheel. It was difficult proposing and driving at the same time. Liz was staring at him, totally confounded. She had always known he had fancied her. But she had never believed that his feelings extended as far as marriage.

'But I'm years older than you. How old are you, Martin?'

'Thirty-two.'

'I can assure you it's a few years since I saw thirty-two.'

'What's so terrific about being thirty-two?'

'Oh, nothing,' she said, overwhelmed.

As they drove for a while in silence, her mind raced. How crazy life was! Jeremy Pascall attacked her through fear of her potential power, And now Martin Pascall offered her, by marriage, the power to thwart Jeremy's attack. Only he had no idea just how far Jeremy had gone. As far as he was concerned, it was a simple matter of office politics, the sort of thing that could happen anywhere. She wondered how he would react if he knew the extent of Jeremy's more criminal activities.

It had turned full circle.

It wouldn't do her any harm to go along with Martin for a while. While Patrick battled and made a lot of noise, here was Martin, quietly offering her a way out.

Pity she found Patrick so devastatingly attractive. He wasn't weak like Martin. She liked Martin more and more, especially now that he had opened up to her, become more easy and conversational. But that was all. Friendship.

For Patrick had grown on her. How he had grown on her!

Still, she didn't need to make a decision yet, did she? God knew her feelings for Patrick were real and intense. Although she was pretty fed up with him always wanting to know this, to know that. At least Martin accepted her on face value.

She would string them both along for a while. See how matters progressed. And then she would make up her mind. Her future and that of her children hung in the balance.

'Please say something, Liz,' said Martin eventually, his voice taut with tension.

'You're a wonderful, kind and sensitive man,' said Liz gently, 'but you've taken me by surprise. Couldn't I have just a little time?'

'You can have all the time in the world,' he replied grandly. 'I am quite prepared to wait.'

It must have been Sod's Law, reflected Martin, that made Alexia especially demonstrative that evening.

He had just returned from the trip to Birmingham, pleased with himself but exhausted, when Alexia ran out to meet him. He had dropped Liz off at home and the promise in her eyes was still imprinted on his mind, so that Alexia's blonde heartiness seemed an incongruity.

Alexia wanted him to go riding with her that evening. Normally, he enjoyed their riding sorties together. It was the only way they ever got any time on their own, since his mother had set herself up as moralist and chaperon to the young couple. Alexia had never been permitted to spend an evening alone with Martin in his own quarters, even though he had his own sitting-room and kitchen.

'I'm tired, Alex,' he said indifferently.

'It'll do you good. You know you always find it relaxing to go riding.' Her eyes were wide, hopeful and trusting, and his sudden guilt for his betrayal of her forced him to comply with her demands.

While he ate, sparsely, since it was not a good thing to ride on a full stomach, Alexia went to the stables and saddled the horses, Martin's big black and Gina's slightly tubby roan for herself. The roan was a little temperamental and needed a firm rider, but Gina had taught Alexia how to handle her.

They trotted sedately until out of sight of the house, but once in the field that adjoined Sir George's land, Alexia kneed her mount into a canter. Martin groaned and reluctantly did likewise, following his fiancée to the copse of trees that sprang from the centre of the field. The sky was pale and the copse made a stark, black silhouette against the skyline.

When they arrived at the copse, they halted, Alexia pulling hard on the reins as the roan was still feeling skittish. Martin

211

dismounted and helped her down, then they tethered the horses.

She wasted no time, pulled him down into the long grass beside her. She was in a kittenish mood, tracing his lips with her fingertips, making soft, mewing noises at him.

He found her faintly ridiculous, but was too much a gentleman to say so.

He wanted, desperately, to be honest with her about his feelings for Liz. Was too much of a coward.

So he suffered her ministrations in rebellious silence, accepting them as a penance for his own inadequacy. But when she tried to push him further, pursing her lips Zadora-style as she undid his shirt buttons, he could tolerate it no longer.

'Alexia! Not here!'

'Why not? No one ever comes here. You've never complained before.'

Like an affronted virgin, Martin sat up, pulling his coat around him. He coughed to give himself time to think. 'I can't,' he said eventually, 'I don't feel well. I think I've got a touch of the flu.' He sniffed a bit and put on a woebegone expression.

'Poor darling,' she was instantly contrite, fussing around him like a mother hen, offering him her pullover to put on under his jacket. He had a sudden, uncharacteristic urge to throttle her. Either she insisted on mothering him, or else she had to be his helpless little girl. She never treated him as an equal. Not like Liz. Liz, who never, ever patronised him.

'Come on,' he said, 'Let's go back.'

But 'back' wasn't much better. In deference to his parents, Martin insisted they pop in for a quick drink. 'Then we'll go back to your place,' he promised. But Sir George was watching snooker in the TV room while Lillian vaguely leafed through *Harpers*. Soon Martin, too, was engrossed in the game. Bored, Alexia snuggled up to him on the sofa, oblivious of Lillian's outraged sidelong glances. She ran her finger in circles around his palm, slipped her stockinged foot up the bottom of his trouser-leg, caressing his skin. Pushed her nose into his neck.

'Good shot,' bellowed Sir George, rising to his feet in homage to Steve Davis, who had pulled it off yet again.

'Sit down, George,' barked Lillian crossly, for he had made her jump, but her eyes still bore dagger-like into Alexia, who had the gall to practically make love to her precious son right in front of his mother's face.

After Martin dropped her at home, Alexia went straight to bed, without seeking out her parents to say goodnight. Home was a large, detached, Tudor-style house in a tree-lined avenue in Chislehurst in Kent. Her room was the smallest in the house by intention, not necessity. Alexia felt cosier, more secure in her tiny box of a bedroom. Claustrophobia was never one of her problems.

She lay down on her back on the top of her quilt. Martin had changed. She did not want to admit it to herself, but he had.

Alexia had always been a big girl, big-boned, a trifle clumsy. During her childhood she had always felt a little inferior to her friends, most of them slim, dainty, feminine girls. Alexia never realised that her own appeal lay in her natural enthusiasm, her openness, her heartiness. So, sometimes, she tried to emulate those friends, softening her voice, dropping her eyes when spoken to, quelling her natual desire to intervene, to make her point when in mixed company.

Of course, she couldn't keep it up all the time. And when she had met Martin, at a dinner party given by mutual friends, he had been entranced by her liveliness and the way in which she spoke up for herself.

Alexia did not know that she had been the one to change first. Martin was the best thing that had ever happened to her and she wanted to keep him. How could she know that he found her independence and capability interesting, that he was enthralled by her lack of guile, that he found it easy to forgive the occasional tactless remark born of her impetuosity?

How could she know that he couldn't see her act for what it was, a mark of her insecurity?

She only knew that somehow she had begun to irritate him and she couldn't think why. It seemed to Alexia he had been particularly depressed ever since. . . ever since that incident

213

when that woman at his firm had been assaulted. What was her name? Liz, Liz Carlton. He had hardly spoken to her that night, and ever since he had not been the same.

She turned on to her stomach, pressing her face into the pillow, refusing to cry. It should have been such a lovely evening. He would never know just how much she looked forward to seeing him, how she lived only for their time together.

She should have felt euphoric this evening, if only it had gone as she had planned it. The exhilarating ride, making love romatically in their favourite spot. They had had everything going for them, the fine late autumn weather, the peace, each other.

But the lightheartedness she had felt at the beginning of their evening had vanished and been replaced by a world-weary numbness that left her weak and longing for her sleep and oblivion.

27

When Patrick telephoned early Thursday evening to ask if he could come round, Liz was half pleased and half apprehensive. Pleased because she had missed him over the past two days, apprehensive that he might find out she was not home the previous night. Hoped that the children would not let anything slip about staying with Mrs Oakes while she went off on her trip to Birmingham with Martin.

She could not bring herself to warn them off telling him. Apart from the fact it was unfair to involve them in such subterfuge, she had vague misgivings about deliberately extending the deception. Deception, somehow, seemed so much more serious when others knew about it, especially if they were closely involved with the deceived party, as the children were with Patrick.

So she kept quiet, crossed her fingers and tried to get the children interested in a TV thriller. Then, by a stroke of good fortune, Charlotte's sometime friend Samantha from the first floor flat telephoned to ask if Charlotte would like to watch a video of a recent gymkhana in which both girls had participated. Robbie said he wanted to go too, and although both Liz and Charlotte knew he was more interested in Sam's younger brother and his collection of dungeons and dragons, he was allowed to accompany his sister.

When Patrick arrived she was alone. He was crazy for her. He made love to her immediately, with a kind of futile desperation, as if he couldn't get enough of her, as if he might never see her again.

She was humbled by the urgency of his ardour, even ashamed for not being worthy of it. She tried to make up for her shallowness by spoiling him. She kissed his face, his body,

215

devoted her whole being to his pleasure and satisfaction. She used every trick she knew, ignoring her own pleasure, yet ironically gaining more pleasure because of her selflessness. It was a new experience for Liz and the novelty of it took her breath away. Yet she was further discomfited when, in the end, overwhelmed with gratitude, he wept his love for her.

'Patrick,' she whispered, 'Don't give too much. Not ever. Not to me. You don't know me.'

'But I want to know you. I want to know everything about you. I could know you, if only you would help me to.'

She quieted him with more kisses, her mouth on his, her tongue probing, her hands fluttering over his body like gossamer wings, delicate and light, so that every tiny nerve beneath his skin throbbed from the sensation of her and cried out for her.

Eventually, satiated, he lay back and began to doze. While he slept, she liked to prop herself up on her elbow and watch him. In sleep, he looked so vulnerable, aroused in her such tenderness. But she was tired now, and although she could not sleep herself, she lay down beside him, her eyes closed. His remark, when it came, caught her unawares.

'I'll stay over with you tomorrow night, so that we can get an early start.'

The weekend! She had forgotten about the weekend at Pascall Lodge. Not so much 'forgotten' as refused to think about it, in the vague hope he might see sense and abandon his crazy scheme. But when Patrick had an idea, he wore blinkers to everything else. His course was set and nothing else mattered until he had seen it through to the end, bitter or otherwise. She sighed and turned her back on him.

He couldn't force her to go along with his plans. He wasn't her keeper. She was an adult woman, with a mind of her own. She was not afraid to face her problems head-on. Their differences were entirely due to the method of approach, not to the validity of dealing with the problem at the first suitable opportunity.

Her way was confrontation. Her way was to storm Pascall House and raise Cain. His way was more subtle and in her view, more dangerous. His way was to wait, to probe, to poke around like a cheap, private detective.

'I can't see any point in my going,' she told him stubbornly.

'But Liz,' Patrick groaned, 'It's all set up, and I can tell you it wasn't easy to invite myself over with just a few days' notice. I sacrificed a lot of my valuable time last week for this weekend. For your sake, Liz, not for mine.' Of course, he knew that was not strictly true. For wasn't her happiness his happiness, her security his security.

'You can't let me down now,' pleaded Patrick.

Liz could feel her face burning, knew she wasn't being fair on him. But supposing Martin was there. Even if he wasn't, he would surely get to hear about it. Martin, her latest would-be protector, whose support might prove critical to her in the coming weeks. Eddie Smith alias William Fraser would be redundant once she had Martin publicly on her side. For if Patrick was right and Jeremy was pulling the strings, what better way to cut those strings than to become part of the family.

In any case, even if Patrick discovered the evidence he needed, how would he manage to convince Sir George, when blood was so notoriously thicker than water.

When a son, a convicted murderer, stood condemned, what mother ever truly believed in his guilt? Whatever the evidence, however incriminating, a mother would always insist her child had been framed. Wouldn't she, Liz, be exactly the same? By the same token, what father would willingly accept that his son, the heir to his business empire, was little more than a common criminal?

Would Sir George?

Never!

Patrick was living in cloud cuckoo land.

On the other hand, with Martin her future would be assured, her children safe from the unwelcome attentions of William Fraser.

Or was Patrick thinking of going first to the police even before he approached Sir George? That would be suicide for Liz, career-wise. Of course, the idea of wreaking vengeance on the unpalatable William Fraser was very attractive, but with Martin's co-operation she was sure she could find some way of crushing that intolerable little creep!

And what about Jeremy. Jeremy ought to be made to *pay*. Married to Martin, she would be in a much stronger position to make him pay, without jeopardising her own security.

Pity she almost loved Patrick!

Even so, although Patrick had proved himself a loyal friend and a fervent lover, he had never actually committed himself verbally to her. Maybe he would want to go onto pastures new in a month or two. Why should she assume they would be grazing together in years to come?

Thus did Liz justify her own divided loyalties.

'I'm so nervous,' she told Patrick pathetically. But he laughed at her.

'Pull the other one! You, nervous! In any case, I'll be right there beside you.'

'I know, darling, but I don't think I can face it.'

'Bollocks!' said Patrick rudely. 'You've never refused to face up to anything in your life. Except your past,' he added nastily.

'All right,' she said, 'What do you want to know?'

Perhaps it wouldn't be such a bad idea to tell him. Even if it alienated him. At least it might get her out of this weekend.

'How did Robbie's father die?'

Eyeing him defiantly, Liz spoke in a deliberate, clinical tone.

'OK, Patrick, here it is, but I don't think you're going to like it. Don't tell me I didn't warn you.'

'Spit it out,' said Patrick grimly, plumping out the pillows behind him and easing himself into a sitting position.

Liz lay on her back, her arms folded over her stomach. The quilt covered her lower body, but from the waist up she was naked. He tried not to look at her, at the way her breasts swelled between her upper arms, the soft smooth curve of her shoulders.

'We had a pretty rough time after Charlotte's father was killed,' lied Liz, 'No money, no future, no status. Charlotte went to the very worst in state schools. Then, when Michael came along, it was like an angel in the midst of hell, an island in a storm . . .'

'All right, Liz, cut out the dramatics. I want the facts.'

She glared at him, and, at the same time, realised he was right. Why was she trying to dress it up for him? Instantly, she recognised her own weakness. She did not want him to think too badly of her. So much for alienating him! So much for getting out of this weekend!

'He was a lot older than me,' she continued in a softer tone, 'If I had not been lonely, I probably would not have married him. As it was, I did, and Robbie was born. But things were so dull. He was so dull. I couldn't bear it. He suffered with his heart and the Doctor advised him against marital relations.

'Patrick, I was only in my early thirties. I just couldn't cope. I began to have discreet affairs. Only once I wasn't so discreet and he found me out. Shortly afterwards, Michael had a heart attack and died. He died, in my arms, in bed. Trying to prove to me that he was as good as my lover.'

'Oh hell!' Patrick buried his face in his hands.

'I'm human, you know,' she said defensively, hating to see him like this, even though she had half-intended it.

'Then why didn't you make sure you didn't get caught,' yelled Patrick.

'So it would have been OK if I hadn't got caught. Honestly, Patrick, what a hypocrite you are!'

'At least Michael would have been spared the pain. I can see it might be understandable for you to have strayed, Liz, that is, if you are telling me the truth. But it was bloody selfish getting caught.'

'*C'est la vie,*' she said sardonically. 'These things happen.'

'Don't you ever hold yourself responsible for anything that happens to you? You're the most determined woman I know, and yet you act as if everything in your life is circumstantial. As if life happens to you without you ever giving it permission.'

This was such a new concept to Liz, that she had to think about it. It intrigued her. Was she *really* like that. Had it been like that with Michael?

219

Michael had been so proud of his bedroom technique.

How could someone be so proud when they were so dull?

Nevertheless, she had recognised the peacock in him, the need to strut, to display his tail feathers in front of her. It was true he had courted her, bought her flowers and chocolates and French knickers of the finest silk. Took delight in slipping his hand up her skirt when she least expected it. Licked his lips suggestively if he spotted a bare breast.

But when he pumped gamely into her, panting, the sweat from him making their bodies slap wetly together in unison, he would give her a sort of half-bashful grin. 'How is it for you, darling?' he'd say then he'd climax before she could answer. 'Wasn't that great?' he'd say, 'Aren't we tremendous together?'

And that would be that. It was never any different. She could have made demands, but what was the point? Some people had their limitations. And Michael was one of those people. No imagination.

She did try to help him after the doctor's warning. Tried to help him to help her. She would tell him she had thought of an exciting new position, and then she would show him a way of making love that was less demanding on him. Maybe they would try it with her on top, or the rear-entry sideways position, so that he could fondle her while he was penetrating her.

Michael complied, enjoying her creativity and the exciting new twists to their lovemaking. As she halved the strain for him, she amused and delighted him, uplifting his spirits and introducing him to new heights of sexual awareness and fulfillment. But on a purely personal level. *His* personal level.

And it hadn't been nearly enough for her.

Not nearly enough.

She still found him inept and clumsy. His fondling was insensitive, sometimes it was so rough her breasts and thighs were bruised for days on end. His kisses were hard, crushing her responses which cried out for the gentle teasing and lightness and control which made lovemaking erotic.

Michael knew nothing of such things.

It was strange, thought Liz, that someone who was academically supreme could be so basic about human relationships.

'This lover,' said Patrick suddenly, bringing her abruptly back to the present. 'Was he another Eddie look-alike?'

'Good gracious, no,' said Liz. 'I suppose that was what hit Michael so hard. He was actually older than Michael.'

'So,' summarised Patrick bitterly, 'You killed your first husband with a dare, your second husband with an insult and your third husband with a challenge.'

It wasn't fair. She knew it wasn't fair. But she wouldn't give him the satisfation of justifying herself to him again. 'That's about it,' she said cheerfully, 'but how did you know about the dare?'

He gave her a sly, knowing look, a look that made her squirm. It angered her that he could make her feel so uncomfortable. She glared back at him.

'An educated guess. I was a young lad at around that time. I knew what went on. And I suspect you must be nurturing a tremendous guilt deep in your subconscious to react the way you do about a husband so long dead. Because of him, you feel guilt about any intense pleasure you receive from any other man. That's about it, isn't it?'

'If it pleases you to think so.'

'Why so blasé, Liz? This isn't you. Why are you deliberately trying to provoke me?'

'I'm not. I just feel that you've condemned me out of court. There's nothing I can say to change that.'

'I am trying to understand, because I care for you. But you're not helping.'

'Suddenly her face softened. She slipped her hand in his and automatically, his large fingers curled around hers. 'It was a strange time, Patrick,' she whispered, 'an enchanted time. I can't explain it. I did love Eddie and I did dare him to race the train, but I never intended for him to die. I didn't believe he would. Our whole lives were speed and glamour and motor-bikes. We thought we were invincible, immortal. It was as if we were on a high, both of us.'

'Thank you, Liz,' he said. 'That helps me a lot.' For a moment, she suspected he was being sarcastic, but she studied him carefully out of the corner of her eye and saw that he was sincere. He really meant it. It helped him to understand, to reassure himself that her warmth was real, that she intended no harm.

Oh God! The weekend! She had burnt her boats now. She could see from the determined expression on his face that he was more committed than ever before.

In a strange way, the knowledge that she had met her match was exciting, strange and infuriating all at the same time. There was no escape. Tomorrow they would be off, speeding along, cutting through, overtaking with sudden bursts and spurts, as if there were a pack of wolves on their tail. Like it or not, they were bound for Pascall Lodge.

For the first time in her life, Liz had no option, had to do something she desperately did not want to do. Couldn't talk her way out of it. Even when she had been cornered by Johnny Morris, she had eventually wormed her way out of it, used his weakness to manipulate him. But it wasn't like that with Patrick. Patrick and his blinkers!

There was no point in fighting any more. She was too tired anyway. Let him have his head. Let him do his worst.

Dear Patrick! She had loved other men, but never in her life had she allowed any of them to influence her the way she allowed Patrick to influence her. Not even John.

It was getting late. The children would be back soon. Had to keep up appearances.

'Come on, Patrick,' she said, 'It's time to get up.

28

At first sight, it was obvious that Pascall Lodge was the focal point of the village, which it dominated on account of its position on high ground, and the height and solidarity of the wall that surrounded it. It was a fortress, this wall, built of rough yellow stone, reminiscent of Patrick's cottage retreat in the Cotswolds.

'They're going to flip when they find out you've brought an unexpected guest,' grumbled Liz. 'Especially when they discover it's me.'

Patrick sighed. She was like a record, being played over and over again. He had never thought she was the type to nag, to drone and complain. Sideways he stole a glance at her. She was dreadfully strained. Hardly surprising really! He had stayed over last night, primarily to ensure that she was available this morning for the trip to Pascall Lodge. He would not have put it past her to have skipped away somewhere for the weekend with the kids, leaving him high and dry.

She had made sure he had suffered for his mistrust of her. 'But we need to make an early start,' he had insisted.

'That's not the reason. You just want your own way. You always think you're right. You're like my gaoler. I'm getting fed up with your bullying, Patrick. I don't know why I put up with it.'

'It's my Irish charisma,' he'd joked, trying to coax her out of her black mood. But she had grimaced and refused to talk to him except to respond in monosyllables to his conversation.

For a sweetener, he had brought her a beautiful bouquet of delicate white roses. White roses for peace. It hadn't been easy to find them, most florists seeming to specialise in the long-stemmed variety. But he had got a bee in his bonnet about white roses and his persistence had paid off in the end.

But she had wakened in the night and had violently roused him, screaming and pounding her fists into his back. Get out, get out, you bastard, she'd shrilled, over and over.

Dazed and bruised, he had sat up. She was sweating, beads of water steaming from her forehead, her black curls damp and flat like a cap against her skull, her face distorted and mottled scarlet. He had eventually managed to calm her.

'It's all right, darling, it's just a nightmare.' Finally, something bordering on sanity and recognition had transformed her features.

After much coaxing, he had ascertained that she had thought it was William Fraser, alias Eddie, in bed beside her.

'I woke up and saw your white roses on my bedside table. I thought they were cow parsley,' she sobbed. 'I thought you were *him*,'

He remembered immediately, as if it were yesterday, that incident back in the summer when Eddie Smith had presented her with the cow parsley in the foyer of Pascall House. Even then he had sensed that the wild roadside plant had some deeper connotation than appeared on the surface.

'What is this thing you have about cow parsley?'

So she had told him.

About that terrible time after the motor-bike accident.

About the railway embankment.

About the twenty-two florets, one for each year of Eddie's short life.

And finally, about the unexpected sprigs of the late, half-dead flowers she had found on Eddie's grave.'

All of which had made him even more determined to get to the bottom of it, once and for all.

'It's a waste of time, this trip,' she'd repeated piteously. 'It's a waste of time because William Fraser is really *my* Eddie and he's trying to pay me back for sending him to his death.'

He'd shaken her soundly. If teeth ever rattled, hers would have rattled then.

'Don't you dare ever to say anything like that again. Honestly, Liz, how can you be so naive? How can you even entertain such ridiculous notions?'

'How can you explain what's happened?'

'I can't be sure at the moment. But I intend to find out. We already know there is a connection between Eddie and Jeremy. I've explained the basis of my theory to you, Liz. All I need is some evidence to substantiate it before I approach Sir George.'

'Patrick,' she'd said slowly, 'you are not being realistic. You are over-estimating Sir George's sense of fair play. For a start, he's not going to believe anything you say against his precious son. In any case, I am far from convinced. It all seems too elaborate a plot to be plausible.'

'In that case, explain the events at the flat,' he'd snapped.

'I can't. But that doesn't mean there isn't a logical explanation.'

'You'd rather believe in ghouls, wouldn't you?' he had muttered contemptuously.

'Oh leave me alone.' She had buried her face in the pillow, weeping silently, shutting him out.

He looked at her now. He had to give her credit. She had made a great effort and was dressed beautifully, the epitome of the English country lady, flecked autumn-coloured skirt, soft wool blouse, brown cashmere cardigan. She looked, for all the world, like the lady of the manor.

'What I need,' said Patrick, as he followed the winding country lane alongside the huge wall, 'is a chance to scout around undisturbed. Jeremy and his wife occupy the apartments in the west wing of the Lodge. There must be something there that I can find to tie things up.'

'What am I supposed to do, Sherlock Holmes? Act as a lookout?' she inquired sarcastically. 'Or am I a decoy?'

'Whatever the occasion demands,' replied Patrick. 'I'm sure I can rely on you, Watson.'

She sniffed, unimpressed. Slowly he continued to drive the circumference of the fortress wall. 'How many acres is this place?' he murmured. 'This wall seems to go on for ever. There must be a way in soon.'

There was something about the wall that filled her with dread. She searched her mind for the reason. Remembered.

It was just like the wall around the cemetary when they had

buried Eddie. So high. So yellow. So solid. As if it had imprisoned all those that lay within its perimeter and was making sure there was no escape.

She thought of the undertaker, standing in the centre of Eddie's parents' cottagey front parlour. Portly, he had seemed to fill up the small room. His pot belly stuck out aggressively so that the waistband of his trousers was by far the widest part of him. His coarse, ginger moustache curled over his fat lips. He rocked back on his heels and remarked that he quite enjoyed his job.

But no one cared.

The undertaker had shuffled his big feet and commented that it was interesting to meet so many people. There were perks. . .

Awaited a response, but none came.

It had been a burial. Eddie's father had insisted. But burials were so hard on the family. There was something so terribly final about the grave, about the coffin so discreetly draped with artificial grass.

The bereaved had sat around in huddles. Liz had known they were talking about her. Talking about the part she had played in Eddie's untimely death. She had clung to her mother, but her mother was angry with her too. She had never had much time for Eddie, felt she was a cut above the Smiths, but she was furious with her daughter for allowing herself to become a butt of contemptuous gossip.

The only person present who did not seem to bear her any malice had been Eddie's mother.

Eddie's mother had flipped!

She was jolly. She was solicitous of her guests, plying them with food and drink.

The sudden song of the ice-cream van was out of context. But Eddie's mother had leapt to her feet. 'I hear Tonibell,' she cried. 'Why don't we all have a nice big Number 99?'

She waved her finger about, counting heads, ignoring any cries of resistance. 'Come and give me a hand, darling,' and she had taken Liz's arm and whisked her away into the street, still weeping, in pursuit of Tonibell.

So it was that Eddie's funeral had been firmly rounded off by each mourner polishing off a 99 cone, with its large piece of chocolate flake stuck like an upended coffin in the soft ice. No one refused, not even the undertaker. The bereaved mother had to be humoured.

Finally, replete, the undertaker had cleared his throat and gone away. Liz had wanted to go away too, away from the taut, condemning silence. Didn't want to think about the undertaker, the coffin, the yellow stone cemetery wall.

'Here we are,' said Patrick suddenly, jerking her back to the present.

The wrought-iron gates were open in readiness for the intended house-guests. Suspended on each side was a colourful hanging basket, from which erupted a profusion of rich purple fuchsia. An explosion of colour like a violent welcome, making the most of the last days of autumn before the frosts came to punish those lovely blooms for their riotous display.

Confidently Patrick drove in, following the road which twisted several times through woodland before emerging into lawns and revealing the Lodge.

At first, Patrick was vaguely disappointed at the insignificance of the Lodge itself. Liz seemed indifferent, but of course, she had been amongst the privileged few Pascall employees previously invited to share the directors' hospitality.

The Lodge was large, low and rambling and all on one floor. Nothing ostentatious, no fancy bits and pieces except for more hanging baskets which gave it a rural, cottagey effect. The plasterwork was beige and on closer inspection looked dirty and flaking. The dark oak beams added to its sombre quality. The windows, lots of them, were small and leaded, with black painted shutters, Continental-style. But as they drew closer, he could see from its depth that it was considerably larger than he had at first thought.

By the west wing there was a small lake, surrounded by reeds and willows.

In the huge expanse of the front lawn, five mature oaks grew

227

and stood guard over the Lodge. Copper beeches modelled their finery with superb elegance.

'It's really quite something,' he said at last, half-grudgingly, as the car drew to a standstill between Jeremy's Porsche and Sir George's Silver Cloud. There was also a Triumph Stag and three Range Rovers.

'I feel like a poor relation,' Patrick jested as he got out of the car and strode around to Liz's door to assist her.

'Come on,' he coaxed, 'put a brave face on it or the whole thing will be doomed before it ever gets started.'

Liz bared her teeth in a deliberately unconvincing distortion of a grin and Patrick cast his eyes skywards.

'Do as you're told or I'll beat you.'

In spite of herself, she had to laugh. 'That's better,' he said approvingly, glad he could still crack that self-imposed barrier she seemed to employ so freely.

She was a little unsteady on her feet, so he took her arm as they approached the Lodge. He had expected a maid to greet them, but instead the heavy, arched door was drawn ponderously aside to reveal Martin's fiancée.

'Hello,' said Alexia pleasantly, then catching sight of Liz, her face dropped slightly. Quickly, she recovered. Liz was taken aback by her fleeting expression of hostility, but Patrick appeared not to have noticed.

'Liz,' exclaimed Alexia, 'how lovely to see you.'

'You're looking well, Alexia. May I introduce Patrick? He is your official guest. I'm afraid I'm the gatecrasher,' said Liz, deciding to brazen it out.

'Really!' gushed Alexia. 'How exciting.'

'What do you mean? Patrick? Or my gatecrashing?'

'Both,' enthused Alexia insincerely, bundling them inside. Liz arranged her face into a smile, quashing a sudden desire to turn tail and run. Apparently unconcerned, Alexia rattled on. 'Come and have a quick drink, if it's not too early for you, then you can go and freshen up after your journey. I'll send Smitherson out for your things.'

As they followed Alexia, Patrick decided that he liked her. The complete opposite of her fiancé Martin, she was hearty and loquacious. Big-boned but not overweight, she was Scandinavian in colouring. He admired the long ash-blonde hair, twisted into a single plait which hung half-way down her broad, strong back. He liked her pretty open face, her wide smile, the sparkling wide-awake grey eyes, the snub nose covered in freckles.

Patrick felt Liz stiffen as suddenly Martin Pascall came striding towards them. He looked every inch the country squire in his riding gear. His hat dangled from his fingers by the strap. As he saw Patrick and Liz, he stopped short and there was no mistaking the surprise and confusion he felt. With considerable aplomb, like Alexia, he recovered, bared his even white teeth in a welcoming smile.

'My dear Liz. I was not aware we were to have the pleasure of your company this weekend.'

'It came as rather a surprise to me too,' replied Liz evasively, not expounding further, as Martin shook hands with Patrick.

'Good to see you,' said Martin stiffly.

But Liz's blushes were not spared, for immediately Alexia chipped in, 'Isn't she a card, darling? She's our first gatecrasher.'

Martin's eyebrows disappeared under the wayward lock of hair that fell across his forehead, as he gave Liz a searching look. Thankfully, she took her sherry from a tray proffered by the maid, and sipped it.

Patrick was admiring the furniture, running his fingers over the red and gold surface of an antique lowboy.

'Netherlands floral marquetry?' he inquired of Alexia. Her face lit up at his interest.

'That's right,' she said. 'It's lovely, isn't it? That's a very fine piece. There's also a matching table in the corner over there and Sir George has the wardrobe.'

'Beautiful,' murmured Patrick appreciatively. 'By the way, is Sir George about today?'

'He's out, shooting at tiny animals,' said Alexia in a conspiratorial whisper. 'Not that I personally approve of such sport, but one cannot keep these men from their little distractions, can one?' Then, mischievously, 'But he's not a

229

very good shot so at least the poor little things have a fighting chance.'

'Alexia!' Liz noted with a start the affection in Martin's reprimand to his fiancée. It fell on deaf ears, however, for Alexia was bent on giving Patrick a blow-by-blow account of every piece of furniture, its history, its production and how the family had acquired it.

It was a lovely room. The light walls were covered in gilded miniatures of the family and its ancestors. Glass-fronted cabinets adorned the walls, containing pieces of china and silver and bronze, all antique. The sofa and chairs were cottage-style and were covered in thick, white, rosebud-material, which fell in deep frills from the seats to the floor. A very ancient-looking tapestry hung from the ceiling over the old marble fireplace.

'Come and see the kitchen garden, Liz,' said Martin suddenly, too suddenly, taking her arm. 'I'm sure you'll find it interesting.'

Alarm fleeted across Alexia's features, a fact not lost on Liz who had glanced at her guiltily. Trying to hide her reluctance, Liz allowed herself to be led outside through the patio French windows. Martin's strides were long and determined so that she had to half-run to keep pace with him.

Suddenly, he stopped, turned on her and she, unable to check her momentum, bumped into him, her forehead making contact with the dark stubble of his chin.

'Careful, Liz,' he said, 'you'll spill your drink.'

'The garden?' she inquired weakly.

'Never mind the garden. That was just an excuse. I wanted to talk to you. What are you doing here, Liz? What are you doing here, with him?' He paused, feeling awkward. 'Don't misunderstand me, I'm delighted to see you and I hope that one day you will be a frequent and welcome guest. But you must realise your timing is not ideal. Jeremy, Alexia . . .'

'I'm sorry, Martin,' she said weakly. There was nothing for it but to be honest. 'Patrick insisted that I accompany him.'

'Insisted! What is he to you?'

'Nothing,' she whispered, 'it's just that he feels bad about taking over my office and wants to talk to your father about it. He felt I should be here.'

'Guilty conscience?'

'I expect so. And anyway,' she improvised wildly, 'it was a chance to get to see you.'

He seemed satisfied. Smiled his dark smile and Liz thought how relaxed he looked when he smiles, how it softened his Arabic swarthiness.

Like a pussycat. Which was all he was. A pussycat.

'I haven't said anything to Alexia yet,' said Martin. 'About us, I mean.'

'Oh!' murmured Liz, staring hard at her feet, clad in their sensible country brogues. 'Look, Martin, I don't want to cause any trouble.'

'Don't even think about it. Alexia is my problem, not yours.'

'Yes. But Martin, we mustn't rush into anything. We have to be sure.' Her face was burning. She hadn't expected him to come on so strong, so soon. But he was hanging on to her every word, couldn't take his eyes off her. Yet she knew he was fond of Alexia. Had heard it in his voice when he had scolded her for her impertinence towards his father.

How would he tell Alexia?

'I so enjoyed our trip to Birmingham,' he was saying softly, 'you were beautiful, Liz, so beautiful. I am privileged.'

She smiled. 'You'd better go back now, Martin,' she replied. 'Alexia will miss you. I'm just going to take a look at the lake.'

'Mustn't start the tongues wagging,' he agreed thankfully, 'At least, not yet. Not till you know for sure.'

He gave her a last, lingering look and she watched him go. Knew that he was basically a gentle and ethical man.

She lingered by the lake, watching grebes and mallards, their tails upending as they sought sustenance beneath the surface of the gleaming expanse. Coots and moorhens scuttled busily amongst the reeds.

Suddenly she felt a grip upon her arm, familiar in its vice-like quality.

'Patrick!'

231

'Et tu, Brute?' Patrick's voice hissed in her ear. 'Keeping all your options open?'

She caught her breath, turned and grabbed desperately at his sleeve, was suddenly afraid to lose him. Knew that she needed him. He pushed her away, but she insinuated herself into his arms. 'Patrick, please understand. Martin's my only friend now among the Pascalls and I can't afford to alienate him. It's just that he's kind to me, Patrick. You're not kind to me, but it's you I love.'

'Do you really think he'd take the chances for you that I do? That he could make love to you like I do?'

'Of course not.'

As he looked into her eyes, he did not doubt that she spoke the truth. She did care for him, as deeply as she was capable of caring for any man. But whether that love was constant enough to turn down a safe bet like Martin Pascall was quite another matter. Could she sacrifice her career and her future for it? Was it trusting enough for commitment?

He knew that sometimes she felt trapped by his possessiveness of her. Resolved to try to give her space, room to breathe.

Slowly, each thinking their own thoughts, they retraced their steps back to the Lodge. Alexia directed her to the guest bathroom and she washed and renewed her make-up. Poked out her hair with her Afro comb.

When she returned to the drawing-room, it was full of people. Sir George was there, holding court over Patrick and Martin. Lillian Pascall, a thin, grumpy-looking woman, was regaling the shining Alexia, and Jeremy's wife Gina, with anecdotes about her recent shopping trip to Oxford Street. Both women looked bored and inattentive. Gina seemed exceptionally tiny and demure as she sat beside Alexia.

Trevor, thin, fair and youthfully handsome, was entwined on a large chair with a glamorous redhead, and they gazed dreamily into each others' eyes.

Only Jeremy saw her enter, and was immediately at her side.

'Liz, how nice. I'd *heard* you were here,' he greeted her with heavy sarcasm. 'You really should have let us know you were coming, my dear. Mummy did not know how many extra pints to order.'

'If I had told you, you might not have let me come,' she retorted with spirit, which seemed to deflate him somewhat.

'Let me get you another drink,' he said smarmily.

As Jeremy retired to the bar, Patrick caught her eye. His deeply meaningful expression as he slipped unnoticed from the room left her in no doubt as to her role.

She was to keep Jeremy involved by whatever means necessary.

It might not be easy. Supposing she failed and Patrick was discovered. Lost his job even. He had taken so many chances for her. Yet he had never been fooled into believing she was anything other than Liz Carlton, with her faults, her problems, her past. And still, he stuck by her. Even now, he was rooting for her, having obviously suspected some deep ulterior motive in her short conversation with Martin.

She wanted to give him her loyalty. But she had given her loyalty to men in the past, and look where it had got her.

John who had been cruel to her. John who had changed her from a woman who needed approval into a woman who did not care.

And Michael. Michael who was only interested in his own gratification. Michael who was too stupid to understand, despite his brilliant mind.

Yet Patrick was different. Different, like Eddie. Just as Eddie had been prepared to lay his life down, so was Patrick. And Patrick certainly did not believe in letting the grass grow under his feet, she thought, with grudging admiration. She experienced a painful twinge in her stomach. She must not let him down.

She took her sherry from Jeremy. 'Thank you,' she said politely. 'Of course, you must realise that I had an ulterior motive in accompanying Patrick this weekend.'

He had not expected her to be so direct. She saw that he was instantly and totally enslaved by his own natural curiosity.

'What do you mean?' he said shortly.

She knew she had to hang it out. Use every delaying tactic

she could think of. 'It's difficult for me to explain,' she muttered, as if regretful that she had mentioned it in the first place.

'Try,' insisted Jeremy, looking as if he thought that, given enough rope, she might hang herself.

'Do you think we could go into the kitchen garden?' she asked. 'I'm a little warm and the air would do me some good. Martin said I might find it interesting.'

Jeremy raised his elegant eyebrows.

'*Martin*, now, is it?' he said, showing his disapproval of her familiarity in dropping the obligatory Mr. But she wouldn't allow him to put her down. 'Yes, Martin, your brother,' she agreed politely.

He followed her outside. 'You certainly seem to know your way around my home,' he said as she led him through the shrubs and rosebushes to the small enclosed area of the kitchen garden.

'I visited once before, but I believe that you were away on a business trip to the Middle East at the time.'

She wandered along the crazy-paved paths, admired the last of the runner beans, the vegetable plot, the stone herb boxes now bereft of their leafy produce.

Jeremy could stand it no longer. Her composure unsettled him. 'My father,' he began belligerently, 'has been considerably upset by recent events. I would respectfully warn you that he needs to relax at weekends without the intervention of problems relating to the company and its employees.'

'I quite understand,' said Liz coolly, sitting down on a loveseat in front of the sprouts, now somewhat gone to seed. Like her! Sir George had not even appeared to notice she was there. Once, in the drawing-room, had looked straight through her. It seemed she did not exist for him any more.

'Are you playing cat and mouse with me?'

'Of course not, Mr Jeremy,' she replied, her eyes wide and innocent. She was beginning to enjoy herself, beginning to feel on top again. Patrick was right. She was born a fighter and she should fight. Look at Jeremy! Clever, devious, cunning

234

Jeremy, completely fooled by her ruse. It would be easy. She would keep him guessing, tantalising him with her bait, the fear of what she might do. She was a woman of mystery, a Mata Hari, a Jezebel. He didn't stand a chance. Like others, could be manipulated.

All the time Jeremy was with her, Patrick was safe from discovery. His wife was unlikely to be aware of what was going on, and, in any case, she would not suddenly abandon her conversation with the other women to return to her apartment.

'I feel I've had a pretty raw deal,' Liz ventured.

'You do?'

'I do. I'm angry about Patrick's displacing me.'

'Patrick is in charge of Robinson's Surgical. You are still Personnel Officer. At least, for the moment,' he added ominously.

'You are wrong. I am Administrative and Financial Consultant.'

Jeremy's eyes bulged. Distractedly he scratched at his crotch, and Jeremy never did anything the least bit vulgar. He was in a state, thought Liz, amused.

'I know Patrick's not after my job,' said Liz. 'I'm talking about my office and my secretary being requisitioned for the new company. Obviously, as you can imagine, I am slightly more upset about my office than I am about my secretary, who, I am sure, can be replaced by a more loyal and efficient girl.'

Jeremy sat down beside her on the loveseat, his eyes sunken, his face haggard, his skin grey. Suddenly he had a headache. A real mind-blowing great granddaddy of a headache.

'Liz,' he said slowly, and the malice in his voice had been replaced by something quite different. His words were hard and positive, yet there was a desperation in them, a sort of cringing whine. 'Liz, I am going to speak to you very frankly. This is just between you and me and if you are foolish enough to refuse, I shall deny this conversation ever took place. Name your price.'

'My price?'

'Your price. To get out of Pascall's, move away, get out of our lives for ever.'

235

Her instinct was to retort 'Never'. But just in time, she remembered the sole purpose of their conversation was delay. So she pretended to consider.

'I don't understand,' she said. 'I don't understand why you are so desperate to see the back of me. I do my job well. Until last week I have never been off sick.'

'For an intelligent woman, you can be pretty obtuse. However, I suggest that you think about it.'

With that, he rose and left her.

She gave him a little time to rejoin the others, hoping against hope that Patrick had finished his research and was safely back with the crowd. Then she too rose.

Just as she got to the kitchen garden gate, she saw that Jeremy had not returned to the drawing-room. He was almost running in the direction of the cars, parked noses in, to the Lodge's east wing.

Her heart jumped as she spotted the red and black motor-bike and the gangly young man removing his red crash helmet.

He was here. Eddie Smith was here.

She watched as Jeremy urgently intercepted Eddie. She still couldn't think of him as William Fraser. To her he would always be Eddie. Jeremy gesticulated wildly then looked back as if to check her whereabouts. She ducked behind the gatepost, out of sight.

As she peeked around again, she saw that Eddie was pushing the motor-bike around to the side of the Lodge, where she would not be able to see it.

29

For several moments, a black hole of terror in the pit of her stomach rendered her incapable of moving. She thought about Charlotte, the look in her eyes when she was day-dreaming about the wonderful time ahead when her breasts had developed and she had grown three inches taller. She thought about Robbie, his expectant, bright face turned up towards hers as he begged for more tales of the Wobblyglucks.

Charlotte, straight-backed, slender hands resting palms down on delicately turned knees. Robbie, his socks at half-mast, his shirt hanging out, his tie askew. Her children. And her life.

Why was she still procrastinating, still floundering?

Dazed, Liz slowly walked back towards the house, but almost instantly Patrick materialised, it seemed, out of nowhere.

'Listen, I've made the excuse I want to look over the stables. Come on, Liz, I've got some news for you.'

'The Pascalls are going to think we are terribly rude guests,' said Liz worriedly. 'They might suspect something.'

'Don't worry about that now,' objected Patrick.

'I've got some news for you too,' she told him as he led her to the back of the Lodge through the kitchen garden, scene of her dramatic interlude with Jeremy Pascall. 'Eddie's here' – there was a note of urgency in her voice – 'and he's got a red and black Norton, just like the one my husband was killed on.'

'That doesn't surprise me in the least,' said Patrick. 'I managed to get into the safe in Jeremy's apartment and I found a whole file on you, Liz.'

'You cracked a safe? What are you, a professional burglar?'

'It did help that I managed to get a duplicate of the key. My father was a locksmith, Liz. There's not much I don't know about safes and locks.'

'You mean you had the duplicate key on you when we arrived this morning?'

'You've got it in one.' He was looking smug again. For once it did not make her cross.

'How did you get hold of the original?'

'Easy. Because of the special key awarded to me by Sir George last week. A key to the executive cloakroom. When Jeremy went into the loo and left his jacket hanging outside on the hook, I found his keys in his inside pocket. A lump of kids' Plasticine, a quick impression of each likely key on the ring and my old man did the rest.'

'Do you usually carry lumps of Plasticine around with you?'

'Not exactly. But I *was* a Scout, so I came prepared just in case the opportunity presented itself.'

'My goodness,' Liz threw her arms around him and hugged him soundly. 'You are the most wonderful man in the world. What did you find out?'

'There were newspaper cuttings alluding to your husbands' deaths. I expect you are aware of the shot taken by a Sunday rag of you sitting by the embankment amongst the cow parsley. And the caption, "A dangerous Game? Who Dares Wins the Girl's Devotion or Loses his Life".'

She flinched but he did not spare her.

'And the one about John. Just a small piece cut out of the local newspaper. It seems that since forensic evidence proved he was sober, suicide was suspected.'

'The inquest returned an open verdict,' she said suddenly defensive.

'So I noticed,' said Patrick, 'but in addition to that there was the obituary notice for Michael. You didn't tell me he was a Doctor of Philosophy in Chemistry.'

'It seems that there's not much you don't know about me.'

'You're not wrong! There are reams of notes about your past, your lovers, your movements. Must have cost Jeremy a fortune in private detectives and research over the past year or two. There were even some casual interviews organised involving your former neighbours and your relatives, all low-key and seemingly innocent, but none the less informative.'

She was silent, overwhelmed by the scale of Jeremy's obsessive enmity towards her.

'There's a whole dossier on you, Liz. And a fully detailed plan. I can even tell you what's next on the agenda. They're about to organise a rail trip for you, and Eddie's going to ride his motor-bike alongside the train, intending to take you back into the nightmare of the past. They want to drive you out of your mind. And it's not actually a Norton, Liz, but it's been customised to look like one. I found the bills in the safe on both counts, one for the purchase of the bike and another for its subsequent. . . embellishment.'

'I don't believe it,' she said weakly, 'it's preposterous!'

'It's true. You're being attacked on all sides, politically at Pascall House and also by the cruellest emotional blackmail. Jeremy actually wants you to think that you're being hounded by your dead husband's ghost.'

'He actually tried to bribe me in the garden. My price, he said, for going away for ever.'

'He's desperate,' said Patrick, 'and he'll go to any lengths.'

'What do you suggest we do? Do you really think we can present this lot to Sir George? Personally, I don't think he'll give us the time of day.' She paused. 'Dare we, Patrick?'

Her face was turned towards him. Her eyes were trusting. She looked. . . helpless. He had never seen her look at him like that before. Had always longed for her to look at him like that. His chest should swell with pride. A few days ago, it *would* have!

But that was before his meeting with Damien Lambert.

'I think you had better see a lawyer first,' said Patrick, 'just in case Sir George lets you down. At least you can prove Jeremy's guilt and you'll be able to sue.'

'But my career! No other company would employ me after a scandal like that.'

'With all the evidence I have here, you might never need to work again,' said Patrick. 'You'd get compensation. You could even sell your story.'

239

'I suppose so,' she said miserably, wondering how he could be so blasé about something that was so important to them both.

'Liz,' absent-mindedly Patrick stroked the long, shiny nose of Jeremy's horse. The horse was restless, wanted to be taken out of his stall, pushed the side of his head into Patrick's arm. 'Liz, there has to be a reason, a good reason, why Jeremy is behaving as he is. His campaign against you, and I don't call it campaign lightly, is hardly a nine-day wonder. It's been going on for some time.'

Liz shrugged, but his sharp eyes noted a guarded glint in her expressive sandy eyes, an almost imperceptible lowering of her lashes.

'I had a drink with Damien Lambert a couple of nights ago. He tells me that Sir George and your last husband were very good friends.'

'That's right.' She had put her mask on now and her face gave nothing away, yet in so doing, gave everything away. 'You're hiding something,' he said.

He waited for her to enlighten him. She did not. He found the long silence uncomfortable. She did not seem to, but as she still had her mask on, he wasn't sure.

'Was Sir George the lover that Michael discovered before he died?'

At last he had said it. She still did not speak. Anger simmered inside him. Anger with her for evading, for lying by omission.

'That's it, isn't it? Sir George has a very guilty conscience about you, hasn't he? The widow of the friend he cheated. I'll bet he feels pretty badly about the kids, too, doesn't he? Especially Robbie, a little boy orphaned as a direct result of an old man's lust. Is that how you got your cushy little job, Liz?' He was shaking her now and the horse whinnied in alarm as the man's body kept thumping against his stall door.

'Yes it was,' she screamed, 'but don't you forget that I started as a minor secretary, not a bloody consultant. I've got where I am on my own merit. Which is more than you can say for the three Pascall brothers.'

'Is that all that worries you?' he snarled and his boyish face became ugly. 'That I might actually think that you got where you are on your back? Are you sure you didn't do anything beyond the call of duty, Liz? No small, extra services to help along your promotion?'

He leaned back against the stable door, his chest heaving, clenching and unclenching his fists, struggling for control. In self-defence she remained silent, giving him time to recover, to regain control of his rage. Her own had evaporated, fear and pain the antidote.

'Is that how you got a mention in the Will, Liz?' There was menace in the softness of his tone. He waited.

If she had screamed invective at him, beaten at him with her fists, called him a bastard, then maybe he could have handled it. He was unprepared for her tears. She tried to hide her face, but her shoulders shook uncontrollably. 'I didn't know, Patrick,' she blurted. 'I didn't know it was relevant. It never occurred to me that Sir George might have mentioned me in his Will. Patrick, you must believe me. I know I've been less than truthful, but this time, you must believe me, because it's true.'

The next moment she was in his arms, believed and forgiven. He could not help himself. And neither could she.

He did not enlighten her about the contents of the copy of the Will he had found in Jeremy's file, and she did not ask. It suddenly seemed irrelevant. They wandered aimlessly around the stables, discretion dispensed with, holding hands because they needed to. Suddenly, Liz halted and tensed. He stared at her stricken face.

'It's him! He's coming towards us.'

William Fraser was approaching them. The angular face she had grown to detest was set, his knees made juts out of the soft material of his trousers with each step. It was almost as if he were stalking them. As he drew closer, she could see the cruel manner in which his upper lip curled, the way that his eyes narrowed like slits. In his dress he was as innocuous as a college boy, the skinny white slacks, a red shirt, a white blazer. She was chilled by his animalistic expression, swayed a bit, felt Patrick's comforting support as his palm slid under her elbow.

'Where is it?' hissed Fraser, confronting them.

'Where's what?' snapped Patrick.

'The file. You'd better hand it over.'

Liz began to shake. This man aroused in her a fear the very thought of which she dreaded. Patrick, however, was not intimidated.

'Get stuffed, you creep,' he said, advancing on Fraser.

'If I were you,' Fraser ignored Patrick, stared hard past Patrick's shoulder, at Liz. 'If I were you, I wouldn't be so surly. You see, I have your daughter.'

'What?' Liz gasped.

'He's bluffing,' Patrick slung the words back over his shoulder, as Liz remained inert, transfixed in terror. She began to shiver. The cold intensified, crept into every cell in her body, greedily sucking in every part of her.

'If you so much as lay a finger on me, you'll never know where she is.'

Patrick let out a sudden terrible roar of rage and Fraser succumbed to fear as Patrick bore down on him. Began to back away, almost stumbled, then turned and ran, hell for leather, Patrick in brave pursuit. But the younger man was wily and athletic, had less weight to carry and easily out-distanced the large, red-haired Irishman. Panting heavily, Patrick was forced to abandon the chase, stopped, waited for Liz to catch up with him.

'Don't worry,' he reassured her, 'he hasn't got Charlotte. I just phoned Mrs Oakes from Jeremy's private line and everything's fine.'

'Then where is the file, Patrick? Can he get at it?'

'It's locked in my car boot. But I suppose he might try to break in. Let's take the car and drive down to the village. I doubt that the bank will be open, but there might be a building society or insurance broker who'll put it in their safe for us.'

They hurried back to the small car park at the front of the east wing. 'Can't we just take off, drive straight home,' said Liz. 'We can't go back into the house and face them after all this.'

'Certainly we can. My own job is on the line, don't forget

that. At the moment I'm Sir George's blue-eyed boy and all the time that situation continues, I'm safe from Jeremy. Jeremy wouldn't dare to say a word against me to his father.'

'What have you got that I haven't?' muttered Liz bitterly, but she realised he was probably right. They had to pretend that nothing had happened, that everything was exactly as it should be.

'Sir George won't live for ever,' she pointed out. 'What then?'

'I don't know,' said Patrick. 'Let's take one thing at a time. OK?'

'OK.'

As they reached the car park, one of the Porsche's engines suddenly roared into life. The car reversed at breakneck speed out of the line of vehicles. A blurred red flash, it spun in a backwards curve on two wheels. The tyres screamed against the tarmac. With a great surge of acceleration, the engine roared again. The vehicle shot forward. A shining, scarlet bullet.

Its low long bonnet bore down on them. Flaring, menacing. The headlights were on full beam, blinding them.

Valiantly Patrick shielded Liz with his body. She did not, could not, move. She was spellbound. He shoved her aside and with the momentum of his action, he stumbled wildly in the opposite direction. The Porsche missed him, passed between them. Did a crazy spin.

'Get between the parked cars, Liz,' yelled Patrick, and to give her time to seek safety, he leapt away from her, drawing the Porsche's crushing wheels towards himself. The red bonnet materialised before him, blazing, and once more, he leapt crazily, fell, narrowly escaping as a tyre passed his eyes, blinding him with dust, missing him by inches.

At that moment Alexia came running out of the house as Patrick stumbled to his feet, wildly looking all around him for the direction of the next attack.

'What's going on?' screamed Alexia.

On his return spin, Fraser hit Alexia with his offside wing. There was a dull thud. Liz caught the look of horror on his face as Alexia crumpled to the ground, face down. Her huge plait stuck out at right-angles to her head. She looked as if she were Rapunzel, fallen from her tower, smashed by her own yearning for escape.

'I'll get him for that,' yelled Patrick, 'see to Alexia, Liz. I'm going after him. Where's the bike?'

He took a chance and raced round to where Fraser had left the Norton. His gamble paid off, for the keys were still in the ignition. He would be faster on the bike. There were no traffic snarl-ups for bikes.

Liz, forgetting about Alexia, followed, watched horrified, as Patrick mounted the huge bike, frantically kicking it over. On the third try, it fired and he wrenched the handlebar throttle into life with his strong grip. As the dust flew beneath the wheels, Patrick vaguely registered a crowd gathering around Alexia's prostrate form, but Liz still stood watching, still spell-bound, at the side of the house, her mouth agape.

As he roared past her, he saw her lips move in a scream. Couldn't hear the sound of her voice above the din of the machine, but knew without a doubt the words on her lips.

'Eddie,' her lips mouthed. 'EDDIE, EDDIE.'

She was still screaming as he sped away, but by now, mercifully, he could not hear her. 'Eddie, you can do it. You *can* beat the train, Eddie. *Faster, faster . . .*'

His brain was misty with the pain of her final betrayal. He centred his concentration on William Fraser, this man who was the epitome of everything he despised. He slewed along the twisting drive, having to put his foot down every now and then to balance the machine as it careered crazily with every turn. When he arrived at the gates, he saw that they had not been hitched back. They swung in the light breeze, indicating that they had been closed and that Fraser had had to get out of the Porsche to open them.

'Good,' thought Patrick, 'that will have slowed him down by several seconds.'

Did he turn right or left into the lane? There were some skid marks on the road, to the left. Patrick shot through the gates and the bike heeled over sideways as he set off in pursuit.

But he didn't know the lane like Eddie did.

He'd forgotten about the hairpin bend.

He flew like a rocket across the curve, into the hedgerow. The front tyre hit the thick bole of a lopped-off hawthorn and the whole bike seemed to levitate beneath him. With a yell of surprise, for he had no time to register fear, Patrick's body took to the air.

His arms reaching forward instinctively, to break his fall, he sailed, head first, over the top of the hedge.

Liz left them clucking anxiously over Alexia and began to run in the direction of the departed vehicles. Even in her distressed state, she did not expect to find anything. Just knew she had to get away from this place before it drove her mad. Through the open gates, hardly able to remember how she got there, and out into the lane, her breath coming in short, sharp gasps, her heart beating wildly.

Running, running, not even sure if she was heading in the right direction. Feeling hot, then cold, her lungs bursting at the unaccustomed effort.

Then she saw it.

The wreck of red and black twisted metal. Its uncanny familiarity struck her first. Like that other time. So like that other time. A wrecked bike. A man she had loved. A man she had sent to his death . . .

She stopped short. Turned aside, leaning against the yellow stone wall. Fell to her knees and vomited into the grass verge. Was so sick that her insides ached with the effort.

She had to pull herself together. Patrick! Patrick needed help and there was only her there to help him.

Determinedly, forcing each step, she made her way along the lane, found a stile and climbed over. Stumbled along the hedgerow on the other side, towards where Patrick must be lying.

The field was blackened because they had recently burned the stubble, was made blacker as, like an omen, the sky darkened. There was a rumble of thunder in the distance. Charred bits of wheat stalk stuck up in stripes here and there, where the flames had failed to consume them.

Please be all right. Please God, let Patrick be all right, she prayed. Normally she did not pray, because she only half-believed. Because she thought that prayer was a weakness, an admission of one's own inadequacy. But now, in her desperation, she prayed.

She almost fell as she drew closer. Could just discern the shape in the blackness. Patrick's large body spreadeagled on the ground.

As her eyes focused, grew accustomed to the sudden gloom, she saw that Patrick's body did not lie directly on the ground. She shook her head, mad with fear, put her hands over her face, unable to take it in. Something awful. Something so awful she could not accept it.

All around Patrick, like some medieval form of torture, framing his body, sprang those black, curved swords.

It seemed that they marched around him like soldiers!

Sinister, evil, unrelenting.

Gloating over their victory.

A naked, guttural sound emanated from deep inside her, encompassing all of her suffering. Crazy, brutal noise like a Satanic requiem.

NO! NO! NO! she screamed, demented. The sense of vibrating liquid flesh deep in her stomach divided, slid down each of her thighs, hit her knees. Her hand shot out uselessly, clutching at nothing. . .

Patrick, God help him, had landed, face-down, on a harrow, left, spikes upwards, alongside the hedge.

She sank to her knees beside him in the stubble She did not weep, was beyond weeping. She sat, it seemed, for ages, a huddle of motionless agony. Unable to move, unable to accept she would never again hear his merry, resonant laughter, see his twinkling hazel eyes approving her, their angry glint when she annoyed him. His sweet, sassy charm was gone for ever. In one fleeting moment, Patrick was no more.

It began to rain. She was oblivious. The rain washed away her tears and her mascara, but could not cleanse her soul.

She was finally aroused by the sound of voices in the lane, the other side of the hedgerow. They were looking for her. Her strong sense of survival overcame her apathy, brought her to her senses. Gingerly she got on to all fours, reached over to the body. Tried to pull his jacket front from beneath the dead weight of him. Fumbled around, feeling for his pocket. Please God, let this be the pocket. After an eternity, she could feel the uneven jumble of Patrick's keys.

Panting, she managed to extricate them from the pocket. Fancied she could feel the cloying warmth of his blood seeping between her fingers. She felt sick. Swallowed.

She struggled to her feet, slipping the keys into the deep pocket of her skirt.

She could hear the procession the other side of the hedgerow making its way noisily to the stile, Sir George trying to insist that the women go back, the gentle, anxious murmur of Gina's small voice, Lillian telling everyone what to do, Jeremy's short rebukes to his mother.

Martin must have stayed behind to comfort Alexia.

Quickly, Liz ran along the hedgerow in the opposite direction, searching desperately for a place where she could break through. Eventually, aware that she was running out of time, disregarding their questing sharp stings, she pushed her way through a large clump of nettles.

Patrick's car.

She had to get to Patrick's car.

Patrick's car, containing the precious file.

She slipped her hand in her skirt pocket, reassuring herself that the keys were still there. Began to run, wet and dishevelled, unevenly up the lane, back to the Lodge gates. Her tights had ripped and fallen about her ankles. The small stabs of pain from the nettles were a welcomed pain, for she concentrated hard on their burning, a small penance for Patrick's own agonies.

30

William Fraser, alias Eddie Smith, was killed at ninety-five miles per hour en route for London in a pile-up on the motorway, in which seven other people were also wiped out and nineteen injured.

Fraser, it later emerged, had been nothing more than an ordinary door-to-door encyclopaedia salesman, but Liz never discovered the basis of his connection with Jeremy Pascall.

He was a nonentity, none the less, a nonentity who had been bent on improving his station in life, by any means it took, no matter what the cost in suffering.

A nonentity who was no more. Which tidied things up nicely for Liz.

She mourned Patrick deeply. The children, too, grieved for Patrick, but with the natural resilience of youth, recovered and got on with their lives.

For the first few weeks, Liz, in her desolation, concentrated only on the essentials.

Like depositing the Pascall file in a safe-box at the bank.

Like firing Dinah. (She also fired Dinah's successor who had the gall to turn up for work in jeans.)

Like collecting her beautiful new BMW.

And like accepting, officially, Martin Pascall's proposal of marriage.

On the day that Liz returned to work, one calendar month after the fateful day at the Lodge, her engagement to Martin was announced in the national press.

Martin was like a dog with two tails.

Gina went home to her family in Milan. Of course she would never marry again, for she was a Catholic and her family and her Church did not recognise divorce. But since she could not have children by her husband, what was the point in staying with him? He had nothing to offer her now, nor she him.

Alexia recovered from her brush with the Porsche, but not from her estrangement from Martin. She took her own life with an overdose of barbiturates.

Liz was sad.

But that was life!

Sir George disinherited Trevor, just as Liz had guessed he would, for Trevor was no good. Sir George knew that. Knew he would not change. Cut him out, as a tumour from an otherwise healthy body.

By unspoken agreement between Liz and his two eldest sons, Sir George was kept in the dark about Jeremy's treachery, mainly for the sake of his health. It would not have served anyone's purpose to have involved him in the grisly details of his son's vendetta and its consequences.

And Sir George soon relented and welcomed his former, favourite prodigy, soon to become his daughter-in-law, back into the Pascall fold. Neither of them ever mentioned their brief fling of long ago. It was past, irrelevant.

To Liz's delight, Sir George took her own children to his heart, especially Robbie, the son of his oldest, dearest friend, the friend he had wronged.

Charlotte and Robbie became his substitute grand-children. Sir George told Robbie all about his stocks and shares, and Robbie showed a healthy interest.

With Jeremy's reluctant agreement, Liz took over Patrick's job of masterminding Robinson's Surgical.

Jeremy smouldered.

It did not worry Liz. She could handle Jeremy. She had the file. Patrick had made sure of that.

Dear Patrick! How she had loved him. She thought of him when Martin made love to her, in his considerate but ponderous fashion. But she was wiser now. She cultivated the habit of making love in silence.

Occasionally she visited Patrick's grave with a beautiful bunch of white roses for peace.

And one long-stemmed red for 'I love you'.